D0720233

Dear Reader:

It is my pleasure to present yet another engrossing novel from bestselling Allison Hobbs. Hobbs is the author of *Double Dippin'*, *Dangerously in Love*, *Insatiable* and *Pandora's Box*; all published by Strebor Books. A "Queen of Erotic Fiction" in her own right, Hobbs now puts a new spin on her previous works by taking on the genre of "paranormal erotica."

Eris is a force to be reckoned with for she is sexy, bewitching and on a path of revenge that spans more than 200 years. Ever wonder about sexual practices in the 1800s? Wonder no more after you read the pages of this quick-paced, thrilling novel.

I first met Allison at the Baltimore Book Festival several years ago and was immediately impressed with her talent. Not everyone has a natural writing ability but Allison was born to create masterpieces such as the one you are about to read. She is ever positive and determined, much like myself, and will go far in this industry as her next three books are already scheduled for publication.

Thanks for supporting Allison's efforts and for supporting my imprint, Strebor Books. I am overwhelmed by the legions of avid readers who genuinely appreciate not only my personal work but the works of the dozens that I publish. For a complete listing of titles, please visit www.planetzane.com.

If you are interesting in making extra income, please email dante@streborbooks.com to be sent an "Opportunity" packet. Now sit back in your favorite chair or, better yet, chill in the bed, and be prepared to be tantalized by yet another great read.

Peace and Many Blessings,

Zane

Publisher
Strebor Books International
www.streborbooks.com

DEC 2010

ZANE PRESENTS

THE Enchantress

A NOVEL

ALLISON HOBBS

PUBLICATION

STREBOR BOOKS

NEW YORK LONDON TORONTO SYDNEY

Published by

Strebor Books International LLC
P.O. Box 6505
Largo, MD 20792
www.simonsays.com/streborbooks

ISBN 13 978- 1-59309-102-6

LCCN 2006928394

Distributed by Simon & Schuster, Inc.
1230 Avenue of the Americas
New York, NY 10020
1-800-223-2336

Cover design: © www.mariondesigns.com

First Printing November 2006
Manufactured and Printed in the United States

10 9 8 7 6 5 4 3 2 1

FOR MY BEAUTIFUL DAUGHTER,
Kyndal Lois Hobbs

Acknowledgments

I'd like to thank all my readers—those who've been with me since *Pandora's Box* and those who've only recently discovered my work. I'm so appreciative for the numerous emails and I feel immense gratitude for your words of praise and continued support.

Thank you to the bookstores and book sellers who've graciously promoted my material throughout the years: Stephanie Wilkerson and LaTanya Townes at Urban Knowledge Books Mondawmin Mall, Zanielle at Black Horizons Gallery East, Melissa at B. Dalton Gallery East, Robin Green at Karibu Books Security Mall, Harriet at Borders Xpress Christiana Mall.

A special thanks to Monique and David Green, Shanee' J. Jones, Locksie of ARC Book Club, Tee C. Royal and Stacey Seay of RAWSISTAZ, Yasmin Coleman, APOOO Book Club and MoNique Nicole and the Circle of Sistahs Book Club.

Much love and respect goes out to my fellow Strebor authors. I have to thank my girls, Tina Brooks McKinney and Darrien Lee for always being there for me. Thanks Harold L. Turley II for playing tour guide, host, and even unwitting driver (when I forgot where I parked my car) in Washington, D.C.

Thank you Charmaine Parker and the Strebor/Atria/Simon and Schuster team.

A heartfelt thank you to my best friend in the whole wide world—Karen Dempsey Hammond.

I want to shout out my new Baby Diva, Kapri Johnson. Thanks Korky and Shari! My nephews and nieces: Sterling Perry, Jalil Perry, Elysha Perry, Kendrick Sealy, and Laila Sneed.

And I thank my phenomenal publisher, Zane.

Chapter 1

The whispered grumblings in the slave quarters on the Stovall Plantation were usually about Eris.

"Now, a gal like dat—black as tar—ain't got no business workin' in de big house," the old man named Make-Do complained.

"You sho' 'nuff right, Make-Do. In all my years, ah ain't nevah seen nothin' like it. Dark-skinded gal wit dem big ol' clumsy feets tendin' to Missus and givin out orders to de cook and e'rebody else workin' in de big house," agreed Peahead. "She sho' got Massuh fooled."

"Hmph! Don't nobody seem to know where she come from, but where-vah dat was, ah bet she wasn't nothin' but a field hand jes' like us," groused Peahead's wife, Florette.

Make-Do scratched his head. "If ah 'members co'reckly, Eris showed up here in de middle of de night. She told Massuh she been on de run from some evil slave owner way down in 'Bama somewhere."

"You mean to tell me dat gal ran all de way from 'Bama to Virginy?" Florette scrunched up her lips and shook her head. "Don't make no kinda sense dem slave catchers nevah got ahold'a her 'long de way."

"Massuh got such a good heart; took her in promisin' to hide her and all. She showed up buck naked—ain't had nothin but a box filled up with potions and such. Told Massuh she was good at nursin' folk. Dat why he keep her up in de big house," explained Peahead.

"Well, it don't look like her nursin's worth mucha nothin'. Missus be gittin' sicker by de day," said a young woman by the name of Willa. "And why somebody blacker den soot talkin' like de white folk? And why she got dem strange-lookin' blue eyes?" There was a collective confused shaking of heads.

"Bet y'all don't know…" Willa paused, waiting to get the group's undivided attention. "Eris done started wearin' all Missus's clothes." Willa's bottom lip jutted out in disapproval.

"Wearin Missus's clothes!" Peahead and Florette chorused incredulously.

"Sho' 'nuff is." Make-Do confirmed with a nod. "Eris done give all her old frocks to Molly and Tookie." Make-Do had been on the Stovall Plantation long before the current master was born. Now, too old to work the fields, Make-Do kept an eye on the children and performed easy tasks that didn't require agility or a strong back .

"I done told dem girls they ain't gon' have nothin' but bad luck from wearin' dat evil woman's clothes," Make-Do continued.

"Uh-huh. I tried to warn 'em, too. Dey so happy to have spare frocks, dey won't even listen. But dey gon' see. Mark my words, dey sho' 'nuff gon' see," Willa said, staring off into space and shaking her head as if a future fraught with unparalleled horrors was being revealed.

"Lawd, look ovah dere." Peahead pointed toward the big house. All heads turned. In the distance, illuminated by moonlight, Eris was kneeling on the ground.

"What she up to now?" Florette inquired in a hushed tone.

Peahead stood up and squinted. "Look like she tendin' to dat garden a-hern."

"At night!" they all exclaimed loudly, then looked around anxiously, hoping Eris didn't catch them spying on her. But Eris was intently involved with gathering the herbs and roots she needed for the mistress's remedy.

"You know dat woman's stranger than a two-headed chicken," Peahead whispered nervously. "Wouldn't surprise me a bit if she diggin' a hole so's to holla down dere and talk to Satan hisself." Peahead gave a shudder. "Come on, Florette. We goin' inside. Ah don't wanna be nowhere near Eris after daylight. And 'specially not with dat full moon burnin' while she dealin' wit' de devil," he said ominously. Peahead and Florette gathered themselves to go inside their cabin, careful not to look in Eris's direction.

Willa latched onto Make-Do's arm and helped him to stand upright.

After he was safely on his feet, Willa respectfully handed the old man his walking stick. She hurried to her cabin while old Make-Do shuffled on down the dusty path to his own shanty.

Edith Stovall, the mistress of the plantation, was so consumed with fever she had no idea that her fine garments had been relegated to adorning a lowly slave. Had she known, she would have diplomatically excused her husband's lack of judgment, but such impudence by a slave girl would have warranted a visit to the whipping post. Nine and thirty. That's how many lashes the ill-mannered, uppity heifer would have incurred if the mistress of the house had her strength and wits about her.

The mistress was stricken with a serious illness and according to her husband, Arthur, she was delirious. Talking out of her head—accusing him of unspeakable acts since she'd been banished from his bed. Having the fever and carrying what appeared to be a deadly and contagious disease, of course she had had to be exiled from the marital bedroom. She was being quarantined until she got better or—God forbid—she died.

Since none of the local physicians could figure out what was wrong with Edith and none wanted to risk catching her strange sickness, it was lucky for Edith that Eris seemed immune. Eris could go in and out of Edith's sickroom and administer to her without so much as a cough or a sneeze.

Arthur was more than grateful to Eris. As master of the plantation, he couldn't afford to come down with the strange illness that had gripped his pitiful wife. Why, he'd lose everything his daddy had left him if he caught whatever was ailing his wife.

It was for the good of the plantation and the future of the Stovall family if Edith stayed far, far away from him as well as any essential slaves whose labor he depended upon. Until her health improved, Edith would have to stay tucked away in that cramped and musty bedroom up in the attic.

But in the meantime, a man had his needs. Manly desires that a sickly wife could not fulfill.

Eris used a sharp-edged rock to grind the mixture that she'd concocted in the moonlight and then carried it up the stairs to the attic. With the wooden bowl and ladle in hand, Eris used her hip to bump open the door to the quarantined room.

"Missus," Eris said sharply. "Wake up, Missus. It's time to take your remedy."

Although Arthur Stovall never came into the room personally, he'd been known to send in slaves whom he considered dispensable to periodically check on his wife and give him a report on her condition.

Eris wasn't willing to risk having unexpected visits from loose lips reporting that she wasn't giving the mistress the best treatment possible, so she set the bowl on the bedside table and used the hem of her apron to blot the perspiration from Edith's forehead. Then, certain that no prying eyes could see her, she roughly wiped the sickly woman's face and mouth, using the lace-edged pocket of the apron,. With a hateful grimace, Eris dug the crust out of the corners of her patient's rapidly blinking eyes. The friction of the stiff lace was painful and caused angry red blotches to pop up all over Edith's frail face.

As far as Eris was concerned, the red blotches further proved that the mistress was contagious and required an extended quarantine. And more doses of her special remedy.

Eris gave a low chortle as she recalled the last slave the master had sent to the attic infirmary. Scared to death, old Make-Do had limped into the room holding a rag over his face. The rag covered his mouth, nose, and eyes.

He wasn't going to be able to give the master a detailed report being that he had neither seen nor smelled anything, so out of pure spite, Eris instructed Make-Do to empty the mistress's almost overflowing chamberpot.

Having to walk with a cane made carrying the *contagious* waste material cumbersome. One would have thought Make-Do had seen a ghost the way he whooped and hollered when bits of loose excrement splattered on his hand.

Imagining he'd been infected by the mistress, Make-Do coughed up blood for a week, but he finally pulled through. Eris found Make-Do's near-death experience extremely humorous and made a mental note to take better advantage of his simplemindedness in the future.

Eris was anxious to report that the Missus's ailment was not better, that she was even more emaciated and pale with a curious eruption of red welts, which were spreading all over her face. The Missus, Eris would sadly state, seemed to be getting worse. Excited, Eris hurriedly left the room, forgetting to administer the poisonous concoction.

Edith was weak and very thirsty. But her heart was filled with relief that the vile black slave had forgotten to force-feed her the twice-daily dosage of poison. Eris's lethal "remedy" was the instrument of the mistress's slow and agonizing demise.

Experiencing an unusually lucid period earlier that day, Edith had kept the poisonous mixture hidden beneath her tongue. She'd spat it out as soon as the slave woman left the room. And now, having skipped the evening dose as well, she was feeling strengthened and hopeful that she might survive this vexation dealt upon her by the hands of a slave. The gall!

Unwilling to risk exposure to his wife's malady, Arthur Stovall insisted that Eris shed the clothing she'd worn while attending to Edith and wash thoroughly before entering his chambers.

The mistress's nights on this earth were numbered. It was just a matter of time before Eris became the Mistress of the House. Although her name would not be affixed to any official documents, she'd be the mistress no less, and she would inform the slaves to address her as such. She'd already begun training Molly, the cook's assistant, to refer to her as *Mistress*.

Hearing her addressed as such would be a problem with the white people, of course. Therefore, she'd have to prohibit visitations by business associates who'd come snooping around. She'd insist that Arthur—yes, she now called him *Arthur*—conduct his business away from the home. She would not kowtow to lawyers, bookkeepers or such. No, Arthur would have to arrange his life to suit her needs.

Feeling powerful, Eris did not cover herself with even a wisp of fabric. Boldly, she glided naked from her room to the master bedchamber. She did not care if curious eyes peered from corners or slightly cracked doors. *Let them behold my beauty—my full breasts and wide hips. Yes, let them admire me from a distance but cower in my presence.* Intoxicated with power, Eris, dark and statuesque, with refined facial features, strode through the corridors with the regal carriage of a queen. Heavy coils of dark hair fell past her shoulders. She did not carry a lantern; the full moon brightened the path to Arthur's chamber.

"My beloved," Arthur said when Eris opened the door and crept to his bed. "I've waited for what feels like ages. Hurry! Come!" He patted the bed.

She peered at him in the dark room. "Wait! I must part the curtains."

"Why, beloved?"

"The moon is full tonight. You've given me many things; but never have you given me the moon."

"Ah, you're a strange one. But I have no power in your presence. Part the curtains if you wish. Have your moon; have the stars as well." Arthur waved his hand extravagantly and laughed.

Eris parted the curtains and for a few moments, stood naked in the window. She threw back her head in ecstasy as she became energized by the light of the moon.

In the cramped slave huts below, candles were quickly snuffed when the slaves saw Eris's naked silhouette. Such a sight seemed unholy and they all wished to escape through sleep as quickly as possible. With prayers on their tongues, they hoped that by morning's light, the chilling image of Eris basking in the moonlight would seem like a bad dream.

Eris walked to the bed. Her breasts were full and tender; a red streak trailed down her inner thigh. Smiling, she pulled back the heavy covers and joined the master whose look of worship assured her that behind closed doors, he'd always be her slave.

Chapter 2

*E*ris awakened at dawn. There was great clattering in the kitchen as the cook and her help prepared the morning meal for Arthur and her.

Molly, an obedient young girl, rapped on the door twice as Eris had instructed her. "Good morning, Mistress," the young girl greeted Eris. Molly did a double-take and looked quizzically at her master, who still asleep, sucked loudly on the knuckle of Eris's middle finger.

"Will that be all, Mistress?" Molly asked, averting her gaze as she set down the breakfast tray.

"No. Go out to the slave quarters and tell that worthless Make-Do to go tend to the Missus. Tell him to empty her slop…" Suddenly remembering that she hadn't given Arthur's wife her evening dosage, she further instructed, "Tell him to add a little water to her remedy; it's in a bowl on the nightstand. He must give her two spoonfuls. Is that clear?"

"Yes, Mistress," Molly said. "Two spoonfuls," she repeated, and whirled around and hurried out of the room. Through the window Eris watched Molly race across the lawn to give Make-Do the distressful news.

Eris was famished and sore. The power she'd derived from the full moon had enhanced her femininity, bringing on her menses and causing her full breasts to lactate although she'd never given birth to a child.

The moon had allowed her to nurture Arthur—to claim him as her own. Last night, she'd encouraged him to suckle her breasts and her bleeding womanhood until he cried from sheer bliss.

Different from other women, Eris's menstrual cycle lasted for just one evening per month, and though Arthur cried and pleaded for more of her delicious dark red nectar, she had nothing left to give; he'd suckled her dry.

Like a fretful baby, he'd cried and whimpered throughout the night. Not wanting to awaken the slaves, Eris had given him her knuckle to suck. This soothed and kept him quiet, allowing him to sleep like a contented child for the remainder of the night.

Depleted and famished from her nocturnal activities, Eris, propped up by three plump pillows, enjoyed her own breakfast and Arthur's as well.

Praying he did not become afflicted again with the doomed Missus's illness, Make-Do hobbled up the flights of stairs, carrying a pitcher of fresh water. When he reached the attic, although it hadn't entered his mind before, the thought of just upping and running away seemed like a better idea than risking another chance with the sick Missus. All that choking and coughing up blood was bound to kill him this time. But trying to run with his bad leg…well, he wouldn't get very far. Nope! The hounds would have a hold on him before he even got close to the river.

Accepting his fate, Make-Do pushed open the door. The room smelled like a pigsty. The Missus looked all dried-up and half-dead, with her thick and cankered tongue hanging out the side of her mouth. Momentarily oblivious of his fear of contagion, Make-Do rushed over, lifted her head and tried to give her a drink of water, but the water rolled off her thick, blistered tongue.

In a quandary, he looked around the room. There was a spoon stuck in the dried-up remedy that Eris had instructed him to give to the mistress. Make-Do cleaned the gook off and began spoonfeeding drops of water to Edith. "Here you go, Missus," he said, carefully aiming the spoon toward her dry lips. His doctoring seemed to work. The Missus began to utter sounds. Incomprehensible noises, but the gibberish was progress nonetheless. Wanting her to get better, Make-Do poured a little water in the remedy and tried to soften it up enough to give to the mistress.

But the mistress started making an awful growling sound in her throat. It scared old Make-Do so bad, he thought she was drowning from taking in too much water. Not wanting to be blamed for killing her, Make-Do slipped out of the room and hobbled as fast as he could down the stairs.

He ran smack into Molly. "Ah give de Missus two spoonfuls of dat remedy jest like you said." He turned to hobble away.

"Did you empty the slop bucket?"

"No, Lawdy, Ah didn't," he said sadly. "Ah sho' is gittin' old and fo'getful. Lemme git back up dere and fetch it."

When Make-Do reentered the infirmed woman's room, she looked surprisingly brighter. Her complexion wasn't as pasty and her tongue didn't look as thick. Encouraged, he picked up the bowl of remedy and started stirring.

Edith Stovall began to moan and Make-Do put down the bowl.

"You don't like dat remedy, do you, Missus?"

She looked at him and grunted.

"Okey-dokey. Ah'm jest up here to fetch yo' slop bucket anyways. So you git yo'self some sleep now, Missus."

Grateful that he hadn't killed the Missus, Make-Do whistled a happy tune as he took care of emptying the slop bucket.

By nightfall, when Make-Do hadn't started choking and coughing up any blood, the slaves breathed a sigh of relief. They loved Make-Do too much to have to beg his pardon and ask him to kindly stay in his own cabin. Yes, they were mighty obliged that they didn't have to turn old Make-Do away.

"Ah's done beat dat ol' sickness," Make-Do told the awestruck slaves. "Maybe de Missus will, too."

The slaves all smiled hopefully. If the mistress recovered, Eris would be put in her place and things would be back to normal on the Stovall Plantation.

Chapter 3

*A*rthur Stovall believed his wife was under Eris's expert care, but Eris, disgusted by the awful stench in the sickroom, preferred the sweet smell of her own quarters, which Molly filled with fresh cut flowers daily.

Expecting Edith to expire at any moment, Eris had stopped providing personal care and now the sickly woman's pasty-colored skin and wildly tangled hair was a completely unappealing sight. In fact, everything about the sickroom and its occupant was unpleasant and not a suitable place for a woman such as Eris, who was living in the lap of luxury.

But with the mistress's unwillingness to just go ahead and give up the ghost, Eris had no choice but to make the remedy stronger—more toxic. She'd left the handling of the infirmed woman up to Make-Do, giving the old slave strict orders to now give the mistress three heaping spoons of the concoction every day.

Eris had custody of every article of clothing Edith Stovall owned. In order to prove his devotion and the sincerity of his love, Arthur had recently given Eris a cameo brooch, and upon his wife's imminent death, Eris fully expected to inherit the woman's entire collection of jewels, especially her beautiful wedding ring. Of course, she wouldn't *wear* the woman's wedding ring; she'd keep it along with the treasure of jewelry she'd acquired and hid in the box she kept buried near her vegetable patch.

Then, when it was time to move on, she'd leave the useless garments, hats and other finery—but the box of jewels would accompany her on the journey to the next plantation.

Eris's plan was to make her way up north. Once settled there as a free woman, she'd cash in her jewelry and live the good life without having to rely on the males that drained her powers with their greedy mouths, depleting her of her womanhood.

Ever so sweetly, Eris persuaded Arthur to take the buggy and meet his banker in town. She considered sending Make-Do along under the pretense of tending to the horse, but she'd instruct him to keep an ear out for any important financial information. However, needing the old man to empty the slop jar and take care of the mistress, she decided Arthur could make the two-day journey alone.

Having not stepped a foot inside the sickroom in weeks, Eris had no idea that Make-Do had stopped administering the lethal potion to the mistress and had been hand-feeding her mashed fruit, soft boiled vegetables, and several glasses of water per day. Thus, Edith Stovall was slowly but surely coming back to good health.

Eris stayed so far away from the attic, she hadn't heard all the laughter and sounds of merriment that emanated from the sickroom. Nor did she hear the Missus clunking around with Make-Do's cane as she taught herself how to walk again.

And so it was a tremendous shock when Eris awakened in her beautiful, sweet-smelling, flower-filled room to an oddly familiar odor. She thought she had to be dreaming when she opened her eyes and beheld the mistress, looking like an old crone propped up with Make-Do's cane, as she observed with increasing rage the splendid surroundings that Eris had become accustomed to.

The wedding ring on the frail hand that gripped the cane caught Eris's attention. She'd wanted that ring so badly; now it was too late. The mistress looked gaunt; her fingers were as thin as chicken talons. Eris could have easily shaken the ring loose from the woman's hand a long time ago and added it to her collection. But it was too late to acquire the prized possession now. She'd have to make her escape with the jewelry she'd already buried.

The mistress cleared her throat, and it was an awful sound. Wearing a mask of hatred, Edith Stovall spat the words: "Get up, nigga wench!"

Young, strapping fieldhands yanked Eris out of the bed.

"Tie her up to a tree. I want y'all to take care of Molly and Tookie first," Edith ordered.

The sounds of weeping had blended into her dream state. But now it was painfully clear that Molly and the other kitchen girl, Tookie, were already tied to the whipping posts outside, weeping and moaning as they awaited their punishment. A punishment that would be dispensed for the crime of wearing Eris's garments and daring to address Eris as *Mistress* while the wanton slave had the audacity to parade around in the real misstess's finery.

Naked as the day she was born, which was how Eris preferred to sleep, she was dragged from her bed, roughly pulled outside and tied to the trunk of a big oak tree. Eris didn't put up a fight. Arthur was due home today and he'd have them all strung up and hung—his wife included—for touching a hair on her head.

Molly's whipping was administered by Willyboy, her very own beau. Willyboy cried with each lash that landed on his sweetheart's once unblemished back. Willyboy, being one of the strongest fieldhands on the plantation, had the task of administering blows to Tookie's back also.

With arms folded and misery lining their faces, the slaves were commanded to stand and witness the whippings or suffer the same punishment.

Willa whispered to Florette, "Ah told dem girls dem frocks wasn't gonna bring 'em nothin but grief."

Naked as a jaybird, Eris patiently waited her turn. Her body was strong and could take the blows that would undoubtedly be weak and without fury as Willyboy became physically exhausted and emotionally worn down from having to whip his sweetheart and her good friend, Tookie.

Without a glint of remorse and for no other reason than plain meanness, Eris had not taken her eyes off the two girls who'd been beaten. Distracted, she hadn't paid attention to the whispered murmurs of the other slaves nor did she notice that their eyes darted nervously toward the gates of the plantation.

The tearing of the young girls' flesh fascinated her, stirred a carnal hunger. Their cries of pain aroused her, filled her with a feeling of raw sensuality. Eris decided right then and there that when Arthur returned—after he'd dealt his wife a sound beating—she'd insist that he stick his manhood inside her throbbing womanliness far deeper and much harder than he'd ever done before.

While in the throes of her lustful imagery, she heard the sound of hoofs. *Arthur!*

But instead of Arthur Stovall, two red-faced, ugly white men galloped on dark horses through the open gates of the Stovall Plantation. This sight did not bode well.

"Get her," Edith Stovall commanded. The two fieldhands untied Eris. She squirmed and hissed at the two men who were eager to show her no mercy.

Shaking with fury and indignation, the mistress pointed at Eris. "Now, tie her to that whipping post."

The post was covered with bloody bits of flesh. Eris recoiled, struggling and trying to break from the strong grasp of the fieldhands. The two white overseers—who had been hired from the Gilbert Plantation, which was a fair distance down the road from the Stovall Plantation—observed the naked Eris with gleaming eyes.

"Give her nine and thirty," the Missus demanded. Molly and Tookie had only been given ten lashes apiece.

The overseers took turns ripping the flesh off Eris's back and buttocks. Each searing blast left Eris bloody and breathless. By the fifteenth blow, she was unconscious, but the men gleefully continued the job they were paid to do. By the time they finished, Eris's back was shredded so badly, it no longer resembled living flesh.

"Now take her and drop her off in the woods somewhere far from this plantation. And you, darkies," Edith pointed menacingly at the cowering slaves—"better not contradict my words. My husband will be told the defiant hussy stole my jewelry and ran off—last seen headed north."

Like a sack of potatoes, Eris was thrown across the back of one of the horses and tied down to keep her from falling off before they reached their destination in the deepest, darkest part of the woods.

Bleeding and naked, out in the woods at night, Eris would surely perish; of that Edith Stovall was certain. It served the hateful slave woman right. But for her husband's sake, she'd have to pretend that his bed wench had tired of him and run off.

Night had fallen. Eris awakened screaming. She lay on her tortured back, upon twigs, dried leaves, and stones, as the two overseers, now drunk from whiskey, took turns having their way with her. Competing with her cries of pain, crickets called out in the night.

"We gonna be in a heap'a trouble if old man Stovall come home and finds us out here," Henry cautioned.

"Then quit actin' dumb. Use your noggin, Henry. We gonna have to pull her deeper in the woods," suggested Bo.

Terror-stricken, Eris begged for mercy. "Don't leave me out here for the wild animals to feed on me. Just take me a few miles out of Roanoke and no one will ever see me again."

"Can't risk that, can we, Bo?"

The man named Bo shook his head.

"Why not?" she asked, looking desperately from Henry to Bo.

"'Spose some do-gooder sees you walkin' 'round naked and all… 'Spose he decides to take you in? Then we got a heap'a trouble on our hands. That do-gooder's bound to declare you a runaway and ol' Stovall will come and claim you. Then it'll be shit's creek for me and Bo."

"Uh-huh, shit's creek without a paddle," Bo added, nodding vigorously.

"Git them old scraps of rags from up under the saddle, Bo."

Bo took his time, but came back with old pieces of wool and cotton fabric. The two men scattered the smelly fabric all over Eris. Her initial thought was that they were covering her nakedness, giving her some warmth and dignity to make it through the long night.

But when Henry told Bo to fetch the lantern, their intentions became crystal-clear.

Eris began writhing on the ground, chanting, speaking in tongues, calling on spirits. Cursing Edith and Arthur Stovall and all their descendants, as well as the two overseers.

The two white men had never seen such a convulsive display of hatred. They'd never heard such evil-sounding words directed toward them. Bo was so spooked by the spectacle, his hand trembled and he dropped the lantern.

The fabric, splattered with oil from the lantern, was instantly set ablaze and clung to her skin. Eris emitted an inhuman wail as she rolled on the ground attempting to extinguish the searing flames. But the dry twigs ignited, consuming Eris in a more intense inferno. She jumped up, streaked through the woods to escape the voracious fire, but the flames, now raging, continued to engulf her.

Horrified, Bo and Henry jumped on their horses and galloped away while Eris ran through the woods burning alive. Her abundant locks went up in flames, then ran down her face like melted wax. The pain was unrelenting. Eris not only felt her body burning, but could hear the pop and sizzle of her flesh.

The woods filled with the acrid stench of charred flesh—human flesh—*her* flesh. The tortured woman's bloodcurdling screams were choked off by smoke filling her lungs, flames licking at her throat.

The gaping red hole that had been Eris's mouth could produce no sound to express the awful, transcending pain. To escape the agony, Eris ran faster but as she raced through the woods clumps of flesh sloughed away.

Suddenly the unrelenting, indescribable suffering ceased, but Eris continued to run in disbelief, preparing for the onslaught of torture to continue. Had the agony really stopped? Eris stumbled to a halt and looked down at her body. Her beautiful silky black skin was unscathed. Running searching fingers from firm breasts up to her coarse tresses, Eris was astonished to discover that her entire body was intact—perfect.

"Wha…What's happening?" Flooded by a mixture of relief and curiosity, Eris turned to retrace her steps. In the distance she saw what appeared to be a smoldering log. As she inched closer, cold dread coursed down her chest and into her loins.

"Oh no, nooo!" Eris screamed as recognition transformed the shape of the still-burning log into the shape of a charred human body. Falling to her knees, Eris cried bitterly. The forest was still, as if holding its breath, while Eris mourned the demise of her body and the death of her ambitious plans and schemes.

"It's not fair, it's just not fair! My jewels, my treasure—gone, all gone,"

Eris wept. "I'm a goddess, with every right to be the Mistress of the Stovall Plantation; how dare they consign me to such a dishonorable end!"

As the stronger emotion of all-consuming rage began to replace Eris's deep despair, a burning desire for revenge infused her, its vile power causing the air around her to crackle with electricity. Arthur Stovall had promised to protect her and he had failed. Oh, he would pay dearly for his fatal indiscretion!

Eris vowed that he and every one of his descendants would suffer for her humiliating and untimely demise. As if in acknowledgment of Eris's vengeful decision, the atmosphere began to coalesce into a dark, undulating, living entity.

Faintly, Eris could hear the mournful moans and howls of the damned as the darkness enfolded her spirit. The unholy screams and demonic clamor grew deafening as the foul void devoured her. Eris was transported to an alternate realm...a heinous realm where crazed and demented souls were condemned to dwell.

Eris's soul had found a realm with others of her kind—confused and angry souls trapped between worlds—a place where they could only dream of vengeance, for the accursed legion was doomed to spend all of eternity lashing out in frustration at one another but never sipping the sweet taste of revenge they so desperately hungered to exact upon those they believed had offended them.

Chapter 4

The Dark Realm

*L*egions of depraved spirits, who while on the earthly plane possessed nefarious characteristics such as jealousy, greed, anger, deceitfulness, lust, and brutality, dwelled together on the Dark Realm—a holding place for corrupt and lost souls. Multitudes of tortured beings that only faintly resembled their former human selves scrambled and snarled for position. The accursed environs resembled mounds of heaving serpents maniacally slithering in a snake pit.

This lower realm was a dismal environment; the landscape appeared as devastated as if obliterated by nuclear war. Sun, moon and stars had abandoned the sky. The forsaken sky was a murky brown with black smudges— a bizarre imitation of earthly clouds. The air was a thick, contaminated mist. Instead of dirt, the ground was covered with razor-sharp obsidian and hot, smoldering ash. There was no greenery in this dark and smoky realm, only dead trees, thorns, and prickly burrs.

And this is where Eris's spirit was contained. Time had no meaning here, and if Xavier, a vicious and shrewd being, hadn't taught her how to use her third eye, she would have spent an eternity bickering and engaging in senseless battles with her unholy brethren. Without cease, soulless beasts fought brutal, bloody battles where there could be no victor and the only reward was unremitting anger.

Eris's third eye provided her a timeless window into the adjacent dimension of the earthly realm from which she'd been dispatched so unceremoniously. The goings-on there, particularly at the Stovall Plantation, were of great interest to her.

The squabbles, shrieks, tormented screams and venomous murmurs were endless, but Xavier was wise and had created with his mind a cavern where he could find solace when he needed to be alone to think.

When his desire peaked, he permitted the most depraved female spirits to share his secluded domain.

Eris joined Xavier in his dank cavern, but was unusually quiet as she kept her inner eye sight focused on the Stovall Plantation. Seething, Eris witnessed Arthur turn his lustful attention to Molly, the kitchen girl. If Eris had had the power to strangle Arthur, the man would surely be dead for having the gall to replace her so easily. However, the delight she derived from witnessing the agony of the betrayed Willyboy, Molly's beau, assuaged her anger…. somewhat.

Molly gave birth to Arthur's son. This infuriated Eris, but again her fury was diminished by the wicked pleasure she derived from watching Edith Stovall's reaction.

Eris's poison had wreaked havoc upon Edith's constitution. Constantly plagued by illness of a female nature, rendered her unable to perform her wifely duties. The humiliation of being openly usurped by Arthur's bed wench, had turned Edith's hair completely gray. Finallly, realizing that she was utterly powerless to keep Molly from Arthur's bed, the mistress of the plantation was forced to swallow the bitter taste of defeat.

Nothing infuriated Eris more than seeing the smile that lit Arthur's face whenever he gazed at his son. Eris's anger was so intense, it became a black mist that swirled about her furiously, sending the nearby wayward spirits into a frenzied fight where they clawed and bit, cursed and spit at each other for what could have been hours or perhaps years if time had existed in the Dark Realm.

Eris made a hissing sound that sent stones and old tree branches hurling when Molly named her little half-breed bastard after Arthur. The little red-head mongrel was nicknamed Artie and ran around the big house as if he owned the damn place.

Edith Stovall, Eris observed, found little satisfaction in life and was becoming sicker with each passing moment. And this time her ailment didn't come from the many elixirs or potions Eris had given her. The fragile woman had taken to bed when Molly first began showing signs of pregnancy and hadn't gotten up since.

Four years passed. Eris knew this because she saw the big birthday celebration in the great yard and watched the little rascal, wiggling as he was turned over his father's knee, while Arthur playfully delivered four birthday spankings and one more to grow on.

Sweet little Molly had turned out to be a seasoned temptress. How had Eris not noticed that the timid little house slave was nothing more than a shameless home wrecker?

Eris could hear Arthur's thoughts and to her dismay, images of her and their nights of passion never crossed his mind. He didn't give Eris so much as a thought—not one second of any day.

On the day that his debilitated wife finally died, Eris watched Arthur slip the wedding band off Edith's skeletal finger. He gave Molly Edith's ring. And although it wasn't a legal marriage, he promised to honor Molly with the same privileges as a legal wife.

Molly was wearing the ring that Eris had coveted. *Molly* was now the mistress of the house—barking orders to the slaves—living the lavish lifestyle that Eris had worked so hard to acquire.

Eris had put far too much energy into her relationship with that weakling, Arthur. She'd plied him with too much of her womanhood for him to have the audacity to forget she'd ever existed. She didn't even entertain thoughts of chastising those overseers who'd caused her to suffer the agonizing death that sent her unwilling soul to a lowly realm most unbefitting a goddess such as herself.

And for that transgression, Arthur and his descendants for generations to come will pay dearly, she vowed.

"What are you going to do about it?" Xavier asked Eris, sensually dragging a long fingernail down her back, splitting the flesh, which oozed a thick pus-like substance instead of blood. Eris threw her head back and emitted a sound similar to a wolf's howl. Pain was pleasure in the Dark Realm. Giving and receiving pain was the only benefit of being held captive on that lower dimension.

"You're getting stronger," he told her.

Eris snorted. "Strong enough to pierce the barrier that confines me to this despicable place?"

"It's possible."

"Then why are you still here?"

"Timing," he advised, arching a furry brow.

"What's that supposed to mean? You're being vague. If there's a way out of here, then tell me. I'm weary of playing the voyeur. The pleasure from that exercise is quickly diminishing."

"Patience." Xavier's lips twisted into a smirk.

"Stop toying with me," Eris warned.

"Or you'll do what?"

"Ignore you," she said haughtily. "Deny you my magnificent presence..." She paused and gave him a malicious sneer. "Without me, what would you do?"

Xavier turned away and snapped his fingers. Within seconds a young girl with only one intact leg appeared. Her other limb was bloody and mangled, having been ripped off at the knee during a recent skirmish. Bringing the amputee down to the serrated and smoking floor, Xavier mounted her from behind. His penis instantly extended to the length and flexibility of a lion's tail; the head formed into the shape of a closed fist. The young girl growled in ecstasy; with each wave of passion, her malformed limb lifted and quivered uncontrollably.

Unwilling to control her jealousy and mounting sexual desire, Eris climbed upon Xavier and savagely sank her teeth into the back of his neck. He didn't respond. Eris dismounted him and wedged her head in between the space where Xavier penetrated the girl, caressing his slippery phallus with her tongue.

Now finding the girl useless, Xavier pushed her away and fed Eris a mouthful of his thick, milky fluid that flowed in a steady stream. When the stream dwindled to a slow drip, Xavier recharged by changing the tip of his phallus from a fist to a pointed arrow, imparting to Eris the most superb pain she'd ever experienced during her captivity in the bowels of hell.

Chapter 5

The Civil War came and went. Slaves were freed and decades upon decades passed; the Stovall family scattered all over the States. Though Arthur had Stovall cousins, nephews, and nieces who were white, the only child he had fathered had been with Molly, therefore, almost every trace of his white blood had been obliterated. Tracking his black descendents was exhausting, requiring intensive third-eye activity; thus, Eris kept her probing eye on the old plantation, making sure her box of jewelry was still buried exactly where she'd left it.

Arthur was long dead and his soul hadn't made as much as a pit stop in Eris's world. If he had, she would have interrogated him about that wedding ring she longed for.

"Who has it? Which of your bastard spawn?" she would have demanded, threatening the simple man with pain he had no idea could bring such delightful pleasure. Ah, but that was just a fantasy. Arthur had gone on to some other place.

"Xavier?" she asked. "How can I keep track of earthly time?"

"Time is an illusion; haven't you heard?"

"Earthly beings believe in the progression of time; I want to view it through their eyes."

"Use your third eye."

"I try, but only certain events are revealed to me."

Xavier lifted a brow. "Many changes have occurred. The black man has been educated. They're business owners, educators and even politicians.

The last time I glimpsed an earthly calendar, I saw the year nineteen hundred and seventy-five."

"How long ago was that?" Eris inquired. "It could have been as recent as the last time I blinked an eye or as long ago as the span of a human lifetime."

"And what is your concern about time?" Xavier wanted to know.

"It seems old houses and buildings are being destroyed while new structures take their place."

"And why does that concern you?" Xavier asked.

"I've got beautiful gemstones, diamonds and gold, a treasure chest concealed in an unsightly wooden box. It's buried in the ground. I must collect my jewels before they're discovered."

"So what is it you want to know?"

"I must claim my belongings. I must get out of here. Show me how!" Eris wrung her hands frantically.

Xavier threw his head back and roared with laughter. When he finished laughing, he took on a serious tone. "It's not that difficult. You could have left long ago."

"Why didn't you tell me?"

"I like your company," he said with sardonic laughter. "I'll tell you this… I'm leaving very soon. Why not join me?"

Eris became so excited by the possibility of breaking out of the prison called hell, black dust swirled and wind whipped around her, making great crashing sounds of destruction.

"Calm down, Eris," Xavier advised.

"I'll join you; what's your plan?" she inquired.

"I intend to be reborn."

Eris scowled. "Reborn? As an infant?"

"Yes. We could emerge as twins or I could find you a human vessel in close proximity."

"Why would you want to risk being a helpless infant?"

"I've got it all figured out. My parents have already been selected."

"That sounds very sweet," she said sarcastically. "But I don't have the time or patience to endure infancy and adolescence. I need to collect my treasures NOW!"

Eris's frustration, like an impending hurricane, caused stones and tree branches to hurl through the air. Xavier gave her a stern look, which she heeded, and aside from the persistent clamor of the inhabitants of hell, calm was restored.

"That bitch, soon to be my mother, was my wife—my queen—before she slit my throat..." Xavier lifted his chin and revealed the scar. "My future father—a cousin of mine who took over my kingdom and sat on my throne."

"How long ago?"

"Thousands of years ago. But I'm a patient man and the time is finally right."

"Ah, so you've been concerned with time also."

"Not really." He shrugged. "I could have left eons ago or I could choose to remain here for several more centuries. Souls jump in and out of bodies, reincarnating at a rapid speed. I happen to like the lifestyle my future parents are living. Thus, the present suits my needs." Xavier gave a satisfied sigh.

"*He* currently has a senate seat; *she* will be the first female Vice President of the United States by the time I'm five years old. Of course, I'll be a precocious child." Xavier rubbed his hands together in glee. "Oh, what a delicious scandal it will be when Madame Vice President is caught in a compromising position with her own child." Xavier exploded in wicked laughter.

While Eris enjoyed the story, she feared Xavier would leave the Dark Realm before she was able. With her thoughts racing, desperate to concoct an escape plan, Eris gave only a mirthless smile.

"She'll be vilified. Branded. Condemned a filthy pedophile." Gazing into the future, Xavier looked enthralled by what he saw.

"Xavier," she said sternly. "I refuse to be reborn. There must be a way for me to abscond from this awful place and maintain the beautiful form I've designed." Her hand proudly swept the top of her head and traveled to her bosom.

Xavier pondered her dilemma. "Hmm. Then you must locate a human target."

"Yes..."

"And begin communication while the human sleeps."

"That's the extent of it?"

"Yes, but you'll be required to dwell between both worlds. You'll dwell on Earth in spirit and here in your true form."

"Absolutely not," she protested as she shook her head emphatically. "I will not exist on Earth as a mere spirit—as a useless puff of smoke. I want to return in human form—my *own* form. I must return as Eris, the beautiful goddess."

Ignoring her, Xavier paced impatiently.

"Do you know who I am?" There was pride in her tone; a suggestion of unrevealed power.

Though his curiosity was piqued, Xavier continued to pace as if he had more important issues on his mind.

"I am Eris, the Goddess of Discord. I was banished from the goddess realm and sent to Earth as punishment. Having to accept the limitations of mortal flesh was intended to be a punishment worse than death, but I quickly learned to enjoy my physical body. Would you believe that I was able to retain limited use of my goddess powers while living as a human?"

Eris smiled mockingly. "The punishment was a mere slap on the wrist. I enjoyed the dim-witted mortals and found living in the flesh to be quite delightful. But when that body was destroyed by fire—" she gave a huge sigh—"my spirit was not allowed back into the comfort and opulence of the goddess realm—my original home."

She gave a bitter chortle. "On Earth, I became comfortable and arrogant, but worse, I underestimated my foes. The penalty was cruel and merciless." She turned her back to Xavier, lowered her head. She studied the ashen ground as she relived her fear, her terror and her rage when her human body was set aflame. It was a harsh and entirely inappropriate punishment—completely unbefitting a goddess.

Shaking away the painful memory, Eris looked up. With her gaze sharpened upon Xavier, she said, "I intend to return and reclaim my jewels. More important, I intend to have my revenge."

"That can be tricky."

"Will you help me or not?"

"To accomplish all of that, you're going to have to consume the life force of a human female."

"All right. How?"

"It's extremely difficult." He stroked her chin; Eris jerked away. Xavier raised his clawed hands in surrender. "Eris," he said in a seductive hiss. "It's so much easier to claim a new body at the moment of that soul's birth. Join me. Earthlings will be nothing more than our personal playthings. Together, we'll reign as the king and queen of terror."

She shook her head vehemently. "Continue your explanation of the alternative."

Xavier sighed long and hard. "Stubbornness does not become you." Growing weary of the verbal battle, he asked, "Your human target will be male, correct?"

"Of course. I intend to seek revenge upon a male descendant of the Stovall family."

Using his thumb claw, Xavier plucked soot from beneath the claw of each finger. "Until you've located your target," he said sulkily, "there's nothing more I can do for you." He turned away, indicating his unwillingness to discuss the topic further.

Agitated, Eris blurted, "How much time do I have?"

Xavier whirled around to face her. "Time! You're much too obsessed with time. My dear wicked one," he said condescendingly, "you're eternal; you have until infinity."

Eris snarled at Xavier and then spoke in a low hissing tone. "By Earth's time measures, when do you depart this realm?"

He looked off in thought. "By Earth's time measures? Hmm. You have just a few days to locate your target. I'll be traveling down a putrid birth canal, with the single-minded purpose of wreaking havoc by the end of the Earth week."

Eris narrowed her eyes. "It's not guaranteed that you'll reach adulthood. The woman you seek to harm may recognize you or catch on to your little scheme. Who knows…she might drown you soon after birth!" Eris laughed. Her laughter, more like a cackle, echoed throughout the smoky abyss.

"You'll need protection during your infancy and toddler years, I could protect you." With eyes that ridiculed him, Eris slithered up to Xavier.

Worry lines formed on Xavier's forehead. "How could *you* protect me?" he asked, attempting to sound superior.

"Perhaps I could be your governess…" She paused and dug her fingernails into his chest. Breaking the skin around his nipples, she pulled him to her. He emitted a low, lustful howl as his male appendage, which had resumed its normal size and shape, once again began to expand. Annoyed, Xavier pressed the pesky tentacle against his leg and held it in place.

"Continue," he demanded, now using both hands to restrain the writhing beast.

"As I said, I could assume the role of governess or even better…I could be your wet nurse as well. What a privilege to be able to suckle these." Eris caressed her large breasts and then squeezed together the beautiful dark mounds of flesh. "Do you think your mother—the future vice president—will spare the time to lend her tit?"

"I surrender, I'll assist you in locating your target and I'll tell you everything I know about sleep penetration and siphoning the female life force."

"Excellent! When?" she asked, delighted that Xavier had finally given in.

Xavier released his throbbing appendage. Although it hadn't grown to its previous length, it was as thick as Eris's forearm and was covered with hardened scabs that resembled metal spikes. "After we attend to this matter of pressing need, I'll combine the power of my third eye with yours and together we'll bring forth a mighty searchlight that will scour the Earth until it shines upon your coveted Stovall male. You'll need the life force of his female counterpart, but in order to siphon her spirit, she, too, will have to be in an altered state of consciousness."

"I don't want to be anyone else. I want to retain my goddess status."

"And you will," he said, patting Eris patiently, all the while thinking what a pity it was that Eris didn't realize she'd lost her goddess status and had been reduced to being a lost soul—a demon—the moment she was cast from the Goddess Realm. To ensure his carnal pleasures be satiated, he decided it would do no harm to placate her, thus Xavier didn't enlighten Eris.

"The woman will become a mere shell of her former self," Xavier went on with passion in his voice. "People like her, who've had their spirit devoured, usually end up in the throes of physical and mental anguish as result of the attack, particularly when attacked by a superior entity with goddess qualities," he added for Eris's benefit. "But be careful! Don't siphon too much. You'll want your victim to survive and continually provide you with her precious life force," Xavier explained wearing a broad smile. He flicked more ashes from his claws.

Eris was elated to get the information. Feeling satisfied, she reclined upon the blistering soot and spread her legs, anticipating the pleasure of the pain that would soon rip through her flesh and soothe her anxious soul.

Chapter 6

PHILADELPHIA, PENNSYLVANIA
PRESENT DAY

*L*ate again, Bryce Stovall parked haphazardly and raced into his office building. He shot into the elevator just before the doors closed, exhaled and checked the time. He was already a half-hour late.

Good morning, Bryce! Morning, my man. How's it going, Bryce? He was greeted by his co-workers with a cheerful enthusiasm that he did not welcome. A man who was a half-hour late and who had been called on the carpet for tardiness too many times to count should have been allowed to slink by and creep into his office undetected—at least until he could spread some papers around his desk and give the impression that he'd been hard at work for the past thirty minutes.

Bryce's new boss, Grayson Swain, was out to get him. And it wasn't just Bryce's imagination. The little twerp had a Napoleon complex and Bryce, a mortgage loan officer, an exemplary employee of five years, deserved better treatment than he'd been getting at the hands of his new clock-watching boss. Since Napoleon had taken over his department, Bryce had been put on probation for excessive tardiness. It was degrading and emasculating, but no matter how hard he tried, he just couldn't get to work on time anymore.

His livelihood was on the line and that was a disgraceful shame.

Bryce had a strong work ethic and had always received sparkling evaluations from his superiors—until now. It really wasn't his fault. He was sleep-deprived. Something continuously interrupted his slumber; this resulted in his getting only a few hours' sleep each night.

He'd gone to his doctor and was prescribed sleeping pills. They'd worked for a couple of nights but now weren't helping at all. Consequently every morning, he endured the same appalling ordeal. The alarm would sound, he'd hit the snooze button. Then five minutes later, he'd hit the button again. Then, in a confused state, he'd turn the blasted thing off, telling himself he'd get up on his own in five or ten minutes.

But by the time he'd awaken, his sweat-drenched T-shirt was the first sign that it wasn't going to be a good day. Shooting a panic-stricken look at the bedside clock, he'd utter a cry of despair upon discovering that an entire hour had elapsed, leaving him only a few minutes to shower and shave and navigate through agonizingly slow-moving morning traffic.

Every morning for the past month, Bryce slung his briefcase in the car, jumped inside and turned the radio to KYW News, listening intently to the traffic report. Should he take the Schuylkill Expressway? Kelly Drive? Should he take the shortcut through Fairmount Park? Depending on the mood of the city, driving through the park sometimes wasn't a shortcut at all.

Sleep deprivation was beginning to show on his face: his appearance was shabby and his work...well....his sales were dropping at an alarming rate. His well-organized life had somehow switched channels and had become a chaotic living hell.

And then there was the matter of Ajali.

An image of his beautiful fiancée caused his shoulders to slump in despair. His soon-to-be *ex-fiancée*, he reminded himself and sank into his swivel chair. He had to cancel the wedding; it was the right thing to do. But knowing that taking this drastic action was going to cause Ajali grief and humiliation was an unbearable burden that was slowly eroding his soul.

He had to call off the wedding! The absurdity of the notion still hadn't completely sunk in. There was no acceptable explanation for what he had to do. There were no words that could explain his reasoning. If he spoke the truth he'd be required to exchange his custom sport jacket for a strait-jacket and a one-way ticket to a mental institution.

It had all started about a month ago. One night as he was sleeping, some-one or some*thing* called his name. The *Voice* was soft and feminine. It seduced him. Lured him away from a peaceful dream. The sound of his name had seemed so close; he could still feel the warmth of the breath that had tickled his ear. His confused mind struggled to rationalize the strange occurrence. Ah—clarity hit him—Ajali must have spent the night but in his disoriented state, he'd simply forgotten. But when he reached out to touch her, there was only emptiness on the other side of the bed.

Refusing to accept that he was alone in the room, he pulled back the covers and even got down on his knees and searched under the bed. Scratching his head, Bryce made a trip to the bathroom and then climbed back into bed. Okay, maybe he was losing it after all; he chuckled to himself and drifted off to sleep.

In the midst of a sweet dream that included Ajali, Bryce found himself suddenly and inexplicably standing alone at the top of a tall building. Curious, he walked to the building's edge and peered down at the busy world beneath him. But he lost his balance and began to fall.

His descent seemed to last an eternity. But instead of crashing to his death he landed on a soft bed of feathers and rolled over into the waiting arms of a strange, but devastatingly beautiful, dark-skinned woman, with eyes, an odd shade of blue. He looked around desperately for Ajali, but she was nowhere to be found.

The woman was naked; her magnificent breasts were so full and perfectly shaped, they looked as if they'd been sculpted. He couldn't take his eyes off the beautiful orbs. She seemed to understand his attraction—his fascination—and gently guided him to her bosom, urging him to part his lips. To suck. And when he did, he was hit with an instant feeling of déjà vu.

He felt embarrassed but couldn't resist the urge to suckle. At first he sucked gently, timidly, taking in just a few drops at a time. The warm liquid was so comfortingly familiar and oh so sweet, that soon Bryce began to nurse with the urgency of a starving newborn.

It was ludicrous…a full-grown man being breastfed, but in the dream state it seemed completely normal and perfectly acceptable.

The woman fondled him soothingly and murmured words he didn't understand; however, as she eased a breast from lips that held a firm suction, she spoke his name clearly and told him: *I'll return on the first full moon.*

Bryce awakened instantly. There was a foul odor in the air and an acrid taste in his mouth. Sleepily, he stumbled into the bathroom, again. After relieving himself, he looked in the bathroom mirror. What the hell? He looked awful. And that taste! It was terrible. He ran his tongue over the roof of his mouth. His tongue felt thickly coated. The taste was disgusting. He grimaced and grabbed his toothbrush and the tube of toothpaste. When he opened his mouth to brush his teeth, he let out a horrible scream. His tongue was completely white; coated with thrush. No, it was beyond thrush. His tongue was covered with thrush that was so thick, clumps had begun to form—clumps that resembled curdled milk.

In a panic, he frantically ran the toothbrush's bristles over his tongue, gagging as he brushed and spit out the despicable clumps. Bryce brushed long and hard—until his tongue was pink and felt tender. And then he rinsed out his mouth at least a dozen times before he returned to bed.

He'd completely forgotten the dream the next morning while on the phone with a client—Arlene Jaworski, a new mother who said she and her husband wanted to get a home equity loan to make an addition to their house for their expanding family. While Bryce was looking over the Jaworskis' credit history and working out some figures, he heard a baby cry.

"Oops! That's the baby," the woman said unnecessarily. "I'm so glad we installed an intercom system. Excuse me for a sec; I have to run upstairs and get the baby. I'll be back in a jiff," she assured him in a merry tone.

"Sure, go right ahead; take your time," Bryce said absently as he pored over the figures on his computer screen.

"Little Tyler must be starving. Luckily, I'm breastfeeding, so I don't have to heat up a bottle," Mrs. Jaworski added cheerfully.

And then he remembered the dream. And the slime balls he'd spit out of his mouth the night before. No wonder his tongue had felt so sore all morning. He'd practically brushed the taste buds out of his mouth.

Oh Jesus! What the hell kind of dream was that? Badly shaken, he told his breastfeeding client that he'd call her back after he crunched some more numbers.

But he didn't. Too frazzled to talk to a nursing mother, he passed the Jaworski account onto Jeri Paynter, a friend and co-worker.

Later that day, Jeri stuck her head in Bryce's office. Bryce was staring at his desk calendar. Jeri cleared her throat. "Hey, buddy. How's it going?"

Bryce looked up. "Good; good. I'm great," he lied.

Jeri nodded politely. "By the way, your clients, the Jaworskis, passed with flying colors. I was able to get them eighty thousand and at a great interest rate."

Bryce nodded and tried to offer a congratulatory smile, but he was deeply troubled and couldn't quite pull off the smile.

"Just out of curiosity," Jeri pressed on, "why'd you pass up that commission? Did a dead relative leave you a fortune?" she asked, laughing.

"Uh, I'm busy right now, Jeri. Can we talk a little later?"

She looked stung by the brush-off. "Sure, Bryce," she said. "Do you want your door closed?"

"Yeah. Thanks, Jeri," he said, finally able to manage a smile. A lopsided sad smile.

He looked at the calendar again. There had not been a full moon the night before; but, checking the lunar calendar he'd found on the Internet, he knew there would be a full moon tonight.

Did this mean that woman—that *thing*—was coming back tonight? Oh God! He couldn't go through that again. It was crazy, but there was no way he was sleeping alone in his apartment when that nightmarish woman had promised to return on the first full moon.

He picked up his phone and called Ajali. "Hey, honey. Whatcha doin'?" He tried to sound upbeat.

"Pretending I'm working, but I'm actually working on our wedding budget, trying to cut the cost of this crazy-high catering bill. Honey, are you sure your distant cousins from Virginia are coming to the wedding? They haven't sent back an RSVP. Maybe we could just take them off the list."

"Sure. No problem. Look, I called to see if you wanted some company tonight."

"Uh…Well, some of the girls were coming over to help me with the wedding favors," Ajali replied.

"They're not staying all night, are they?"

"Of course not. What time do you want me to put everybody out?"

"Around nine?"

"Okay, baby. See you at nine. Smooches." Ajali kissed into the phone three times.

Bryce didn't reciprocate, but he'd make up for it when he kissed her on the lips tonight in bed. There, he'd already forgotten that he had to cancel the wedding. He loved Ajali, but this night creature was confusing him, playing tricks with his mind.

Chapter 7

*H*is overnight bag was packed. A fresh shirt and suit hung in a zippered travel bag. He checked his watch; it was only seven o'clock so to pass the time, he watched a repeat episode of *Law & Order*.

Lying across his bed as he watched TV was a grievous error. Bryce got too comfortable and fell asleep. Deeply asleep. He didn't hear the phone ring at nine-thirty and he didn't hear Ajali's urgent voice on his answering machine.

But he heard *The Voice* whispering his name. In that in-between state of consciousness when one is not quite asleep and not quite awake, Bryce struggled to become fully alert. He was almost there, but something was overpowering him, pulling him back into that dark dreamy place that he now feared.

The Voice cajoled him, calling him sweetly. Invisible fingers drew him deeper into the abyss. But he fought the overwhelming dark force that tried to lure him back to sleep. Bryce thrashed and kicked; he would not surrender. He tried to yell for help, but no sound escaped his lips. He banged his head against the headboard, but was still held in the dark and powerful grip.

He slapped and scratched his own face; he'd do anything to wake up. More frightened than he'd ever been in his life, he stopped fighting for a split second and tried to gather his thoughts; maybe he was going about it all wrong. Furious, he began cursing in his mind: *Let me go, bitch!* The darkness persisted and grew stronger. *Get the fuck off me!* The invisible force became excited; gleeful, in fact.

By the time Bryce realized that his anger and the use of profanity strengthened his enemy, it was too late. His eyes opened wide. Floating above him was a smoky outline of the woman in his dreams. She lowered her beautiful ethereal body over Bryce and looked him directly in the eye, mesmerizing and paralyzing him at once with her intoxicating beauty. His eyes, the only part of his body able to move, blinked in terror.

No longer able to put up a fight, Bryce's consciousness was being slowly and seductively dragged into a place where he and Eris would engage in unspeakable ghostly sexuality.

For a brief moment, just before he was engulfed by the darkness, he shifted his eyes toward the bedroom window and caught a glimpse of the bright full moon.

Cradled by limbs that felt more like tentacles than arms, Bryce screamed to be released. But Eris held him tight and nuzzled him, speaking seductively in his ear. When she pushed her heavy breasts against his face, Bryce clenched his teeth and pressed his lips together until they felt as if they were sealed shut. He refused to be enticed again into drinking this creature's foul curdled milk.

Oddly, he could feel her hot flesh against his. And to his horror he discovered he was naked. What happened to his clothes—the jeans, T-shirt, and sneakers he'd been wearing? Oh, dear God, why was this happening to him?

Eris kissed and licked at his tightly closed lips. A shiver of pleasure ran up his spine, but Bryce fought temptation and kept his mouth clamped shut.

Then Eris lowered her mouth and began to nibble at Bryce's neck. He shuddered involuntarily but remained unyielding and rigid. Until she slithered down his body on her belly and began sucking his balls. He cried out in passion…he cried out in fear as her hot tongue darted out and traveled from his scrotum to his aching manhood.

His frazzled mind couldn't begin to comprehend what was taking place. The woman was giving him an indescribable feeling of intense pleasure. It felt so good; he began to babble. Hearing incoherent nonsense pouring from his lips frightened him. Then Bryce suddenly realized that he wasn't babbling. He was speaking in a foreign tongue.

It was an ancient language he had no conscious awareness of knowing. Yet he fully understood every strange syllable that came forth from the depths of his soul to gush from his lips: a plea to the gods to spare him—to save his soul, for he felt that his very essence was being sucked away as the strange woman undulated on her belly like a snake, darting out a long and fiery forked tongue.

His face contorted into a pre-ejaculatory grimace and then he woke up.

"I was worried sick about you. I called all night and I've been trying to reach you at the office all morning. Didn't you get any of my messages?" Ajali shouted.

"No, baby, I'm so sorry. I had a headache and took something for it and the next thing I knew, I was out like a light. When I woke up, it was time for work." Bryce whispered into the phone, "I slept so hard, I overslept. I was late for work again. Real late."

"Oh honey, that's a shame. I'm sorry. Did you get in trouble?"

"Not yet. But Napoleon wants to have a word with me. I'll call you later, okay?"

"Okay, sweetie. Smooches."

Bryce quickly clicked Ajali off the line. He couldn't get into their smooches ritual. Not today. He was a troubled man, being haunted in bed at night and abused on the job by day. Giving out smooches over the phone was entirely out of the question.

But aside from that, the nocturnal activity had him feeling like he was cheating on Ajali. Maybe he was having a hard time distinguishing between illusions and reality. One moment he felt strongly that he had to stop the wedding and the next moment everything seemed fine.

The condition of his dick, however, was real. It was raw. Red and chafed as if he'd been fucking all night long. If Ajali had just a glimpse at what she liked to refer to as *her* love tool, she would have had serious doubts about his fidelity, too.

It was all so absurd. He felt like he was going insane. He thought about seeing a psychiatrist, but the escalating penile pain convinced him that he needed to get an appointment with his family physician.

Napoleon's secretary broke into his thoughts, informing him that "Grayson Swain will see you now."

Bryce looked at the piece of paper and couldn't believe his eyes, and when his boss started talking, he couldn't believe his ears.

"I don't know how my predecessor ran things, but I run a tight ship," Grayson said smugly. "When you've finished reading that, sign it so I can send the form down to Human Resources. Consider this a verbal warning. But the next time you're late, you'll get a written warning. And if the tardiness continues...well, look at your employee handbook and you'll see that the next step is security escorting you out the front door. I don't want to have to resort to such extreme measures; so do us both a favor, pal, and start getting your ass to work on time." Grayson Swain chuckled and then offered his hand to conclude the humiliating encounter in a gentlemanly fashion.

Bryce was six foot three and could have picked the little dwarf up and rammed his head into the wall. But, of course, he restrained himself and actually accepted the hand that was extended, shook it like a man and walked out of his boss's office feeling like a two-inch prick.

He needed the comfort of Ajali's love more now than ever. His ego was badly bruised and his nights were being haunted by creepy illicit sex. But he felt so unworthy, so unclean. His penis was covered with strange welts. He gingerly ran a finger over his impaired member and winced. His dick hurt like hell. No, he couldn't go near Ajali—at least not sexually until he sought the help of a physician. For a man who planned to be married in less than a month, his life had certainly taken a horribly strange turn. There was no joy in his life. And until his problem was resolved there was nothing that could make him smile.

He called his doctor's office and made an emergency appointment for that evening after work.

Frowning down at Bryce's chart, the doctor entered the examining room. "So what are your symptoms? Do you have a discharge?"

"No," Bryce said, his eyes darting nervously. Having to explain his predicament was extremely embarrassing. "I've got some...um...strange welts...scratches...burns or something," he said, feeling mortified.

"Does your partner have a yeast infection? If so, your symptoms could be the result of—"

"Uh, no. I don't think so."

"Herpes?"

"Of course not!" Bryce said vehemently, but worry filled his eyes. Ajali was as pure as the driven snow, but that night demon... He thought about the slimy milk curdles. Ugh! Who knew what diseases she was infested with?

"Okaaay," the doctor said, sounding doubtful as he gave Bryce a significant look.

Feeling more humiliated than he could ever recall experiencing, Bryce opened the gown and revealed his limp penis.

With a surgically gloved hand, the doctor examined Bryce's limp member, which embarrassingly began to spring to life in the doctor's hand. The doctor pulled it to the right and then the left. He lifted it and checked the underside as well as the scrotum. "I don't see anything," he said as he scooted backward on the wheeled stool, removed the gloves and tossed them in a waste can.

Shocked, Bryce examined himself. His penis was smooth, even-colored and flawless. "There were welts and something like little blisters when I woke up this morning..."

"Are you under some kind of stress, son?" The doctor's tone became gentle—concerned.

"No. Well...yes. I'm getting married soon..."

The doctor erupted into laughter. "Last-minute jitters, huh?"

Bryce joined in the laugher, but his chuckling held a nervous edge. "Look, Doc, I'm having some trouble sleeping. Do you think you could prescribe something that will help me get through the night?"

"Sure. But if you saw visible lesions, we could be talking about herpes."

"I didn't say lesions," Bryce said indignantly. "I said there was something that looked like welts or scratches."

"Well, it would probably be a good idea for me to draw some blood and you know—run a few tests."

"No, that's okay. The marks are gone. It probably just caught in my zipper or something," Bryce said, unconvinced. Feeling relieved that his now unblemished penis no longer looked as if it had been scratched and burned, Bryce gratefully stuffed himself back inside his pants.

"Well, Mr. Stovall," the doctor said, "if your upcoming marriage is causing you this type of trouble, causing you to exhibit psychosomatic symptoms, it might be wise to get some type of counseling before the big day. You know what I mean?"

Bryce nodded dumbly.

Clutching a prescription for sleeping pills, Bryce headed for the nearest Rite-Aid pharmacy. He now had some protection. The pills would help him sleep without interruption. *The Voice* could call all she wanted, but he wouldn't hear it. No more forced feeding on sour milk, no more hot licks from an amazingly long and fiery forked tongue. No more waking up to semen-stained sheets. The pills would knock him out completely and give him some badly needed, peaceful sleep.

Chapter 8

THE DARK REALM

"He's blocking me; I can't get through!" Eris screeched.

Xavier shrugged. "I've told you everything I know. You've had fun with your target; stop obsessing, wicked one. Move on to someone else."

"Someone else!" she shouted incredulously.

"Yes, surely there are other male descendants of Arthur Stovall," Xavier said, maintaining a tone of calm indifference. "After all these years, there must be hundreds of them. Hundreds of nocturnal playmates—all yours for the taking," he said; now placating her as he seductively clawed a trail of broken skin down her arm. His male organ began to pulsate.

Disgusted, Eris jerked her arm away. She laughed at him; it was a guttural malicious sound. "I'm not interested in lying in the soot with you. I've acquired a craving for human sex; nothing else can satisfy me now."

"Is that so?" He tried to sound unconcerned as he covered his shrinking appendage.

"Yes, and I've been doing some seeing of my own," she said snidely.

"Oh really? You've actually been snooping around behind my back?"

"That's right. I'm a goddess, remember? I have powers far superior to your half-blind third eye."

Xavier flinched. "How did you know my third-eye vision has become impaired?"

Eris responded with mocking laughter.

Recovering from the insulting blow to his ego, Xavier continued to query her. "If you possess such superior power, then why are you disturbing me?

If you were using your third eye properly, you'd know that I'll be departing this realm shortly. Ah! I forgot! Despite your unique *goddess* qualities, you have no concept of time! How interesting," he added with a roar of spiteful laughter.

"Touché, Xavier."

"Leave me," he hissed at her. "I'm mentally preparing for my important journey into the physical realm. A place, I might add, that *you* can only experience by creeping like a thief into the bed where an unsuspecting innocent sleeps."

Eris's narrowed eyes gave off angry azure-colored glints, which set off sparks inside Xavier's cavern. She closed her eyes and calmed herself.

"That's better," Xavier said. "I'm in no mood for stamping out flames."

"Xavier." Eris softened her tone. "Forgive my temper and unkind words."

Reluctantly, Xavier nodded. However, he sensed she had more to say and was curious.

"I've been shut out by a force that I don't understand; I cannot penetrate the dreams of my Stovall man."

"As I said," he bellowed, "find another! I don't have the time or the inclination to help you with this obsessive search. And as you so unkindly reminded me, my vision is not what it used be. Thus, you're limited to using a single searchlight as you scour the Earth once more for the prized Stovall kin."

"I discovered something," Eris said in a whisper.

"What?" Xavier sarcastically mimicked her whispered tone.

"Bryce Stovall is not an ordinary descendant. He's not even kin."

"So why the big ado about nothing?"

"In desperation, after being locked away from Bryce's dreams, I borrowed some of your vision..."

He jabbed the middle of his forehead, the site of the invisible third eye. "*You* caused this impairment? *You* stole the vision from my third eye?" Xavier waved his arms around in a fury, causing a tremendous storm of dust.

"It was an accident. I planned to return your vision, but I couldn't. I never meant to harm you," Eris said regretfully.

"Luckily for you, where I'm going, I won't need my third eye."

Eris bowed her head, relieved that she'd been forgiven. "Unable to penetrate Bryce's dreams, I decided to halt further dalliance with insignificant kin and place the focus of my revenge upon the true perpetrator—Arthur Stovall.

"Using our combined vision," she said softly, apologetically, "I discovered a very tiny portal that I could slip through for limited visitation to other realms. To my great dismay, Arthur Stovall was nowhere to be found."

"You're confusing me, wicked one. But I'm enchanted by your tenacity; your strong desire for revenge is...stimulating." Xavier had to use his forearm to restrain his manhood, which had sprung up to the size and density of a wooden club. "Please go on," he encouraged, with an uncomfortable scowl as he wrangled with his male appendage.

"I began my search on the lower realms. Beneath this realm, there are five others, but he wasn't on any of those levels. Next, I ascended to the higher realms—and, I might add, gaining admittance was not easy." Eris looked away briefly. "A rival, Tara, the Goddess of Peace and Protection, had the audacity to block my entry into the fifth dimension, a higher realm where I once enjoyed the freedom of coming and going at will."

Eris looked mystified. "Oddly, I couldn't overthrow Tara; her strength was far superior to mine. Isn't that peculiar, Xavier? And standing close by was the Goddess Kali, a ferocious and most unattractive goddess. Kali stood in a combative stance as if to back up Tara if I gained admittance." She shook her head, confused. "Why would the goddesses prevent me from seeking information? I've served my time on Earth. I should be able to dwell among my own people now. No offense to you, Xavier, but I don't belong in this hellhole with you degenerates."

He shrugged and smiled innocently. "No offense taken. I rather like it here, but I like Earth better. But back to the topic that concerns you...I don't know how to answer those questions. What do I know of goddess matters? I've always dwelled on this dark, lower realm."

Eris nodded; she understood that Xavier knew nothing of the Goddess Realm. Still, she was insulted and would soon deal with the Goddess Tara. She'd prefer not to battle the Goddess Kali, who was known as being a mighty goddess who could easily overcome obstacles and who had a particular fondness for children, saving them from physical and spiritual danger. Just the thought of the meddling Kali caused angry sparks to appear and crackle in the air. What was Kali's business with her? There were no children involved in Eris's diabolical plan.

In due time, she would wage war against Tara and Kali as well if she had to. Then, she'd regain admittance to her true home. But in the meantime, she had pending business on the earthly realm.

Xavier interrupted Eris's vengeful thoughts. "Please continue," he said impatiently. "What were your findings regarding the Stovall man?"

"Arthur Stovall wasn't on any of the realms but there was a record of his existence and the time he'd spent there."

"Oh! They keep records, do they?" Xavier stroked a doubtful arched brow.

Eris ignored the sarcasm. "The records are kept in a place that's between the higher and lower realms. There is a book of life called *The Akashic Records*. That book holds not only man's collective consciousness, but the entire history of every individual ever born since the dawn of civilization."

"Fascinating, do go on," Xavier said.

"I discovered that Arthur Stovall was reborn in 1981 and returned as Bryce Stovall," Eris said excitedly. "Although it's rare for a soul to return within its own family, Arthur was a white slave owner who felt he owed a karmic debt to African Americans."

"To whom?"

"Slaves. The former slaves are called African Americans now."

"I see. And that would include you, correct?"

"There's no record of my birth; I've assumed many forms, but never have I experienced birth," she said haughtily. "I am a goddess. A goddess who's unjustly trapped in this hellish place," she yelled.

"So tell me more about this human you're so obsessed with."

"Arthur chose to reincarnate as a black man so that he could overcome poverty while experiencing racism, social injustice, intolerance and a host of other undesirable circumstances."

"What on Earth for?"

"For spiritual growth, I suppose. He was always a weak and spineless creature.

After pledging his undying love, he left me to burn, you know. Maybe he reincarnated to finally try to develop a set of balls. Quite frankly, his reason doesn't interest me. I'm beside myself with malicious pleasure. Can you believe that instead of dallying with some watered-down descendant, as I assumed I had been doing, I've actually been causing the original Stovall man to suffer?" Eris rubbed her hands together. "And now I can finally settle the score."

Xavier was quiet—pensive.

"So, I've told my tale. Now I beseech you to assist me. More than ever, I'm determined to break through the barrier he has put up."

"Wicked one..." Xavier spoke gently and shook his head sympathetically. "I have no knowledge of what barriers modern man has developed. But if you'll just be patient and wait until I'm reborn, I'll allow you to penetrate my dreams. In my human form, I'll have a better understanding of the modern day advancements. Now come...." Xavier reached out to Eris. "Come lie with me in the soot."

"Lie with you in the soot!" Eris kicked a clump of ashes that swirled in the air and landed in Xavier's face. Her fierce anger caused his mentally constructed cavern to shake as if being rocked by an earthquake. Wind whipped, water splashed; there was a hurricane inside. Rocks and stones hurled against the walls, cracking the foundation until Xavier's home crumbled to the ground, resuming its original composition of dead leaves and ashes.

Caught up in the whirlwind of Eris's temper, Xavier became so distracted, he withdrew his close attention to his soon-to-be Earth mother and was unaware she had gone into labor. Feeling the pull of a body in need of a soul, Xavier recognized the sensation and quickly transformed himself into mist and whooshed through a tight, dark tunnel until at last he entered a tiny human form.

But something was wrong. In his haste to enter the body, he'd flipped it around and the body was now facing backward. The obstetrician was completely puzzled as to how a normal birth had suddenly changed to a breech. Scratching his head, he ordered an emergency cesarean section.

During the ensuing chaos, a foul odor filled the air in the delivery room, but no one associated the smell with the dark mist that was Eris, who cleverly, albeit uninvited, had also transformed to mist and attached herself to Xavier, accompanying him through the voyage down the birth canal.

Finally free from his mother's womb, Xavier emitted an enormous scream. The doctor was pleased that the child had such healthy lungs, but the poor birth mother could not take her eyes off the dark mist that slowly glided above her and then swirled above the baby to whom the doctors were administering. The dark mist taunted the baby, hovering closely, causing him to howl. Then the mist switched directions and headed for the window.

The baby screamed, there was rage in the sound as he, too, watched the fleeing dark mist. The next sound he released was clearly a word: BITCH!

Eris laughed to herself; she'd been called far worse. Free as a bird, she slipped through the window and streaked across the sky.

Chapter 9

When the smiling faces of the ten o'clock newscasters appeared on TV, Ajali Logan took the remote from Bryce and hit the power button. She tossed the remote on the floor. She hadn't made love to her man in ages, and she'd be damned if they were going to waste another precious moment listening to detailed accounts of other people's lives.

Ajali began the love ritual by smoothing the hair on Bryce's face, and then she began raking her nails through his beard, which she knew would calm him and slowly get him in the mood.

Bryce pulled her hand away and kissed her palm. "I love you so much, baby. I swear to God, I'd die if I didn't have you."

Though she appreciated hearing the words, there was something a little unsettling in his tone. Determining that her uneasy feeling was unfounded, she lightened her mood by suddenly straddling him and playfully pinned down his arms.

"Bryce, I'm not going anywhere. And you better start working out a little harder at the gym because if you ever try to leave me, you're gonna be in for a hell of a fight."

Bryce wrestled Ajali off of him and then pinned her down. She struggled until both hands were free and then she wrapped her arms around his neck and pulled his lips to hers. His kiss was different. He kissed her with his mouth shut; she had to use her tongue to part his reluctant lips, but after a few awkward moments, they established a groove and fell into their usual rhythm. Ajali moaned loudly as the headboard banged against the wall.

Bryce reached for a pillow and placed it between the wall and the headboard to eliminate some of the commotion that was an announcement to his neighbors that he was sexing his baby girl down.

Ajali turned over and got on her hands and knees, pushing backward, inviting Bryce to take her doggy-style. As Bryce positioned himself behind her, she grabbed the other pillow to muffle the screams of passion she'd soon be unable to control.

Afterward, he kissed her and told her good-night, but as she was drifting off to sleep, she felt Bryce get out of bed and plod to the bathroom. In her hazy state, she listened to the medicine cabinet slide open and heard the sound of a cap snapping open and pills being shaken, no doubt into Bryce's hand. Then there was the sound of running water, and the glass door sliding back into place.

Bryce hadn't mentioned anything about being on medication. She found that curious and made a mental note to ask him about it in the morning. When he returned to the bed, he automatically pulled her to him. Lying close to her, he whispered in her ear, "I love you so much, Aj."

"I love you, too, Bryce. Everything's going to be okay." After soothing him with encouraging words, she wondered why she'd felt the need to reassure him. She hadn't a clue, but knew she was responding to some plea from deep inside him; she was merely doing what a loving woman does—giving her man the peace of mind he obviously needed.

"Good-night, baby," she said drowsily and then settled into a comfortable position and fell asleep. As Ajali snored softly, Bryce tossed and turned. The pill wasn't working or maybe her snoring was keeping him from falling asleep. He gently slipped his arms from around her and rolled to his side of the bed. With his back turned to her, he curled in a fetal position and finally drifted to sleep.

Bryyyyyyyyyyce! Terrified, he bolted upright. *The Voice* was back. He shot a glance at Ajali, hoping against hope that it was she who had called his name. "Aj," he whispered, shaking her shoulder just to be sure, but she was in a deep sleep, snoring louder than ever. Torturous memories of the last encounter with that *thing* sent him rushing into the bathroom, where he hastily gulped down another pill. There was no way he could endure a night of depraved sexual activity with a fucking ghost. The double dose of his sleeping medication had an immediate effect. As wonderful sleep began to claim him, he turned toward Ajali and draped an arm around her; inching closer he sniffed the fruity fragrance of her hair.

Then he saw something strange in the dark room. It was just his imagination, he told himself. It had to be. Maybe Aj had left a dress or a jacket draped across the bedroom chair. However, just before sleep claimed him, Bryce saw a misty, ethereal form of a woman. She seemed to be sitting in the chair, leaning forward with glowing eyes that glared at him and Ajali. He could have sworn sparks flickered from the eyes of the ghostly being, briefly lighting the room.

And then Bryce descended into the darkness of sleep. Mercifully, he was able to sleep though the night.

Ajali awoke feeling sexually satisfied, invigorated, happy and in love. Swinging her legs off the bed, she trotted to the kitchen and made a pot of coffee.

Complaining that the cup she made was too weak, Bryce poured it down the drain. He'd been so caring the night before and after hearing him express such sweet words of everlasting love, Ajali was surprised and disappointed that Bryce seemed to have awakened on the wrong side of the bed.

"Do you want me to make another pot?" she offered.

"No, I don't have time; I'll pick some up on the way to work," he said, frowning. "You know what I'm going through with my boss. I can't risk being late."

His words sounded accusatory, as if she'd been the cause of his problems on the job. "Bryce. Sweetie, what's wrong? You were so loving and warm last night. Now you're acting like a grumpy old bear." She lovingly rumpled his sandy-colored hair but Bryce shrank back as if tousling his hair might cause its permanent ruination.

Sighing, he went to the bureau mirror. He wore a scowl as he finger-combed his sandy coils back into place.

"Baby," he said with a forced patient tone. "I'm running late and you know I'm on probation for tardiness, so please don't play in the morning. Okay?"

Ajali felt like a child who'd been scolded. His words hurt, but she nodded agreeably. Then she remembered the pills she'd heard him take out of the medicine cabinet last night. She wanted to ask him about it but changed her mind. She didn't feel like having her head bitten off again. She'd ask him about the pills later—when he was in a better mood.

That new boss at the mortgage company was really driving her man crazy.

For the fourth day in a row, Bryce made it to work on time. But groggy from doubling his medication, Bryce felt like shit and could only grunt in response to all the cheery morning greetings from his co-workers.

When he strode into his office, he was greeted by the aroma that wafted from a steaming cup of Starbucks coffee. There was a Post-it on the cup: *Thanks for the Jaworski account. I owe you one, but consider this a small token of my appreciation. Jeri.*

The cup of good ol' Starbucks was just what the doctor ordered. "Thanks, Jeri," he said aloud, giving her an imaginary toast as he guzzled the hot but comforting caffeinated elixir. The grogginess lifted perceptibly and in a matter of minutes he was back to his normal self.

Guilt hit him like a ton of bricks. He'd treated Ajali terribly that morning. Picking up the phone, he called her at work.

"Hey baby."

"Oh, it's baby now?" Ajali said in an unpleasant tone. "The way you treated me this morning I thought my name was Mud." Then she laughed, letting him know that all was forgiven.

"I'm sorry, Aj. I wasn't feeling too good this morning," Bryce explained.

"Yeah, I meant to ask you about the pill you took last night. What's going on, honey? Are you all right?"

Caught unaware by her knowledge of the medication, Bryce was quiet while he gave himself time to think. Breaking the uncomfortable silence on the line, he cleared his throat. "Uh, I'm taking something to help me sleep," he said unsteadily. He was embarrassed; taking sleeping pills didn't seem very masculine.

"How come you never mentioned it? It's not like you to keep something like that to yourself?"

"I don't know. It's the job, baby. With all this lateness and the threat of getting canned, I had to take drastic measures to make sure I get a decent night's sleep."

"Did the doctor say how long you'd have to take them? You know those pills can be addictive."

"Aj, can we talk about this some other time? This isn't the time or place to be having this discussion. Look, I'll talk to you later." Bryce hung up, feeling annoyed with Ajali. Again. Her need to pry was irksome. Why couldn't she have just accepted his apology and left everything else alone?

During the course of the workday, Bryce was able to forget his nocturnal problems. He and Jeri had lunch together. She told him the most hilarious story about her latest date from hell, which had him laughing so hard his sides hurt.

But he could not conjure a humorous thought on the drive home. Night was sure to fall and with darkness came the eerie whispers and depraved dreams.

Feeling desperate, he mentally counted the remaining pills in his medicine cabinet. There weren't many. The doctor had only prescribed fifteen pills and hadn't made getting refills an option. He'd said he wanted to see if the medication agreed with Bryce.

The sleeping pills weren't working; he'd have to take at least two just to get to sleep. And now the *thing* had made an appearance in his bedroom. How many pills would he have to take to prevent himself from having to see that sight again?

Maybe he didn't need a regular doctor; he probably needed psychiatric help. But the more he thought about it, a psychiatrist probably couldn't help him either. Bryce wasn't a religious man—not in the sense that he regularly attended church—but maybe his predicament required the services of a priest, like in the movie *The Exorcist*. Or one of those hoodoo women who were capable of undoing a hex. But where could he find such practitioners in an urban city like Philadelphia?

For the help he required, most likely, he'd have to travel to the backwoods of Louisiana or Haiti or somewhere like that. It was crazy: the life he'd once known was rapidly unraveling, and he was being driven insane by an insatiable apparition who was coercing him to participate in unspeakable acts of sex.

Chapter 10

*E*ris made herself comfortable in Bryce's apartment. When he and his mealy-mouthed little fiancée left in the morning, Eris explored her new environment. It was a strange place with unusual mechanisms, but she had all day to understand the inner workings of the gadgets created by modern technology.

By reducing her hot temperature and allowing herself to become a cool mist, Eris discovered that she could enter the device that controlled the voice and picture box, from which Bryce seemed to derive such pleasure. Breezing through the openings of the device and moving her airy body in a circular motion, she could turn the contraption on and off at will.

After mastering that, she moved on to gain knowledge of the functions of the other contraptions in the apartment. Tinkering with the light switches and operating kitchen appliances was child's play. Moving objects, however, was going to require hard work and concentration. And hard work was the last thing on Eris's mind.

She wanted to have fun and could hardly wait for her playmate to come home.

Bryce stuck his key in the lock. It wouldn't turn. Annoyed, he jiggled it for as long as his patience would allow. He took a deep breath, frowned down at his watch, snatched the key out and tried to figure out what he should do. He was scheduled to meet his trainer at the gym in a half-hour and he'd promised to take Ajali to dinner at eight.

Blowing out a frustrated breath, Bryce tried the key again and to his dismay, it still wouldn't turn. Angry, he kicked the door.

Inside his apartment, Eris languished seductively on Bryce's bed. His anger at her little trick with the lock excited her. Though she did not possess flesh, bones or blood, she'd attempted to fashion her ethereal composition into the shape and density of her former human self—but mirrors didn't reveal her reflection, so she had no idea that the look she'd crafted was a disfigured and most hideous sight.

Her neck and head were positioned too far to the right, giving the impression that her head was attached to her shoulder. She'd been in such a hurry to have Bryce see her reclined in a sexy pose, Eris forgot to give herself two arms. The one arm she'd focused her attention upon was draped sexily across plumped-up pillows on the bed. She hadn't, however, used good judgment in the proper length of a woman's arms—the limb was elongated and hung over the side of the bed with talon-like fingers that swept the floor.

Her breasts were enormous and pointed out as sharp as daggers with tiny knobby attachments that masqueraded as her former nipples. Eris was so aroused by the anger that emanated from the man on the other side of the door that the gaping hole of her womanhood began to ooze and emit a foul and inhuman odor.

Satisfied that she looked ravishing, Eris allowed the key to turn the lock.

Bryce sniffed the air the moment he entered. He must have forgotten to take out the trash. He flung his briefcase and headed for the kitchen, but the trash container, lined with a fresh green plastic bag, was empty.

He sniffed the air again and grimaced. His kitchen really stunk. Had a mouse gotten inside and crawled behind something and died? Determined to find the source of the odor, he pulled the refrigerator away from the wall. Nothing.

If he didn't get a move on, he'd be late for his appointment at the gym. Shrugging, he hurried from the kitchen, but the stench—much stronger—was in the hallway as well. He stopped mid-stride and sniffed the air. What the hell? Maybe there was a population of mice living in the walls.

Bryce shuddered and continued toward the bedroom. He'd call the rental office and make a strong complaint in the morning. In the meantime, he'd have to pack a bag and spend the night with Aj.

Packing a bag would slow him down and possibly cause him to miss his appointment with his trainer. But hell, he didn't have a choice. He went into the bathroom to get some sleeping pills. Even if he downed the entire bottle, he knew he still wouldn't get a wink of sleep in his foul-smelling apartment. Shaking two pills into his hand, he frowned into the container. There were only four pills left.

He rushed into the bedroom and started slinging personal items into his overnight bag. The disgusting odor was so strong here, Bryce began to choke and gag.

In his present state of fury, he found himself unable to control facial tics, grunts and compulsive utterances of obscenities. It was as if he were afflicted with Tourette's syndrome.

Oh, how he pitied whoever answered the phone in the rental office in the morning. He'd be so self-righteously angry that he knew he'd be unable to censor the string of cusswords aimed at the innocent receptionist who'd have the misfortune of working for a company that allowed disgusting rodents to run rampant in a high-rent apartment complex.

With a T-shirt covering his nose and mouth, he picked up the phone to call Ajali. Damn, no dial tone. What was going on? He slammed down the receiver.

A second later, his cell vibrated inside his pocket. He took it out and looked at the name. A big smile broke out on his face.

"Hey, baby," he said. "You must have ESP."

"Why do you say that?" Ajali asked.

"I was going to call you."

"Hold up," she said, sounding suspicious. "I don't want to hear it."

"What?" he said innocently.

"Don't tell me you were going to break our dinner date."

"Nothing of the sort. I wanted to ask if I can spend the night. I've got to make some quick amends for my bad behavior this morning."

"Well, I hope those amends aren't too quick," she said, joking. "I'm in the mood for a very long ride tonight. Think you can handle that?" she asked in a sultry tone.

"Uh-huh. So, look... Why don't we skip the dinner date so I can get an early start on making amends? I can pick up something to eat after I leave the gym. Want some Chinese?"

"Sounds good. But don't forget to bring some chocolate. I'm having a craving and you know how chocolate hits my spot."

"Oh really? Okay, what kind of chocolate?" Before Ajali could respond, Bryce said, "Please don't say Godiva; I don't feel like driving all the way downtown. Can you settle for a Snickers bar, baby? Or something else I can pick up at the Chinese store? I'll get you some Godiva tomorrow."

"Promise?"

"I promise."

"The multilayered, big box?"

"The biggest box in the shop," he assured her.

Ajali started laughing. "Baby, I was just kidding. The only chocolate I want is you. You've got the only brand of chocolate that can hit my spot. Now hurry up with your workout."

"I'm there," Bryce said. "Damn, I love you, girl."

"Love you, too. Now hurry up!"

Bryce clicked off his cell with a smile plastered on his face.

"Bryyyyyyyyyce," Eris called. She undraped her long arm from around the pillows, pulled her hand from the floor and dragged it across the bed and up to her face. Sexily crooking a talon, she called him again. But he didn't respond. He just kept stomping around the room and muttering profanity.

"Bryce," she said, using a sharp tone. Still, he ignored her.

Preoccupied with gaining Bryce's attention, Eris lost her concentration and her malformed human shape returned to the ethereal mist—the Earth form to which she'd been diminished. Infuriated, Eris leapt from the bed. An effusive streak, she shot across the room.

Thankfully, Bryce couldn't see the malformed atrocity that had been propped up against his headboard in a disgusting manner that was intended to seduce him. Nor could he see the agitated mist that was swirling around him at that very moment. For in his fully awake state, he couldn't see or hear Eris. Aside from leaving her stench, she had no power over him.

Then she remembered the activities that had kept her busy while Bryce was away at his place of employment. Since she was unable to capture his attention with her feminine wiles, she had no choice but to manipulate the electrical mechanisms that she'd played with all day.

And for a brief moment she felt powerful again. But then the spark of power flickered and dimmed as she recalled the little talking device Bryce had used to communicate with his meddlesome fiancée. In a flash of pure hatred, Eris spun in a circle of fury that emitted a flurry of sparks.

As she regained her composure, she realized she'd have to study the little talking gadget that didn't require electricity and figure out a way to block Bryce's communication with that interfering but insignificant slut.

As Bryce headed for the front door with an overnight bag slung over a shoulder and his gym bag in his hand, the television suddenly popped on. Stunned, he stood frozen, staring at the TV. His eyes swept the room as he forced himself to locate the remote. It was on top of the nightstand. As if it had been stored in the freezer all night, the remote chilled his hand. He abruptly hit the power button, rushed out of the bedroom and began to run down the hallway toward the door that would lead him to the safe sanity of the outside world.

Chapter 11

"He laughed! The baby actually laughed," Catherine Wallingford said to her husband, her voice filled with wonder as she looked down at her infant son.

"Honey," Dorsey Wallingford said with a tinge of condescension, "the baby is less than a week old. I doubt if he actually laughed. He's probably hungry; he's just working himself up for a hearty bout of that insufferable crying."

Catherine elbowed her husband teasingly. "You're so cynical. It really sounded like he chuckled."

Unconvinced, Dorsey gave a snort.

She shrugged. "Well, you know what they say...Babies laugh when the angels are talking to them."

Xavier—now known as Dorsey Wallingford, Jr. (a name he detested)—had indeed chuckled. But his laughter was not provoked by angels. Any angel worth her wings would steer clear of a demonic child like him.

When he and that conniving Eris entered the Earth realm together, he entered as a physical being and she emerged as a puff of smoke. Ha! Without a physical body, there was nowhere to fit a third eye, thus the miraculous return of his vision. That, of course, was merely Xavier's theory. It didn't matter how he had reacquired his sight. The important thing was that he had been able to view Eris while she made a complete fool of herself.

Eris hadn't a clue of how utterly horrid she looked, with a lopsided head, one upper limb missing and the other deformed to the point of resembling a five-foot tentacle—and she'd completely forgotten to give herself a pair of legs. And the vagina she constructed! Why, it looked as if it were stretched as wide as the Panama Canal.

Such a look would have been quite fetching on any of the lower realms, but here on Earth...Xavier *tsked*. Why, she looked like someone's worst nightmare.

But the most hilarious part of the entire comedy scene was watching Eris's reincarnated lover's reaction. With all that coughing and retching, it appeared he found the stench of "the goddess" absolutely revolting. Pity he hadn't been able to actually see the vile vixen as she posed on his bed, writhing and salivating as she flicked her lips with a forked tongue. The sight of her accompanied by the smelly hole she intended to offer him would have been more than enough to send the weak lad over the edge. Yes, Eris was right about one thing—her Stovall man was weak, weak, weak.

Eris had finally figured out that Bryce hadn't been able to see her or sense her presence. Had he known she was there, surely he would not have fled to the arms of that revolting other woman. Playing second fiddle to another human irritated her. She'd dallied long enough with the former Arthur Stovall, now it was time to get serious.

But getting serious required a human body. Hadn't Xavier mentioned something about siphoning the life force from a female being who shared the Stovall man's life? Well, at least she knew the source of the life force she required. But how to go about getting it was quite a different subject. Oh, where was Xavier? Hadn't he said he was being born to an important woman? She'd just have to do some research and find him.

Drat! Even if she located him, how could she communicate with an infant? Eris thought hard and then smiled. Telepathy! She'd find Xavier, penetrate his sleep—disrupt his blissful dreams until he gave her the information she needed.

Feeling much better, Eris swirled around happily, traveling from room to room. Something caught her attention in the bathroom. An open container sat on top of the sink. Four tablets were inside. Using her superior mental aptitude, Eris concluded that these tablets placed a barrier between her and Bryce during their special time.

Turning up her temperature until she transformed from a cool mist to hot steam, Eros entered the container and heated the tablets until they liquefied and eventually evaporated.

Tomorrow night she'd have her lover all to herself. Even if his arms were wrapped tightly around his betrothed, Eris would still penetrate, seduce and claim him. She'd implore him to travel to Roanoke and there she'd lead him to the spot where her treasures lay and insist that he dig and dig until her precious jewels were unearthed and returned to her.

Chapter 12

*A*jali set out her best plates in preparation of the Chinese food that Bryce would soon bring over. Certain that their wedding gifts would include elegant dinnerware, she saw no reason to save her good dishes for company.

Being with Bryce was more special than any company she would ever entertain. And with that thought in mind, she replaced the paper napkins next to the plates with gay floral-print cloth ones. Her man deserved the best she could offer.

It was close to eight o'clock. With a tingly feeling of excited anticipation, she took a quick look in the heavily carved French walnut mirror that hung in her living room. The old-fashioned mirror didn't fit in with the modern décor but she'd seen it in a thrift shop, and feeling drawn to it, made the whimsical purchase. The mirror gave the room an eclectic look that wasn't really her style; still, for some unknown and extremely quirky reason, Ajali displayed the mirror prominently.

She gazed in the mirror and smiled. Ajali held no illusions about her looks; she was pretty enough—she certainly got her share of compliments—but she felt she was far from being a beauty queen. Whenever she complained about her looks, her best friend, Tee, said she was simply being modest. "Girl, you got it going on. I'm just grateful that with your good looks, you don't walk around acting like a diva."

A diva! Ajali felt she was far from diva material. She supposed she did have flawless cinnamon brown skin and pretty doe-shaped light brown eyes, and if her nose weren't so broad, and if her chin wasn't so pointy, perhaps she'd agree with the consensus.

But what the hell, Bryce loved her just the way she was. And in his presence, she felt beautiful. In fact, his pet name for her was "Beautiful." She didn't think she'd ever stop blushing when he called her by that name.

Bryce arrived looking as handsome as ever. Ajali loved the way he wore his hair—a rebellious natural style that wasn't quite locked but didn't require combing or regular visits to the barber to keep it trimmed and neat. The look was easy maintenance—shampoo, a little gel and finger-combing. Bryce was so good-looking, with his dark brown eyes and chiseled features, that when he first entered her life she felt as if someone had given her a gift.

Although she knew he loved her dearly, she couldn't help feeling lucky to have him. Bryce was the prize and she was the luckiest woman in the world.

After dinner, they lounged on the sofa; Ajali rested her head on Bryce's lap while he flicked through the channels with one hand and massaged her forehead and temples with the other. Feeling relaxed but desiring more of his touch, Ajali moved his free hand to her breasts.

As if his hand had just been raked over hot coals, Bryce jerked away. The remote flipped out of his grasp, flew up in the air and then crashed and skidded across the floor.

Ajali sprang to her feet in an instant. "What the hell just happened?" she inquired, her face anxious for an explanation.

"I'm sorry, Aj. You took me off guard."

"I took *you* off guard?" She shook her head uncomprehendingly. "You just scared the shit out of me. Why would touching my breasts startle you to that degree? I mean...your reaction was just crazy. What's going on, sweet—"

"Don't call me crazy," he said defensively. "I said you took me by surprise. Stop making a big deal out of nothing." Bryce got up and retrieved the remote. Ajali didn't know what to do with herself. After his strange outburst, rejoining him on the sofa and settling back into position with her head in his lap seemed inappropriate and out of the question.

Her nerves were frazzled; she needed some space and was sure Bryce could use some time, too, so she decided to go to the kitchen to clean up the mess they'd made earlier. Before stacking the dishwasher, she began to pace vigorously as she tried to make some sense of the scene that had just transpired in the living room. Ajali replayed in her mind their lovemaking the night before at his place. To her chagrin, she realized Bryce had not touched her breasts; he'd avoided them, actually.

After she finished cleaning up, Ajali cleared her throat nervously. "Honey, I'm gonna take a shower and call it a night," she said, trying to sound casual despite the tension that hung in the air.

"Oh, okay," Bryce responded, also trying to inject a natural quality into his tone.

In the shower, she rubbed a soapy lather over her body with a bath sponge. She put the sponge down and suspiciously kneaded and squeezed her breasts. Had Bryce located a lump during one of their lovemaking bouts? she wondered. Now terrified, she performed a breast exam; thank God, everything felt normal.

So what was the problem? She'd let it drop for the night. But Bryce's strong aversion to touching her breasts had to be brought out into the open. Soon.

After her shower, Ajali entered the bedroom and applied a fragrant lotion. Bryce went past her into the bathroom. The sounds of the shower curtain being pulled aside followed by running water informed Ajali that Bryce was wrapping up a night that had suddenly turned disastrous. He was ready to retire early also. Perhaps together in bed, they could work through what she hoped was just a misunderstanding and not a major relationship issue.

Replaying the episode in her mind, Ajali decided that she'd overreacted. It made no sense for her future husband to suddenly become repelled by touching her breasts.

Lying on her back looking at the ceiling, thinking, Ajali sat up when Bryce came into the bedroom. With the remote in hand, he got in bed beside her.

She assumed her body language spoke loudly of a woman with troubles on her mind, but Bryce seemed oblivious as he propped his head up with pillows and chuckled along with something stupid on Comedy Central.

By the time Ajali had formulated the words she felt would launch, hopefully, a civil discussion regarding the breast issue, Bryce's breathing had become shallow and quickly progressed to snoring.

Feeling undesirable and disrespected by Bryce's lack of concern for her emotions, Ajali was close to crying. But she didn't. Instead, she sought comfort from the warmth of his body as she inched into a spooning position. As if on automatic pilot, Bryce's arm went around her waist and pulled her closer.

Chapter 13

There was nothing for Napoleon to complain about. Bryce was seated in his office and hard at work an hour before his workday officially began. He skipped lunch in order to close a deal and by three o'clock was close to securing another. Not bad, he thought with pride. But feelings of pride swiftly changed to shame when he thought about the night before and his dramatic and negative response when Ajali had prompted him to fondle her breasts. He'd behaved like an asshole.

He could have at least tried to make amends but instead, he'd taken the cowardly route and guzzled down the sleeping pills so he wouldn't have to deal with the issue. What could he say? *Uh, I'm sorry but I'm really not into tits at the moment. Maybe in the future when I get my head together and can get rid of these haunted breastfeeding dreams I've been having, perhaps at that time I'll be able to get back into that whole mammary gland thing. But until then.. Well, I hope you don't take this the wrong way, baby, but, right now I'm going through something and...um...you're seriously going to have to keep your fucking boobs out of my face.*

He knew if he had expressed his true feelings, Ajali would suggest he have his head examined. Couldn't blame her. So in the meantime, Bryce decided that he'd visit his primary physician in a couple of days and let him know the pills weren't working. He needed something stronger.

Maybe the creepy feelings and dreams were actually brought on by some type of prewedding jitters. Bryce thought about the marks that had appeared on his penis— psychosomatic symptoms, like the doctor had said, he told himself. Deciding he'd done enough work for one day, he began to clear off his desk.

The phone rang.

"Hey!" Ajali said cheerfully as if he hadn't acted like a weirdo the night before.

"Hey, Beautiful, how's your day going?"

"I've had better. This one could have been a little better if I'd heard from my fiancé."

"You're right," he said uncomfortably. "I should have called; but honey, I've been crazy busy all day. Closed one deal and damn near closed a second. I've been on the phone with clients all day."

"When the alarm went off this morning, I was shocked that your side of the bed was empty, that you'd already dressed and gone to work. No good-bye, no kiss—nothing. That was rude, Bryce. You could have left a note or something."

Damn, he hated being chastised. Particularly when he didn't have much of a defense. Truth was, he'd left early because he'd needed to get away from Ajali. He knew questions about last night were still in her mind and until he had some clear answers or a solution, he had to lie low.

"You're right," he said to Ajali. "But I'm really busting my ass trying to improve my relationship with Napoleon. With the wedding fast approaching, I'm trying to make sure I'll have a job after we're married," he said with forced humor.

"Well, what are your plans tonight? Are we getting together?"

Damn! He'd hoped to avoid her until he'd talked to the doctor about increasing the dosage of his medication or trying another brand of sleeping pills.

"Aj, I think I'm just gonna chill at home tonight. I want to finish up some work and then hit the client hard in the morning with an offer he can't refuse." He chuckled uncomfortably; Ajali didn't join in.

"Okay," she said without emotion, but he knew she was hurt.

Putting his baby through this hell—*his* hell—was killing him. Still, he couldn't risk being with her. In his current state of mind, there was no telling what new phobia he'd developed; he couldn't risk another unpleasant episode with her. Hell, suppose his dick just refused to get hard? How would he explain that? Yeah, it was best to stay at his own apartment tonight. With the assistance of the sleeping pills, he wouldn't have to worry about hearing *The Voice* calling him and he wouldn't have to endure any deviant sex with a damn ghost.

To ensure his peace of mind, he'd take an extra pill tonight. He didn't care how fucked up he'd feel in the morning. Getting through the night without a ghostly encounter was all that mattered.

"Can I get a rain check?"

"Sure, baby," she said, feigning nonchalance. "I'll see you tomorrow. Love you."

"Love you, too."

When he arrived home, Bryce decided against listening to the evening news. Admittedly, he was a news junkie, but today he felt as if he needed something tranquil. And there was nothing tranquil about any of the up-to-the minute news reports that so easily kept his attention.

He stuck a Wynton Marsalis CD in the player, pulled out his laptop and began to work on his new account. With his brows scrunched together he compared property values within a ten-mile radius of his client's home. Hmm. Everything looked good so far. A home that had been purchased in the area for $120,000 had sold six months ago for $257,000. Now *that* was good news.

Wynton was blowing and although Bryce's eyes were on the computer screen, his mind was with the music—peacefully trapped inside the notes. And in that state—wide awake but altered—Eris was able to slip in.

Riding on a musical note, she appeared in his mind. She danced and swayed in time to the beat. Aside from body jewelry: a gold ring, which dangled from her navel, and wrist and ankle bracelets that clinked and tinkled, adding a feminine element to Wynton's song, she was completely naked. And her body was perfection. She was a hand-carved ebony priestess crafted by a highly skilled master. Too beautiful to remain inanimate, she had come to life and now danced for Bryce, undulating to the rhythm of his favorite song.

She was just a sexual fantasy, Bryce reminded himself as he allowed her to pull him in deeper. This ebony queen was not the nightmare woman who'd invaded his sleep—this woman was every man's highest sexual dream. Seemingly in the throes of ecstasy as she danced, she swept up her heavy hair, lifting it high and running the fingers of both hands through the long, coarse tresses, then letting the hair fall seductively over her face and across her shoulders.

She performed an erotic dance that held him entranced, aroused him to the point of pain. It was a love call that he was compelled to answer as she gazed at him with smoldering eyes that emanated hot sparks of desire.

The scenery around her changed from ordinary grass and trees to a sandy tropical beach scene with beautiful blue water splashing behind her. The music seemed to pour from the ocean and from the swaying palm trees.

She beckoned him. Bryce was not afraid as he speedily joined her on the sand. Anything is possible in a fantasy, and thus a towel to lie upon instantly materialized. Long, nimble fingers unsnapped the button and unzipped his pants. His pants and his shirt vanished in a blink of an eye. Now as naked as she, Bryce relaxed, closed his eyes against the glaring sun and cradled his head with interlaced fingers.

His fantasy ebony goddess did not speak, but she did things with her mouth that words could never describe. Fighting the intense pleasure, he bit down on his lip. Though tears of passion and pain moistened the corners of his eyes, he was a man and he refused to cry. When she released him, he cried out, "No, please. Don't stop." Panting, he reached for her, but she slipped from his grasp, eased away from his lower body and inched toward his face.

As he continued his pleading protest, she silenced him by placing her sex upon his lips. Bryce explored her with his tongue; he probed as deeply as his fleshy, muscular organ of taste would permit. But there was simply not enough length to get to where he wanted to go and so he allowed his lips to pucker and take in her juices, which tasted as sweet as nectar from an exotic piece of fruit. He sucked greedily, hungrily...like a starving man.

Abruptly snatched from the island, Bryce found himself once again sitting in front of his laptop. He felt dazed as he observed his fingers, placed calmly on the keys as if they'd never left, had never gripped the kinky wild hair of the fantasy woman who'd relieved him of so much sexual tension that he felt drained and lifeless.

Amazingly, the Marsalis CD was ending. How much time had elapsed? he wondered, looking over at the clock. Before he could make an accurate deduction, the player had switched to another CD and John Coltrane burst from the speakers, distracting Bryce as he became hypnotized by the crying sound that poured from Coltrane's soprano sax. The rhythm changed within the song and became fast, free, uneven, and open. Being in the midst of the brilliantly abstract Coltrane song, he felt further confused and disoriented.

Trying to get his bearings, he glanced at the computer screen. The many columns of numbers had been replaced by something else. Something that felt vaguely familiar—like the feeling upon awakening of trying to hold on to the last piece of a dream. Just before the image faded, Bryce caught a fleeting glimpse of the ebony goddess traipsing naked into the crashing waves of the ocean. As the blue water devoured her, she looked over her shoulder and gave Bryce a gleaming, triumphant smile.

Bryce, suddenly remembered everything; the hairs stood up on the back of his neck. Terrified of what he'd find, he drew a trembling hand to his face and allowed his frightened fingertips to inch slowly toward his eyes. He felt something sticky, pulled his hand away. Daring not to conduct the examination with the full vision of both eyes, he closed an eye and with his other eye cracked open to just a slit, he inspected one of his fingers.

"Aagh! Oh God!" he yelped and fell forward, causing the laptop to crash to the floor. Feeling nauseous, Bryce touched the other areas that had been in contact with her sex: the soft hairs of his mustache, his chin, and lips. He jumped up and sprinted to the bathroom with such speed, he was practically airborne.

He groaned at his reflection in the mirror. A sticky red substance covered his face and hands. Frantically, he searched his memory bank, praying to God he'd messily rushed through an extra-large order of French fries, a couple hot dogs, a double cheeseburger or some type of meal that would require the pouring of extremely generous amounts of ketchup.

It has to be ketchup, he told himself as he washed his face with scalding water. Feeling violated and dirty, a washup at the sink would not suffice. Nauseous and afraid, Bryce stripped out of his clothes, slid back the glass door of the shower stall, turned the nozzle to red hot and stepped inside. With much trepidation, he watched the red-tinted water wash down the drain.

Chapter 14

"Bryce?" Ajali spoke his name questioningly only because she'd called both his phones over a dozen times during the past few hours and continually got his voice mail. It was nerve-racking and frightening at the same time. That he was safely at home filled her with both exasperation and relief, but, she could no longer dance around the subject. Something was going on with Bryce. Another woman?

"Bryce!"

"Yes, sweetheart. Is something wrong?"

"I should be asking you that question. You're the one who's been behaving strangely. You've been vague and distant. And last night on the sofa, you acted...um, wary of intimacy. That's not like you, Bryce."

"I know, Aj," Bryce cut in. "I wanted to talk to you about it, but I couldn't get into it on the phone today at work—"

"Oh God! Bryce, what's going on? Are you seeing someone else? Do you want to call off the wedding?" Panic caused her voice to rise, and the thought that her worst fear had been realized caused the tears she'd been holding back to pour down her face.

"No!" he shouted. "There's no one else. I love you too much to ever cheat on you. I love you, Beautiful. You know I do."

"Then tell me what's wrong," she said, still sniffling and crying pitifully. "I'm trying to be understanding, Bryce. I've tried to give you your space, but you've got to help me out. Any time my own fiancé acts like I'm a pariah and can't touch me, then something is terribly wrong."

Guiltily, Bryce thought about the night before and how in a matter of seconds he'd gone from warm and affectionate to squeamish about touching her. To be completely honest, as he and Ajali had lain together on her sofa, he'd behaved outrageously—like an inhibited lunatic—a man terrified of a pair of tits.

"I'm really starting to feel like I'm the only one in this relationship," she continued. "You've changed, Bryce. You're starting to avoid me. It...it feels like you've already left me. I feel so all alone," she said, expressing her pain with a whine that changed to a gut-wrenching sobbing session.

"Baby, please don't cry. Please," he pleaded.

Ajali tried to shut off her lamentations. Choked whimpers issued from her lips and though the sounds she made were softer, the pain was just as apparent and equally heartbreaking.

"Is it okay if I come over? I know we need to talk. Can I come over, baby?" he asked.

Ajali didn't answer; she couldn't, between crying and sniffling and blowing her nose. To Bryce's relief, the crying stopped. "Okay," she finally said as she emitted a residual sniffle.

"I'll be over as soon as I can pack an overnight bag."

Eris had become cool and vaporous as she drifted into the holes in the mouthpiece of the phone. Once inside the mechanism she had heard both sides of the conversation and she wasn't happy with the outcome. Not one bit.

Then, as she departed the cramped talking device and filtered back out into the open air of Bryce's living room, she came up with a brilliant idea.

Bryce hung up the phone. Folded his arms as he considered what he should pack. He cut his eye at the mess he'd made when he'd dropped his laptop. Stepping around the mangled apparatus, he decided to leave it for now and investigate the extent of the damage tomorrow.

He threw toiletries inside his bag, then remembering his sleeping pills, he grasped the bottle as if it were a life raft and he was a drowning man. In his haste to get to Ajali, he failed to perceive that there was no sound of pills jingling together. The pills had evaporated but he didn't detect how light the bottle had become. Without giving it a thought, he tossed the empty bottle inside the overnight bag along with the rest of his things.

Eager to take the journey that would place her inside her weak and ineffective adversary's dwelling place, Eris swirled excitedly inside Bryce's bag. Feeling an early thrill of victory, her excitement caused a slight change in temperature. As Bryce stooped to zip his bag, a gush of heat hit his face.

Beads of sweat broke out on his forehead. He dreaded having to confess to Ajali that he was experiencing something supernatural that seemed to have sexual undertones. Oh hell, the sexual nature of the haunting was more than a mere undertone—it was major and was making his life a living hell during sleeping hours. And to his horror, now his time awake was being haunted as well.

The heat, emanating from the bag, intensified. Bryce wiped his forehead and zippered the bag. He clicked off the lights, shut the door behind him and then carefully double-locked his apartment.

Ajali answered the door wearing a simple teal-colored satin negligee. She didn't risk wearing anything sheer or too revealing. Nothing that demanded: *rip through the fabric and fuck me hard*; nothing that revealed what her body was really craving. She didn't want Bryce to feel ill at ease—like he was obligated to get in bed and make love to her. Instead of showing her true feelings, Ajali smiled and said, "Would you like a glass of wine?"

"No thanks, Beautiful. You know I'm taking that medication. I shouldn't have anything to drink."

Ajali smiled in understanding but was seething inside. Damn! Their relationship had certainly taken a terribly horrible turn. Her man couldn't touch her breasts, and he had probably become too timid during sex to hold her legs high up in the air and hit her spot hard the way he used to. No more caressing, no more wild sex, and now, he couldn't even have a damn drink!

Although people told her she was quite pretty, Bryce's drastic change was wreaking havoc on her self-esteem. And even if she was as pretty as people said, what did it matter? Bryce certainly didn't care. He called her Beautiful but with the same tone he would say "buddy" or "pal." Lately, whenever she and Bryce were together, she felt so undesirable; she might as well have been downright ugly.

"Bryce," she said softly. "So much has changed; I need you to explain as best you can exactly what's going on."

"It's not you, Aj, I swear; it's me. But...uh, I think my problem does have something to do with the wedding."

Ajali gulped and looked around uncomfortably at the stacks of beautifully wrapped wedding gifts that had already begun to trickle in. "Cold feet?" she asked, terrified that he was about to reveal that he no longer wanted her to be his wife.

"No. No. Nothing like that."

"Then what is it, honey?" She was growing both frightened and annoyed.

"It's my job; some kind of fear of failure issue. I guess I'm worried that once we're married and have a child, I may not be able to hold up my end and be the kind of provider that you and our child would deserve."

"Oh, Bryce," she said, pulling him close. "Please don't torture yourself worrying about some dreadful future event that has no bearing on our relationship right now. Why can't we just enjoy the moment?"

"You don't understand. My boss is a short, sadistic tyrant and he enjoys threatening my livelihood. Knowing that my wedding is only weeks away, he's really messing with my head."

"And you're as guilty as he."

Bryce stared at Ajali, waiting for an explanation of her absurd comment.

"You're giving him permission to torment you. Ignore him, Bryce. Stop letting him get to you. Deluxe isn't the only mortgage company in the city. Hell, if you ever need to find another job, we'll move to another state if we have to."

Feeling as if the problem was solved, Ajali lifted her head and puckered her lips. Bryce gave his best imitation of a passionate kiss, but he didn't fool her. She recognized the gesture for what it was—nothing more than a half-hearted brush against her lips.

"Wanna lie in bed and watch the news...Or we could watch one of those crime shows you love," she offered, trying to sound cheerful.

"I didn't come here to bore you."

"I'm never bored with you. Look, I'm glad you're here. We don't have to do anything. We can just lie in bed and cuddle. Okay?"

The look of relief that crossed his face hurt Ajali badly—cut her to the core, but she wore a stoic expression and pretended to not notice. She quickly manufactured a smile that appeared selfless. Her smile expressed the assurance that everything was fine and dandy. Bryce needn't worry about his masculinity, their sex life was healthy and there was no reason to fear that acts of intimacy might possibly become nonexistent. The twitch in the corner of her lips began to betray that she'd faked the smile and her selflessness was bordering on unhealthy martyrdom.

She loved Bryce too much to cause him more grief. He was just going through a phase and she would have to ride it out. The wedding was only weeks away; what choice did she have?

After *Law & Order* went off, Bryce stole away to the bathroom to take his sleeping pills. Ajali heard him gasp. "What's wrong?" she called.

He came back into the bedroom looking grim. "Honey, what's wrong?" she asked again.

"I'm out of pills. I thought I had at least three or four left."

She propped herself up, trying to give the impression that she might have a solution, but she knew she didn't have any type of sleeping aid. Then it hit her. "Honey," she said, wide-eyed as she twisted from beneath the covers and got out of bed, "I have just the thing that'll help you."

"What?" Bryce asked desperately.

"I'm going to make you a cup of Sleepytime tea. You'll be sleeping like a baby in no time."

He smiled and nodded in acceptance, but the moment she turned around, if looks could kill, Ajali would be dead on the floor. Shot in the back with multiple bullet wounds before she'd could even make it to the bedroom door.

A cup of tea *instead of pills!* It was going to be a long night. Bryce fell back on his pillows in despair as he waited for Ajali to return with the useless potion that would have no effect on the nocturnal sex fiend that would soon make an appearance and lure him into dreadful dark places.

"I used honey; sugar might keep you up," Ajali said brightly.

Bryce nodded. Looking morose, he blew on the hot tea. Unlike Ajali, Bryce couldn't keep up a brave or cheerful front.

A gloom and doom atmosphere permeated the bedroom. Feeling helpless, Ajali silently rubbed Bryce's back in a circular motion. She intended to soothe him, but being rubbed made it difficult for him to drink the hot tea, so he gave up and put it down on the nightstand.

Ajali coaxed him to lie on her chest. She cradled him, massaged his scalp and gently rocked him until she heard the familiar sound of his snore.

"Bryyyyyyyyyce."

He jerked awake and tore himself out of Ajali's arms. "Did you hear that?" he asked, his eyes ablaze.

"Hear what?" Ajali was frightened. It occurred to her that perhaps Bryce was really going insane.

"Somebody keeps calling me. Night after night. And now it's happening right here while I'm lying in your arms."

"Calm down, baby. Please. You're scaring me."

"Oh, *you're* scared?" He hopped out of bed and began to pace. "Try hearing some ghostly bitch calling you night after night. Try getting up and going to work after being sexually abused all night."

"What? Bryce! What are you saying?" Ajali wondered if Bryce was suffering from a serious psychological disorder. Had he suddenly become delusional?

"You wouldn't understand." His eyes were darting about wildly. His hair, mussed from lying in bed, was sticking out every which way, giving him the look of a true madman.

"I'm going home. If I have to go crazy, I'd rather be alone. You don't need to have a front-row view of this bullshit."

"You're not going anywhere." Ajali tried to insert strength in her tone. "I'm not letting you leave this time of the night." She blocked his path.

"Oh, no? What's out there that can cause me any more harm than what's already being done? If there's somebody out there that wants to jack me, if some nut comes up to me and puts a gun up to my head, I'm gonna thank him and say, 'good lookin' out, my man.'"

Ajali started crying uncontrollably. She held on to Bryce's arm and pleaded with him to stay. But he pulled away from her, struggled into his clothes, grabbed his bag and stormed out into the night.

Chapter 15

*B*ack in his apartment, Bryce slung the overnight bag on the sofa. In a rage, he paced aimlessly. When he stumbled upon the laptop, he gave the equipment an angry kick; broken pieces went scattering in different directions. "Worthless piece of junk," he muttered.

"Come on, witch, you want some of this?" he yelled, grabbing his crotch crudely. "I'm tired of you; I'm sick of living like this. So come on, let's get this shit over with. I'm not scared anymore." Looking crazed, he went from room to room in search of the nightmarish being. Still clutching his crotch, he called out tauntingly, "Why are you hiding now? Don't you want some of this? Come on out; you can get it!"

Now in the bedroom, Bryce stepped out of his pants; he snatched off his shirt. "You're kind of quiet there, witch lady. What's the problem? You don't like aggressive men? Oh, I see," he said sarcastically to the silence. "You like creeping up on a brotha when he's half-asleep. Got me doing all that nasty shit while I'm half-asleep and helpless. You wait until I'm deep into a dream and then...here you come pushing up on me with demon sex. Why don't you try sticking your foul pussy up in my face while I'm wide awake..." Bryce bit down on his lip. He balled and cocked both fists as he recalled the sticky red substance that had been embedded in his facial hairs and on his lips.

He flopped on the bed. "I'm not medicated and there's not a chance in hell that I'm going to fall asleep. Guess it's gonna be a long night, so when you're ready to get your freak on...Bring it! I'll be right here."

He didn't turn on the TV or play music. *Fuck a psychiatrist and fuck sleeping pills. I got this.* Feeling more empowered than he'd thought possible; he lay in the dark in complete silence, ready to do battle with the unknown.

Bryce's tantrum amused Eris. However, he'd called her bluff, challenged her to come out of her hiding place. Being challenged riled and exasperated her. But it aroused her as well. He'd never shown such spunk as Arthur Stovall.

Existing as a gaseous vapor, her powers over Bryce were limited when he was fully awake. In her current form, she could only toy with him while he was in a relaxed state. Eris was growing tired of having to wait for him to essentially lose consciousness to impose her will upon him. She desperately needed a physical body.

In the meantime, as he lounged on his bed, feeling puffed up and powerful, Eris decided to remind the Stovall man that he was nothing but a man. A mortal man at that.

He hadn't turned on that blasted picture box. Excellent. During those times he was far too alert—too focused, making it extremely difficult for Eris to slip into his consciousness.

She'd had the great pleasure of discovering earlier that day that listening to music took him to another place. A place where he lingered for long periods with his guard down. In such a vulnerable state, it was easy for Eris to slide into his mind.

Using one of her recently acquired skills, she clicked on the CD player. Startled, Bryce shot upright and fumbled for the chain of the bedside Tiffany lamp.

Bryce got to his feet and crept up to the stereo component as if expecting the object of his haunting to jump out from behind the system and yell, *"Boo!"* Bryce did a thorough search of the bedroom. Satisfied that he was alone, he allowed himself to believe that he'd accidentally programmed the system to turn itself on.

On high alert, he lay back on the bed. He became engrossed in the complicated music of John Coltrane; he listened intently, but didn't fall into an altered state.

Impatient, Eris used her power to silence Coltrane and switch to the next shiny circle of music that lay in its own individual sphere inside the music box.

Bryce was briefly startled when a Phyllis Hyman CD suddenly began to play, but shrugged it off as an electronic glitch. His eyes shifted to the lamp and was comforted in knowing the glow of the lamplight would illuminate that witch bitch if she tried anything sneaky.

The richly textured vocals of the songstress were so soothing; Bryce couldn't help but close his eyes. Although he fully intended to open them, he never got the chance. As he concentrated on one of Hyman's lush notes, something happened inside his mind that sounded like a door closing softly. In an instant Bryce was pulled into a trance, trapped inside Eris's world.

But it wasn't a nightmare. Although disoriented, in this dream-like state, Bryce did not fear the ebony-colored woman. In fact, he was tantalized as she graced the stage of a smoky nightclub. Clad in a sexy sequined gown, she caressed the microphone, moistened her lips and began to sing.

Her voice was sultry and hypnotic. Amazingly, she sounded exactly like Phyllis Hyman as she crooned, "The Answer Is You." And even more amazingly, out of all the faceless men in the crowded club, her indigo eyes were fixed on him as she wailed: *Where have you been?*

Oddly, Bryce could still hear her singing as they left the club, hand in hand. "My name is Eris," she said. And even as she spoke, he could still hear the song. Hearing her singing in the background of his mind while she simultaneously spoke was weird, but extremely erotic.

"Bryce," he said, offering a handshake. "Have we met?"

Eris clasped his hand loosely. "Probably," she said, releasing his hand when the limo driver opened the door. "I travel a lot, what about you?"

"Me? Naw; I'm just a hood rat. I don't stray too far from home."

"We'll have to do something about that," she said as she turned her back to him. "Unzip me, would you please?"

Without hesitation, Bryce unzipped the sequined dress. Her back was so smooth and beautiful, he gasped. Eris pressed her back against his lips. As if responding to an unspoken request, he kissed each shoulder blade and placed tiny kisses down her spine.

Eris shuddered as his mouth and hot lips reached the barrier where the zipper stopped.

"You're so beautiful," he declared as he pulled the dress over her luscious hips and watched with excitement as she kicked it to the floor. Feeling suddenly prudish and desiring privacy, Bryce closed the window, preventing the driver from having a private peep show.

Out of her dress and naked, Eris turned her back to him again. Picking up where he left off, Bryce continued to kiss and bite her back while cupping and squeezing her enormous and firm breasts.

Eris moaned and jerked with pleasure as he covered her back with kisses. Her sounds of passion encouraged him to give more. The hands that had held her breasts now cupped and squeezed her butt cheeks. The lips that kissed her back traveled as if ravenous to the uncharted territory of her magnificent black ass. And when her soft cries of pleasure became loud and demanding moans, she abruptly turned, unzipped and lowered his pants. The denim fabric dangled around his ankles.

In a breathy rush, he tried to kick his pants off, but couldn't manage the task as Eris took his rigid manhood inside her mouth and held him there until he admitted in an anguished whisper, "I can't hold it."

She let his penis fall from her mouth.

"Do you still love me, Arthur?"

Though his name was not Arthur, he was comfortable with the sound of it. Hearing it was as welcome and as familiar as coming across a favorite old coat.

"Yes, I love you," he gasped. Being on the brink of an orgasm, he really didn't care what name she chose to call him.

"Are you sorry for leaving me?"

"I'm so sorry," he said to appease her. His heart was pumping from excitement; he wanted to feel her tongue licking his shaft and teasing the head of his dick. He'd say anything to get back into her warm, wet mouth.

"Look at what they did to me," Eris said sulkily. She twisted around to reveal her back.

Bryce let out a fearful yelp. He cringed and recoiled; his stomach lurched. Eris's back no longer resembled smooth mahogany; it was bloody, ripped and charred, and smelled like rotting flesh. Gagging, he slid away from her and bent down to pull up his pants.

She grasped his hand before he could get to his pants. "Do you still love me?" Her voice had changed from soft and sexy to a low snarl.

"Y-yes," he stammered quietly, hoping there was a sincere quality in his tone that would inspire her to loosen her grip. He really wanted to pull up his pants—the urge to cover himself and run for his life was extremely powerful.

With his free hand, he pecked on the window that he'd closed for privacy earlier. He needed to tell the driver to pull over and let him out at the next light. He didn't have a clue where he was but he didn't intend to stick around and ask for directions. Naw, he was straight; he'd find his own way home.

"Prove that you love me," Eris insisted, pulling his hand away from the window. Like a pair of handcuffs, she held both his hands in a tight grip.

"How?" he asked, feeling terribly uneasy. Feeling captured.

She turned completely around, again fully exposing her torn and burned back. "Make it better; kiss my wounds." And once again, she pressed her back against his lips.

Bryce screamed, pushed her away. With flailing arms, he reached for the door handle. There was a crashing sound and the limo went black.

The lightbulb smashed when the Tiffany lamp hit the floor. Bryce leapt from the bed and tripped as he frantically searched for the light switch on the wall.

Lying in a heap on the floor with his pants gathered around his legs, Bryce took deep breaths as he tried to calm down. But he couldn't. He gave in to the fear; the futility of trying to fight something that the medical profession would tell him was all in his head. And maybe it was. Maybe he was stark, raving mad.

Yes, I am quite mad, he finally admitted to himself and then curled into a fetal position and wept.

In the dark room, Phyllis Hyman's beautiful, haunting vocals echoed from the speakers, providing background music to Bryce's lamentations in the dark.

Chapter 16

*A*jali knew what all the whispering was about. Tee had invited her to dinner, but every time the phone rang, Tee would turn her back and lower her voice to a whisper.

Unusual names such as "The Lion," "Cream" and "Tank" crept into the hushed conversation Tee was having with her co-conspirators. It sounded to Ajali like Tee was rattling off names of male exotic dancers.

It didn't take a rocket scientist to figure out that Tee was planning a surprise bachelorette party for her. Under normal circumstances, Ajali would have been flattered and even would have assisted in the espionage by finding an excuse to leave the room; but she was under so much stress and was so fearful that her wedding plans might not come to fruition that the best she could do was try to twist around in her chair, stretch her neck toward the TV in the living room and pretend to be interested in the latest news flash.

Tee hung up and picked up a chicken wing. "Girl, if we plan on fitting into our gowns, this has to be our last fattening meal before the big day." Ajali nodded and absently observed Tee tear the meat off the wing.

"What's wrong?" Tee asked, suddenly noticing how quiet Ajali had been.

"Nothing," Ajali said unconvincingly.

Tee looked at her skeptically. "Now that I think about it, you've been acting funny for the past few days. What's up, girl? You and Bryce going through something?"

"No!" Ajali protested too loudly.

Tee gave her another skeptical look and then wisely changed the subject. "Girl, let me tell you what my crazy boss did today..."

As Tee launched into the latest unbelievable antics of her boss, Ajali's thoughts drifted to Bryce. Something really terrible was going on with him. She strongly suspected that he had conflicted feelings. She believed he loved her, but her instincts told her Bryce was having an affair.

Someone had captured her man's attention. Was the affair based on sex? What had she done or not done that had sent him into the arms of another woman? Ajali wondered grimly. Was his heart involved; was it possible he had fallen in love with this mystery woman? These appalling thoughts continued to flit through her mind. It wasn't fair that she, a bride-to-be, should be so unhappy and filled with doubt.

"I swear if that bitch don't get some dick soon," Tee continued griping about her boss, "I'm gonna pay somebody to tighten her ass up because she's driving me crazy. Damn, ever since her divorce, she's been acting like a damn demon from hell."

Divorce! Oh God. Ajali wasn't even married and yet she flinched at the mention of the word *divorce*. She took it personally, as if Tee and the entire universe were conspiring against her—setting her pending marriage up for failure before it had even begun. Oh, what a terrible turn her life had taken!

On the drive home, Ajali called Bryce from her cell. She hadn't spoken to him all day. She was really and truly trying to give him some space but damn, they were getting married soon and she had a right to expect some kind of communication.

A quick phone call certainly shouldn't be too much to ask. Ajali sighed. What she wouldn't give to hear him say: *Hey, how ya doin', Beautiful? Look, I'm busy, but I'm just checking on you. You all right?* Seemed like a lifetime ago that Bryce was thoughtful and considerate. Now, when she needed him the most, he was grumpy, sensitive, easily irritated and was having sleeping problems and sex-related issues. It was so damned unfair.

She counted each ring of his phone and prayed she didn't get his voice mail. It would not be wise for him to see her name on the caller ID and decide to ignore her call. At a time like this, when she was feeling vulnerable and unloved, he didn't need to add insult to injury by obviously ducking her. If he was planning to dodge her calls, Ajali would be left with no choice but

90

to run red lights all the way to his apartment and bang on his door with the heel of her shoe while yelling his name. Yeah, it would get real ugly if he didn't pick up the damn phone. She deserved at least that much respect.

"Hullo," he said sleepily.

"Were you sleeping?" Wasn't he supposed to be suffering from a sleeping disorder? She wondered what kind of lie was he was about to tell and sucked her teeth audibly.

"No, I'm awake."

Well, at least he didn't lie. "What are you doing?"

"Just lying here listening to music." His voice held a strange, unfamiliar quality. He sounded distant, distracted...and there was something else in his tone that she couldn't quite place.

"Did you go to work today?" she inquired

"No."

"Why not?" She felt ridiculous. So far, making Bryce participate in the conversation was like pulling teeth.

"Sick," he said in a monotone. His one-word responses were starting to really irritate her. Then it dawned on her; he said he was sick.

"Sick? What's wrong?" she asked, alarmed and then instantly felt stupid. She was really starting to sound like a broken record. *What's wrong... what's wrong?* Those two words were being uttered far too often and Bryce continually gave vague or complicated responses.

"Nothing serious. Came down with something. I should be better in a couple of days."

"Do you want me to pick up something from the pharmacy?"

"No."

Ugh. Another one-word response. She fought the feeling of agitation. "Should I come over?" she asked desperately.

"Not tonight, Aj. I'll be all right. Okay? Look, I have to hang up; I'll talk to you tomorrow."

Click! Just like that he terminated the conversation. The dial tone blared. Incredulous, Ajali still held the phone to her ear. She wondered if she should put her plan in motion. Should she push her foot down on the gas and screech into a parking space in front of his complex, use her key to get past the security door, run up the flights of stairs and kick down his fucking door? She gave a heavy sigh, pulled over to the curb, broke down and cried. She was too weak for a confrontation.

Bryce had another woman; she knew it. Throughout the conversation, she could hear soft music playing; the kind of music a man would play if he had a woman lying beside him in bed. The blurry image of Bryce's new woman lying happily next to him made Ajali's temples throb.

The stereo system seemed to have a life of its own; it had been playing the same five CDs that were already in the player on the day that the ebony woman first discovered that she could use music to lure him into a peaceful state. Since he no longer controlled when or how long the system played music, he could at least exercise some control over the type of music she used to seduce him. Yes, he was on to her but, drained emotionally and physically, he couldn't put up even a weak fight.

Robotically, Bryce arose and put five different CDs in the slots and returned to the bed. He knew the ebony woman's arrival was inevitable so in the meantime, as he waited, he decided to listen to Billie Holiday. He commiserated with Billie and concurred with every pain-filled note that streamed from the speakers.

Chapter 17

*E*ris delighted in exploring Bryce's personal areas—his drawers, closets, shelves. Interesting items were secreted away in corners and beneath things. She uncovered photographs of former lovers that the sentimental fool refused to throw away, all manner of sappy, overromantic items, such as greeting cards and old love letters; but the greatest find of all was the discovery of the ring!

What a stroke of luck to find the very piece of jewelry she'd coveted over two hundred years ago. Out of all the Stovall descendants, it turned up safely in the custody of a man whom she once had bewitched and now possessed—body and soul.

Now more than ever, Eris was motivated to reconstruct her body so that she could walk down the aisle with the former Arthur Stovall and become the legal keeper of the ring instead of having it end up on the finger of his simpleminded little fiancée. The woman was useless to Bryce.

Bryce needed a powerful woman with unusual beauty, who was also cunning and wise. He needed Eris, the Goddess of Discord, who could shake things up and restack the deck in his favor. Since he was incapable of putting his pint-sized boss in his place, she'd handle the matter and give Shorty a taste of what it felt to be at the receiving end of harassment. Otherworldly harassment. Harassment so severe the miniature man would behave so erratically that the employer's security team would be called to escort *him* off the premises. In a headlock!

Yes, Eris would inspire Bryce to reach for the best this Earth realm had to offer. She'd move every obstacle out of his way. To settle for mediocrity was unthinkable; she deserved a wealthy man who gave orders to others and commanded respect.

With her superior intelligence, of course, she'd be the real power and he'd be merely a puppet—her mouthpiece. She'd insist that he build her a show-place; larger and far more elaborate than the old Stovall Plantation. She deserved a palace filled with servants who'd be at her beck and call twenty-four hours a day.

Finally, she would become the mistress of the house, as she was intended to be. The Stovall man owed her that and it was time for him to settle his debt.

So, instead of coming to him through music, she decided to allow Bryce to sleep. During his slumber, she'd infiltrate his mind, his heart—his soul.

She had the ability to make him love her...adore her. And so she began her work. As he slept, Eris whispered subliminal messages in his ear. "You'll never marry her. You cannot. You've kept me waiting for many lifetimes; you must marry me." After hours of these whispered messages, Eris began to insert images into his mind. She forced him to not only view but also feel the brutal whipping and murder she'd endured at the hands of his hired men. When she felt he'd suffered enough unpleasant imagery, she gently took him by the hand and led him into the moonlit nights when they used to lie together in his bedchamber. She re-created the scene, allowing him to suckle once more. Cradled in her arms, he felt as safe and content as a newborn.

When Bryce awakened on semen-stained sheets, her name issued urgently from his lips, his hands groped wildly in search of her. He could still feel her presence, smell her scent and taste her lips. She was no longer a nameless something that came in the night. Her name was Eris and she was his beautiful queen.

Although Eris was pleased with Bryce's unwavering devotion, she yearned for a body; she yearned to walk this Earth as human with the powers of a goddess who could make grown men weep.

But first things first. On the top of her list of priorities was to strengthen Bryce with nourishment. She'd deliberately depleted him just to keep him weak and dependent. But now she wanted him to get up and out of bed. She wanted him to inform Little Missy—the bride-to-be—that there'd been a change in plans; the wedding had to be cancelled.

While Bryce slept, Eris encouraged him to eat and take in liquids when he awakened. He needed fortification with earthly nutrients. Her personal nurturing served his body only while in an altered state, endowing him with the superhuman stamina he required to even attempt to satiate a goddess such as her.

A vision of Ajali lurked in the corners of Bryce's mind, and he felt—fleetingly—a deep love for her. And then an overwhelming sorrow. That pang of strong emotional attachment toward Ajali passed quickly and was replaced with passion.

Hot passion. For Eris. But a rendezvous with Eris could only take place in his dreams. For that reason, Bryce craved sleep and the unlimited carnal possibilities that came in the form of dreams.

Suddenly ravenous, Bryce padded to the kitchen to fix himself something to eat.

While Bryce mixed together the ingredients for an omelet, Eris streamed into his mobile talking unit. She tinkered with it and in just a matter of minutes she knew the intricacies of its inner workings. As utensils clattered in the kitchen, Eris sent a text message to Ajali:

Meet me at Thai Palace tonight at 7. Bryce.

Eris was such a clever goddess, she wondered if the Goddess Tara was looking upon her with envy as she again maneuvered with such ease on the Earth plane. Indeed, Tara would have her hands filled trying to protect the Earthlings who had the misfortune of crossing Eris's path.

Chapter 18

*T*he text message, as cold and impersonal as an e-mail blast, should have put up a red flag. But Ajali was so happy to hear from Bryce, she didn't heed the warning. Instead of surrounding herself with a protective emotional barrier, she sat through the meal smiling and laughing—leaving herself unguarded and vulnerable.

They had dinner at their favorite Thai restaurant in University City. Afterward, as they walked to Bryce's car, Ajali was still in a blissful haze, unaware that her world was about to collapse.

Throughout the meal she'd kept up a steady stream of one-sided conversation interspersed with cheerful anecdotes that should have exhausted her. It was a wonder she didn't have a pounding headache from putting forth so much effort along with a tremendous amount of forced laughter, which now echoed loudly in her head.

She'd overextended herself and continued to persevere, talking a mile a minute about the wedding as she lovingly clutched Bryce's hand. They appeared to be quite the lovely couple as they turned the corner on Thirty-eighth Street onto Spruce.

Then Bryce stopped suddenly. Elated by the assumption that Bryce had been overtaken suddenly by a moment of overwhelming love for her and was unable to contain his need to publicly display his affection, Ajali turned to him expectantly, lifted her chin and closed her eyes dreamily. But instead of the anticipated kiss, she felt Bryce's hands cup her face. Seconds passed without a kiss. Feeling foolish, she allowed her eyelids to flutter open.

Bryce's pain-filled eyes instantly filled her with anxiety. "What's wrong?" Now that she thought about it, Bryce had been as distant throughout the meal as he'd been for the past week. "Oh, my God, Bryce, what is it?"

Then it hit her. He'd been fired! Bryce needed to concentrate at work but his sleeping disorder had negatively affected his job performance. He'd complained about the flack he'd been taking from his boss over tardiness and dwindling sales. But she'd been so caught up in the wedding, she hadn't been listening, nor had she offered any advice or sincere words of comfort.

Shocked, she gasped and covered her mouth. She'd been so absorbed in what she believed to be his detachment from her that she had never actually been there for him. Selfishly, she'd viewed his sleeping problems and job problems as an inconvenience in her life. Never had she really felt his pain. She just wanted him to hurry and resolve his issues and get back on the wedding planning bandwagon.

Ajali felt so ashamed. She shook her head in dismay. She was so self-absorbed. She'd have to work on that aspect of her personality. Marriage, after all, required being considerate of one's spouse.

But losing a job wasn't the end of the world, she reminded herself. They could both make it on her salary until he found another position. The perfect life they planned together would not be interrupted for one moment. Feeling better, she asked in a much calmer tone, "Bryce, what is it?"

"I'm sorry, Aj. I just can't go through with it; I'm not ready for marriage." His voice filled with anguish.

"You're not serious," she said in disbelief and then broke into a nervous chuckle, hoping a little humor would prompt Bryce to admit he was only joking. He *had* to be joking.

But his pained expression remained in place.

"You're not ready? What do you mean you're not ready? Have you lost your mind? Everything is in place; we're getting married in two weeks!" Her voice was shrill and hysterical. And to Bryce's credit, he didn't look around in embarrassment or ask her to lower her voice.

"You have no idea how hard this is for me," he said softly—patiently. "But I've made up my mind. I don't want to get married. At least not yet."

"Not yet? Then when?" She screamed at the top of her lungs, alarming the many passersby in the bustling University City area.

Ajali began to softly weep as she and Bryce continued the walk to his car, which was parked three blocks away at a meter on Spruce Street. With Bryce plodding along beside her, her quiet sobs escalated to a full-blown wail. Ajali, normally a dignified and self-respecting young woman, didn't care that she was making a public spectacle of herself. When her legs suddenly buckled from shock and grief, she didn't put up any resistance as she felt herself plunging toward the pavement.

Assuming she was drunk (a normal occurrence among the University students) apprehensive pedestrians stopped in their tracks and rushed to offer assistance. Bryce lifted a wobbly Ajali from the sidewalk and with an embarrassed and apologetic smile, he assured the well-meaning crowd that he had everything under control.

Wanting to walk on her own, Ajali jerked away from Bryce's supportive hand, but her feet wouldn't cooperate. Bryce had to half-carry; half-drag her the remaining blocks to the car.

Aside from her wracking sobs, partially muffled by the palms of her hands, the drive to her apartment was silent; the mood understandably solemn.

"Do you want the ring back?" she asked, sniffling when Bryce double-parked in front of her building. The honking horns of a trail of impatient motorists urged him to either park or be on his way.

"No, I don't want it; you can keep it," he said in a glum tone, still wearing that pained expression Ajali now wanted to slap off his face.

There was an awkward silence as Ajali considered his offer. "Keep it for what?" she finally shrieked, twisting the ring off angrily.

"I don't know." He shrugged uncomfortably. "Maybe you can sell it or something. I have no use for it."

She wanted to throw the ring in his face, but held on to the hope that Bryce was going through a bad case of last-minute jitters. Hoping it was a temporary matter from which he'd recover in a day or so, she put the ring back on her finger.

Later, alone in her bedroom, shocked by the sudden and tragic turn of events, she sat twisting the engagement ring as she stared into space. *It's another woman*, she resolved. *Bryce is a moral and decent human being—what else could be the reason for him to abruptly, callously stop our wedding?*

It was a sad, heartbreaking and irreplaceable loss. She flung herself across the bed and sobbed in abject despair.

Feeling overwrought and too emotionally impaired to function, Ajali realized she could not handle the daunting task of canceling a wedding. She picked up the phone and called Tee. Wiping her eyes, she told her friend the tragic news.

Tee expressed shock, sorrow and then rage. Hurling a long stream of expletives, she threatened Bryce with bodily harm. "I just can't believe Bryce would put you in such an embarrassing position. What's wrong with him? Has he lost his fucking mind?" Tee asked at the end of a lengthy rant. "I'm here for you, girl," Tee said, her tone softening. "Just tell me what you want me to do."

"I don't know what I want you to do," Ajali confessed, crying softly. "I really can't handle, this, Tee." She paused to blow her nose. "Do any of those wedding magazines or etiquette books make any mention of how to handle a cancellation?" Ajali asked in an embarrassed voice that sounded scratchy and nasally. She cleared her throat and then took on a sudden sarcastic tone. "Do the professionals provide a list of do's and don'ts on what to tell your guests if you get dumped right before the big day?"

"Don't worry, girl. I got you covered. I'll go through the list and contact everyone who returned an RSVP. Oh, by the way," Tee said, nervously. "Um..."

"What?"

"If I'm not mistaken, Aj, I think you're supposed to return the wedding gifts that you've already received." Tee gave a heavy sigh.

Her words were a jarring reminder of the finality of her situation. "Okay, I'll get everything together in a couple of days."

Two days after the breakup, holding on to the hope that Bryce would come to his senses, Ajali continued to wear the engagement ring. She held out her left hand and examined the round two-carat diamond as if viewing it for the first time. The loveliness of this symbol of love still amazed her as it had on the day Bryce proposed.

She turned her hand slightly to the left and then the right admiring the brilliance of the stone. Though modern, the gold bezel setting was a perfect match to the hand-crafted antique wedding band that Bryce had intended to place on her finger on their wedding day. The wedding ring, Bryce had proudly told her was a family heirloom, over two hundred years old.

Bryce was raised by a neighbor after both his parents were killed in a car accident when he was only eleven years old. Before his death, Bryce's father had told him all he knew about their family history. He'd told Bryce that his own father—Bryce's grandfather—had died a mysterious death. Bryce's father said he'd heard hushed murmurs that a curse had been put on the Stovall family during the time of slavery.

Bryce, however, didn't believe in a family curse. He was far too grounded and sensible to feed into family superstitions. Such talk was merely rubbish. Illogical hearsay. Thus, despite his parents' sudden and tragic death, Bryce held no beliefs in anything even remotely paranormal.

Abandoned at birth and never adopted, Ajali was a survivor of the foster care system. She knew her mother's name, but that was it. At eighteen, she'd thought about looking for her mother, but changed her mind. Her mother had never once bothered to look for her. That she came into adulthood unscathed and well-adjusted was a miracle that she could attribute only to her own inner strength.

Neither she nor Bryce had any immediate family; it was one of the things they'd had in common, one of the things that had drawn them together. Two people determinedly making it through life alone had connected with each other; she'd always considered their relationship something of a miracle— a blessing from above.

Bryce's family situation, however, wasn't quite as desolate as her own; at least he'd known his parents and still had a few distant relatives—some black and some white. His African American family members were scattered throughout the north while his Caucasian relatives remained down south in Roanoke, Virginia.

From what Bryce had told her, the two races had never gotten along and for generations had bitterly squabbled over some land in Roanoke where a grand mansion had once stood. That mansion, Bryce had told Ajali, was now just a crumbling shell, but it was still a source of contention.

Bryce was the descendant of a slave owner who had stipulated in his will that he would not leave his property to any of his white kin—his only son and direct heir was born to a slave. He'd specified that the property was to be passed down to the eldest male Stovall child in each generation.

The old man's will was ignored for years; distant white cousins, nephews and nieces had squatted on the property for generations. The only visible black faces seen on the land were a few hired hands. But over time, the plantation lost its glamour. It was expensive to keep up; therefore, it had been vacant for decades.

The white Stovalls insisted that the property belonged to them, but after the civil rights movement, the black Stovalls (Bryce's grandfather and a few of his cousins) had heatedly disputed their claim. After a drawn-out court battle, it was determined that the property belonged to Bryce's grandfather, the only direct descendant of Arthur Stovall, the original plantation owner.

Bryce's grandfather was willing to share the property with his cousins who were all living in different parts of the north; but the cousins had been involved in the lawsuit on general principal only and didn't actually want any part of the neglected plantation, which they knew would cost a fortune to restore.

And so the property sat, empty and abandoned. Before Bryce's grandfather got a chance to rehabilitate the property, he became another victim of the alleged Stovall family curse. dying mysteriously before Bryce's birth.

Bryce's father was the last surviving Stovall man and had been wise enough to continue to pay the taxes. He'd told his son that one day the property value in those parts was going to appreciate and he wanted his son to reap the benefits of the blood, sweat and tears of his ancestors' hard work.

Bryce had never seen the property and had grown up not even giving it a thought. The taxes, however, continued to be paid out of the small trust fund left to him by his parents.

On a lark, he did a property search and discovered that the value of the Roanoke land had appreciated considerably; Bryce told Ajali the land was worth several million. He'd said he wanted to take a trip to Roanoke in order to decide whether he should restore the mansion or simply sell the land.

Since Bryce had expressed no sense of urgency as one would expect of someone who'd just discovered himself to be the recipient of a sudden windfall, Ajali never invested any interest in the matter.

Talking about the Roanoke property, its history and their future plans for it had seemed like a fairy tale to Ajali—something fun to dream about but nothing to really take seriously. Bryce couldn't possibly be the owner of land worth millions, as he'd claimed. If so, why was he taking so much guff from his boss? Why not just quit and go live off the land?

Owning a mansion on an old plantation seemed nothing more than a fantasy, thus she humored Bryce but didn't really have faith in the Roanoke multimillion dollar property deal. She was braced for there to be a catch—some clause that would necessitate her having to comfort Bryce after he discovered the land really wasn't worth a plugged nickel.

Reluctantly, her thoughts turned to her present situation; she covered her mouth in despair. Her thoughts became torturous and willfully returned to the night her world collapsed; tears began to slide down her face.

Bryce was gone and it was no fairy tale. It was real life. Mournful sobs pushed against her throat. Unable to contain the strong desire for release, she dropped her head and wept. Through her tear-clouded vision, Ajali fixed her eyes on her left hand and resignedly twisted off her engagement ring. She rose and walked to her dressing table, opened the top drawer and, with utmost care, she replaced the ring in its elegant velvet case.

Her wedding gown, preserved in a zippered plastic bag hung on a hook on the back of her closet door, seemed to mock her. She yanked it off the hook, pushing hangers and clothing aside as she stuffed the gown into the back of her closet.

A decision had to be made soon. Wedding gowns, she'd heard, should not be exposed to sunlight for an extended period of time. She'd have to either sell the gown or have it professionally packed and preserved. The chance that Bryce would soon come to his senses made the latter choice far more appealing.

Invitations announcing the wedding of Ajali Logan and Bryce Stovall had been sent a month ago, and RSVPs along with gifts from their registry were still coming in. Unable to muster the strength to tell the invitees that the wedding had been called off, Ajali was relieved Tee had taken responsibility for that unpleasant task.

She took extended sick time from her job. To ensure she wouldn't have to communicate with anyone, she turned off the ringers of both her home and cell phones, but checked the caller ID a million times a day, hoping to see Bryce's name and praying he'd had a change of heart.

Chapter 19

On the Saturday that she should have been standing at the altar with Bryce, Ajali mechanically browsed the aisles of the self-help section in the Borders book store in Bryn Mawr. The downtown store was closer to her apartment, but she didn't want to risk bumping into anyone she knew on her intended wedding day.

Too embarrassed to face anyone, she was using the three months' sick time she'd accrued on her job at Deluxe, the same company Bryce worked for— but luckily, a different branch. Still, everyone knew about the humiliating breakup. Most likely, Ajali would resign from her administrative assistant position when she ran out of sick leave.

She wondered if she'd ever stop feeling so bad. The pharmaceutical industry could make billions if they'd come up with a pill for love sickness. A pill that would immediately stop the pain, remove the self-doubt, remove the yearning from your heart. Yes, it would be nice if there was a quick remedy for what ailed her.

In the meantime, self-healing was her top priority. The pain of losing Bryce was unbearable. She hadn't a clue as to how to begin using the pronoun *me* when she was so accustomed to being part of a *we*.

Most nights were spent tossing and turning, crying and screaming, "why?" Once, during a particularly restless night, she'd jumped in her car and drove to an all-night pharmacy where she purchased an over-the-counter sleeping aid. The pill took care of the torturous nocturnal hours; however, upon awakening she felt groggy, grumpy and more depressed. The pain of her loss seemed heightened, more acute. Angry and frustrated; she'd thrown away the remaining pills.

The pain would have been no less excruciating had she found out Bryce had fallen for another woman. If that were the case, at least she'd have an explanation for being tossed out of his life at the worst possible time. Bryce refused to be specific about why he had ruined her life.

A chatty couple joined her in the aisle where she was browsing. Standing close—too close—they discussed authors and book titles. Annoyed, Ajali moved to another aisle, but when the happy couple ambled into her new-found territory, she'd had quite enough. Without even looking at the title, she grabbed a book and stormed away to a bench in a quiet corner.

Her head ached, her body ached and oh, how her heart ached. Needing to ease the pain, Ajali dug into her purse and pulled out her cell phone. Without any preparation or knowledge of what she'd say, but holding on to the hope that he'd miraculously come to his senses and realized that he loved and couldn't live without her, she called Bryce.

His phone rang four times and then his voice mail picked up, which meant he'd seen her name and chose not to answer. Hurt, she felt the tears begin to well. She sought refuge in the restroom and cried until there were no tears left to fall. Dabbing her swollen eyes with a moist paper towel, she went to the cashier and paid for the book: *Self-Healing Through Meditation*. She shrugged; it was worth a try.

For the most part the book was boring. There were long passages about alpha states of consciousness, opening chakras—stuff she'd never heard of or had any interest in. Cutting to the chase, Ajali flipped to the middle of the book.

Lighting a white candle for protection was suggested. She scoffed at the notion that she'd need protection. Protection from what? Boy, what a crock. But she'd spent fifteen bucks on this foolishness, so she'd try to get a portion of her money's worth by at least trying to reach the peaceful state the book promised. Peace from the all-consuming yearning for Bryce was all she asked for.

Following the author's instructions, Ajali sat in a comfortable position and began breathing deeply and telling every part of her body to relax.

Talking to her toes made her feel like a complete idiot but by the time she'd reached her eyelids, she had to admit she was feeling relaxed. So relaxed, in fact, she sank into the cushion and thought about absolutely nothing. Her mind was blank. She felt free. And then the darkness behind her eyelids became a shade darker, as if someone had suddenly turned off the lights. That was a bit unsettling so she opened her eyes. The lights in her apartment were on. Okay. She decided to try it again. This time, her body relaxed easily and in no time at all she was back in a state so relaxed she no longer even felt her body.

In the meditative state, there were no worrisome thoughts. She was not plagued by impossible decisions. She was pure consciousness—peaceful and free

Then something odd occurred. She felt herself lifting from the chair. Rising upward. But how was that possible? More curious than afraid, Ajali decided to go with the flow and remained calm as she allowed her spirit to rise and separate from her physical body.

Suddenly, she was flying. Well, not actually flying, it was more like floating in the air—bobbing along the walls and softly brushing the ceiling. Although she was unable to control the direction in which she floated, she felt happy. Happy! That realization made her think of Bryce. Just the thought of him instantly catapulted her to his living room.

She felt wonderful electric currents flowing through her as she bounced and bobbed in the air. She reached out her hand to touch his ceiling. Amazingly, her finger went right through the surface. The sensation was incredible. Eerie, yet magically exhilarating.

From a corner near the ceiling, Ajali hovered over Bryce. She felt his emotions: sorrow, deep pain. She saw him pick up his cell phone and scroll down to her name. He looked disheveled and forlorn; his suffering was palpable. He slammed the phone shut, tossed it aside and gripped his head in anguish.

She tried to will her body to float down so she could sit next to him. She wanted to comfort him, but she had no control over her movements. He couldn't see her and he didn't seem to sense her presence, so Ajali decided to test her vocal cords. Perhaps he'd be able to hear her.

"Bryce," she whispered. "Bryce, can you hear me? I'm here. I'm right here, honey." She tried to will him to look upward, but he didn't so she pressed on. Trying to get his attention, she spoke louder. "I don't know why you've pushed me away, but I do know you still love me. I can feel it. Do you hear me, Bryce? I love you and I know you love me."

Bryce's head lifted. Hopeful that he'd heard perhaps a snippet of her love call, she tried to edge closer, but couldn't. Her ethereal body continued to bounce around aimlessly.

Determinedly, Ajali tried a different tactic. Instead of trying to attract his attention vocally, she called Bryce's name in her mind. His head jerked up. But a dark mist formed and hovered directly over Bryce, distracting him and seeming to deepen his profound pain.

Ajali mentally called Bryce again, but got no response from him. The dark mist, however, swirled furiously and then began to move away from Bryce and toward Ajali.

The mist did not evoke feelings of peace within Ajali; it seemed to emanate animosity and ill will. Its movement seemed threatening. Suddenly fearful, Ajali jerked backward. In an instant she found herself transported back to her living room, sitting peacefully in her overstuffed chair with her hands folded in her lap as if she'd never moved a muscle.

The only sign that she had come into contact with something unnatural was the frantic pounding of her heart. She'd encountered something she didn't understand and couldn't begin to express to another living soul without the possibility of exposing herself as a nutcase.

She'd have to keep the experience a secret and come to terms with the fact that she'd seen and felt a presence that was dark and possibly evil. A presence that had scared her out of her wits.

Ajali cracked opened the meditation book again and nervously ran her finger down the table of contents. Her finger froze at chapter six. *Out-of-Body-Experiences.* The words put a chill down her spine. She quickly turned to that section and by the end of the chapter she'd learned that what she'd experienced was called astral traveling.

The average person rarely experienced this phenomenon, but numerous people have claimed that after many months of practice, they finally achieved this ability.

Ajali's out-of-body experience had been instantaneous; she hadn't properly prepared herself for it, but she was confident she could do it again. But did she dare? Her feelings were conflicted. If she tried it again, she could see Bryce and perhaps come to an understanding of what had gone so terribly wrong that he'd cancel their wedding. But on the other hand, if she went back, there was the risk that that scary black vaporous thing might come back.

Pondering the out-of-body event, she remembered that the mist that hovered over Bryce had seemed more than just a smoky substance; it seemed alive and appeared to pulsate with a threatening energy. When it perceived Ajali's presence, the dark vapor had advanced toward her.

Ajali suddenly recalled a chilling aspect of the experience. The dark mist didn't merely move forward—it slowly glided and then suddenly lunged at her, and worse...it emitted a loud hiss. A warning to keep away from Bryce.

Chapter 20

*S*earching for more information that would explain how she ended up bouncing around her ceiling as well Bryce's while her body never left the cushy living room chair, Ajali picked up a handful of books on astral traveling. In addition, she scanned a local New Age newspaper that advertised everything from aromatherapy to relationship therapy. In between there were ads for breath work, dream therapy, energy healing, feng shui, reflexology, just to name some of the therapies touted to heal whatever needed fixing.

Though she doubted her problems could be resolved easily, the ad for relationship healing struck a chord. It was worth looking into. She quickly picked up the phone before she allowed herself an opportunity to change her mind. She spoke to a woman who called herself Madame Alvenia and made an appointment for the next day.

The woman gave Ajali directions to her home in a town called Marcus Hook, Pennsylvania, which was an approximate forty-five-minute drive from Philly.

It was pouring on the day of her appointment and it took Ajali over an hour to get to Marcus Hook. When she arrived, Madame Alvenia was standing at the door waiting for her.

"I was hoping you didn't get lost in all this rain," she said as she opened the door wide. She looked to be in her seventies or so; her hair, completely gray, was trimmed short and worn naturally. Madame Alvenia lived in a tiny, ramshackle, wood-frame house. The woman was obviously impoverished, which bothered Ajali a great deal. How could someone living in substandard conditions offer helpful advice?

It occurred to Ajali that she should bolt for her car, but Madame Alvenia had kind eyes, which encouraged her to stay and at least listen to what the woman had to say about relationship issues.

Additionally, after driving in pounding rain for over an hour, Ajali decided it would be ridiculous to turn back around just because the woman appeared underprivileged. Did only the rich have healthy relationships? Of course not, she told herself as she stepped inside Madame Alvenia's tiny house.

"Would you like a cup of hot tea?" Madame Alvenia asked with a warm smile. As Ajali considered the offer, the woman reached to relieve her of her dripping umbrella.

"Have a seat." She pointed to the minuscule dining area. "I'll be right back with your tea."

Ajali sat at the table and surveyed her surroundings. Surprisingly, the raggedy old house was very neat inside. Actually, the house was spotless. Listening to the woman putter around the kitchen had a calming effect and Ajali relaxed her shoulders and pressed against the padded back of the dining room chair.

But instead of enjoying the peace, her restless mind wandered to Bryce— the breakup—the pain and the humiliation. As she began to ruminate on the embarrassment of being dumped just before her wedding, Madame Alvenia strode into the dining room with a cup of tea and a pack of cards. Ajali eyed the cards skeptically. Did the woman presume that she could heal Ajali's problems with a deck of tarot cards? Oh well, she only charged twenty-five dollars, so what the heck?

"Here you are, dear." Madame Alvenia set a dainty bone-china cup and saucer with a white-on-white etched floral design complemented by platinum trim in front of Ajali. It appeared to be part of an antique set—a very expensive set of china. Madame Alvenia was full of surprises.

"You're wondering what I'm going to do with these cards, right?" asked the woman.

Ajali nodded sheepishly.

"Well, Angie..."

"Ajali," she politely corrected.

"Beautiful name. Well, Ajali," Madame began again, "this is a Goddess tarot deck, with cards representing forty-eight goddesses from around the world. Each goddess has a specific specialty. For example, Aphrodite is Goddess of Sexual Love, and then there's Bona Dea, Goddess of Fertility."

Ajali nodded in understanding, but wore a perplexed expression.

"When you seek advice from the Goddess Realm," Madame Alvenia explained, "you are reconnecting with ancient female wisdom, intuition and truth. Now tell me, who could give you better advice for your relationship problems?"

A marriage counselor, Ajali wanted to say, determining that she'd wasted her time. Only pathetic and desperate people came out in the pouring rain and expected results from a pack of playing cards. This poor old woman didn't have any answers for her, but out of respect for Madame Alvenia, Ajali decided to sit through the ritual or whatever it was called, pay her the twenty-five bucks and be on her way—back out in the rain, suffering through slippery expressway traffic while clutching her chest, trying to hold together a heart that felt as if it were splitting in a million different places.

As Ajali took the last sip of tea, Madame Alvenia scooted her chair away from the table. "Finished, dear?" Ajali nodded and Madame, surprisingly spry, was on her feet to remove the cup and saucer. She returned from the kitchen with a dish towel and wiped the moisture ring left by the saucer.

When she finished tidying up, she sat down and looked at Ajali intently.

"I won't pretend that these cards can heal what's wrong in your relation-ship. However, the card you draw will be the Goddess with the abilities best suited to your particular problem."

Madame Alvenia began shuffling the deck. The cards were bright and color-ful. As they flashed in Madame's wrinkled hands, Ajali felt an electrical current in the air.

Madame Alvenia placed the stack of cards, face down, in the middle of the table. With one hand, she spread the forty-eight cards out like a fan.

"Pick one," she instructed Ajali.

"Just pick a random card?"

"Select the card that you're drawn to; the card that calls you."

And sure enough, Ajali felt a pull toward one of the cards. Hesitantly, she reached across the table and gingerly touched it. It felt alive. Startled, she withdrew her hand.

A knowing gleam appeared in Madame Alvenia's eyes. She turned the card over and studied it for a few moments. Then with a solemn expression she turned the card around. Clipped between both thumb and index fingers, she revealed the card to Ajali.

"This is the Goddess Kali. She destroys ignorance, but assists those who strive for knowledge. Her name means 'The Black One' and the city of Calcutta is named in her honor. And Kali's also called Mother, the source of fertility."

Ajali wanted to turn her nose up at the card. The woman who appeared on the card did not fit Ajali's vision of a goddess. Kali was quite ugly.

She looked fearsome, wild eyed, her tongue hanging from her mouth; she was wielding a bloody sword and holding the severed head of what appeared to be a demon. She was also wearing a belt that dangled the severed heads of her victims.

With her mouth agape, Ajali looked at Madame in shock. Kali didn't fit the profile of being a relationship healer. Ajali wanted to ask if she could put the card back. She preferred the assistance of someone who looked more goddess-like. The Goddess Kali looked like a monster.

"Don't let appearances fool you. You've drawn this card because you are in need of her help."

Ajali considered the woman's words. Well...of course she was in need of help, otherwise she wouldn't have driven to a little hick town during torrential rain, and so Madame Alvenia's deduction didn't have much bearing on her credibility.

Ajali studied the card. She didn't like the look of it and decided she didn't want to continue with the session, but when she raised her head to speak, she was so startled her mouth hung open wordlessly.

Madame Alvenia stared at Ajali with wide unblinking eyes. She was stock-still with her back, shoulders and neck erect. Her unmoving hands were placed on the table in front of her.

"Madame Alvenia? Are you okay?" Ajali reached to touch the woman, hoping to God the woman wasn't about to have a heart attack or a stroke. Ajali patted her hand several times, but she didn't flinch. She appeared to be in a trance.

Then Madame Alvenia's mouth opened wide—wider than Ajali thought humanly possible. It was a disturbing sight. Ajali was ready to make a run for it but she didn't want to leave the poor woman unattended if she was in need of medical assistance. From Madame Alvenia's open mouth, came an explosion of air that sounded like howling wind during a hurricane.

"Oh, my God," Ajali cried. "What's wrong, Madame Alvenia? Should I call 911?" Ajali twisted around to locate a phone. When she didn't see one she started rooting around inside her purse to find her cell phone.

"I am Kali," Madame Alvenia said in a voice that commanded attention. The voice was strange but powerful and spoke in a dialect that Ajali didn't recognize.

"Madame Alvenia?" she said again, hoping this was a prank. Madame Alvenia apparently had a sense of humor but Ajali didn't think it was funny. Not one bit. She shut her purse and stood, deciding she'd call 911 from the safety of her car. As she rushed to the door, the voice said, "The Stovall man called Bryce is in grave danger!"

Those words stopped Ajali cold. She'd never spoken Bryce's name to Madame Alvenia. Taking slow steps, she returned to the table and fell into her seat.

"What did you say, Madame Alvenia?"

"I am Kali, Goddess of Destruction," the voice insisted in a stronger tone. "I am known for many things. I am the destroyer of ignorance. I am the mother of the universe and I am the protector of children. I have come to advise you that the time is come for you to face your fears."

"Goddess of Destruction?" Ajali asked in a quivering voice. She didn't like the sound of that. She'd come looking for relationship healing or at least advice. Now, Madame Alvenia was looking and talking like someone delusional. It was clearly time to stop being polite. It was time to go. Ajali stood.

"I destroy evil and restore peace. You have summoned me."

Shaking her head in denial, Ajali said, "No, I came to visit Madame Alvenia for relationship healing, but I see I made a mistake, excuse me. I'll pay you now; I really have to go."

The so-called Goddess Kali pounded her fist on the table, making Ajali jump. "Through this one, you summoned me." The alleged goddess drew up her lips angrily and pointed at her chest as if Madame Alvenia was no longer present.

"There is another who wishes to bring harm to you and your loved ones."

The reference to Ajali's loved ones was puzzling. Tee was Ajali's girl and all—her best friend—but since Ajali had no family, Bryce was really her only loved one, which proved this goddess woman was totally off the mark.

"The dark entity thrives on chaos and has exceptional dark powers," Kali went on. Her eyes protruded frighteningly, looking as if they were about to pop right out of her head. "You have opened a portal and are now unprotected," she said and pointed a finger at Ajali. "She will not stop until she has siphoned your life force and has depleted the last breath from the one known in this life as Bryce Stovall."

Ajali gasped at the sound of Bryce's full name coming from the lips of this bizarre so-called goddess who shouldn't have any knowledge of either her or Bryce.

Chapter 21

*T*aking the woman more seriously, Ajali sat up straight and asked, "What portal did I open?"

"When your spirit separated from your body and traveled to the place of your loved one, a portal between worlds was opened. During your journey across realms, the silver cord that connects body to spirit was damaged."

Ajali looked stricken. "Damaged? Am I going to be okay?" She patted herself to make sure everything was intact.

"When you were jolted back into the body, a portion of your life force seeped out and was siphoned by the evil one, a former goddess called Eris," Kali continued without responding to Ajali's direct question.

Beneath the table, there was quite a racket as Ajali's knees knocked together in uncontrollable fear. She thought she'd been feeling a little weak after the astral traveling incident but had attributed it to being stressed-out and unable to eat.

As if reading her mind, the goddess spoke. "At this time, your physical condition is not affected by the loss of life force. This is a spiritual loss."

"What should I do?"

"You must protect your life force as you attempt to save your loved one. The entity known as Bryce is possessed by a demon."

"A demon!" Ajali shouted. She thought about the evil black mist that had chased her away from Bryce and realized that this Kali person was quite possibly speaking the truth.

"Eris was once a goddess who was cast down to Earth to live in the physical and hopefully amend her wicked ways. She did not make the required amends. Thus, when her physical body was destroyed, she was forced to dwell with wayward spirits on a lower realm very close to hell. Using feminine guile and the goddess powers she retained, Eris slipped back into the earthly realm.

"The Goddess Counsel did not sanction Eris's reappearance on the Earth plane. Stripped of her goddess status, she is now a violent spirit, surrounded by darkness. She is considered succubus—a sexually insatiable demon that violently seduces a chosen man as he sleeps, draining him of energy and his desire for anyone other than her." Kali closed her eyes and muttered a chant in a language Ajali didn't understand. "Unfortunately, this demon is so corrupt she can reverse her malignant spirit from succubus to incubus at will."

Ajali nodded dumbly, making a note to look up the two Latin-sounding words: *succubus* and *incubus*. Hmm. She had no idea what they meant, but she knew it was something vile and reprehensible.

That information about Bryce being seduced by a demon explained his sudden disinterest in sex. Even though the words she was hearing sounded crazy and scary, discovering that Bryce didn't break up with her of his own free will made Ajali feel much better.

"It is in the nature of the succubus to kill her prey after an allotted time," Kali continued ominously.

"Kill?" Ajali's voice was filled with alarm.

"Eventually, she will also kill his female counterpart from whom she must siphon the life force that will allow her to prowl in female human form."

Nothing the woman said made sense, but Ajali did hear the word *kill* quite clearly. "Me?" she asked, poking herself in the chest, her gaze darting from side to side. "This dangerous entity wants to kill me?" It was all truly crazy, and perhaps she would have scoffed at the notion that an "entity" was out to get her had she not encountered the dark vaporous thing during her out-of-body experience.

"Your life is in peril," Kali said simply.

Ajali's lips began to quiver and then she broke down and cried.

Kali remained stoic and waited for Ajali to compose herself. "There is no time for tears. You must take action," she said.

"What can I do?" Ajali asked, wiping her eyes.

Kali leaned in. "You must learn how to travel safely between realms. You entered the invisible realm without protection; you weakened your spirit and lost precious life force that is being misused at this moment by another."

"I was just trying to meditate," Ajali said defensively. "I never meant to travel anywhere."

"You must protect the being known as Bryce. Your presence shields him."

"But he refuses to see me; he won't even speak to me on the phone."

"Visit him in spirit. Meditate."

Ajali scowled and shook her head. "I don't know. That thing really scared me."

"You must," Kali shouted, her eyes bulging wildly. She no longer even remotely resembled Madame Alvenia, nor did she have the woman's sweet temperament. Minus the sword and the dangling skulls, she had gradually assumed the ferocious attitude and appearance of the goddess portrayed on the tarot card.

"Without your help, your young man will meet his demise."

"Oh God!" Ajali broke down in wracking sobs, again.

"Silence!" Kali's tongue protruded as if to emphasize the severity of her words. Then she retracted her tongue and spoke. "Light two candles before you meditate. One black, the other white. The white candle will protect you and keep you connected to the silver cord that is your life force, and the black candle will summon me."

"Then what?"

"We will journey together to the invisible realm to reclaim your soul mate." Kali drew in a deep breath, closed her eyes and shuddered. When the woman opened her eyes, Ajali was looking into the kind face of Madame Alvenia.

After Ajali explained everything about her relationship with Bryce and recounted her experience with Kali, she looked at Madame Alvenia expectantly. There was a sense of disquiet before Madame Alvenia spoke. "I'm sorry your encounter with the goddess Kali was so unsettling. However, it would be wise to heed her advice."

"But she wants me to travel out of my body..." Distraught, Ajali covered her face with her hands.

"Kali is wise," Madame Alvenia soothed, leaning forward and patting Ajali on the shoulder.

Ajali took her hands away from her face. She bit her lip nervously, and then after a heavy sigh said, "I don't know if I can face that evil thing again."

"Do you love him?"

"With all my heart."

"You mentioned that your young man suddenly broke off your engagement." Ajali nodded.

"And it was not in his character to behave so irresponsibly?"

"Not at all."

"You admit to having seen a dark presence hovering over him as he appeared to be in despair?"

"Yes, but—"

"Were the words *'til death do us part* included in the vows you were prepared to take?"

"Yes." Ajali's voice was a whisper.

"It is not your young man's time. However, his fleshly limitations prevent him from overcoming the dark force. You have somehow stumbled upon the portal between worlds and are able to astral travel."

"Yes, but I can't really make my spirit body go where I want it to go. It just sort of bounces around. And when that thing came after me, I don't know what would have happened if I hadn't landed back in my real body. If I can't protect myself, how can I protect Bryce?"

"Kali will guide you. Have faith. And most important, know that love does conquer all," Madame Alvenia said knowingly.

Ajali stood up and began to fumble in her purse. She pulled out her wallet and opened it to retrieve the money to pay for Madame Alvenia's services.

Madame Alvenia held up her hand and shook her head. "I didn't help you. Not yet. Bring your young man to meet me after the wedding. I'll accept my fee when your relationship is healed."

"Oh, Madame Alvenia…You are so sweet. Thank you for believing that there's hope for Bryce and me."

On the drive home, Ajali braced herself for another encounter with the dark force known as Eris. Feeling deeply troubled, she wondered how many astral trips she'd have to make to save herself and Bryce.

Chapter 22

On her way home, Ajali exited I-95 and turned off on Island Avenue. Penrose Plaza was on her right. She had a white candle at home, but she needed to pick up a black one to perform the dreaded ritual that would save Bryce. *And me*, she reminded herself.

She pulled into the lot and parked in front of K-Mart. Putting up her umbrella, she dashed inside to find a black candle. She perused the bright array of candles in that department. Every color in the rainbow was represented, but there were no black candles. Desperate, she asked an apron-wearing attendant, "Do you sell black candles?"

"We have only what you see," the man said without breaking his stride.

She searched the candle section again and then, crestfallen, she left the store. There was a dollar store a few feet away. With great hope, she went inside. Again, no black candles. Frustrated, she flipped open her cell and called Tee. "Hey, girl. Listen, do you know where I can find a black candle?" she asked in a matter-of-fact tone.

"A black candle? What for? You planning on working some roots on Bryce?"

"Stop playing, Tee. I, uh...need the candle for..."

"Need it for what?"

Thinking fast on her feet, Ajali convincingly told Tee that in her quest to get over Bryce she had started a new hobby—collecting candles—and she had every color except black.

Feeling sorry for her poor jilted friend, Tee tried to be helpful. "Um, you may be able to get a scented black candle at a Hallmark gift shop. They sell Yankee candles."

"No, I don't want it in a jar. I need an *unscented* black candle." Ajali didn't mean to shout, but she was desperate.

"Well, I know for a fact there's an occult shop on South Street that sells black candles. But to drive that far for a damn candle—"

"What's the name of the shop and where is it located on South Street?" Ajali interrupted.

"Um, I think it's around 10th and South. I forget the name. But if memory serves me correctly, it's a man's name. Something like Jim's Occult Shop, Mike's Occult Shop, or maybe it's Bob's Occult Shop. I forget, but look in that area, you can't miss it. The shop looks real spooky. So, be careful."

"Okay, I'll talk to you later." Ajali hung up. She knew Tee felt sorry for her and was trying to indulge her because of what Bryce had done. But Tee had no idea of the trouble both Ajali and Bryce were in—and there was no way she could explain it.

Ajali was wet from the rain and exhausted, but she pulled out of the Penrose Plaza parking lot, headed for South Street and determined to find a black candle.

Ajali slowed when she neared 10th Street, looking on both sides for the occult shop. She spotted it on the corner of 12th, but parking on South Street was next to impossible. The only available space was next to a fire hydrant. Ajali didn't care if she got a ticket. Defiantly, she pulled up next to the hydrant, parked and dashed into the shop.

Tee was right. The shop *was* weird. But the man who ran the place was very friendly. Ajali felt uncomfortable asking for a black candle, but the man didn't bat an eye. He produced six black candles of various shapes and patiently waited for her to make a decision. There was no telling how many astral trips she'd have to make; not wanting to run out of the necessary equipment, she selected three tall black candles, paid the man and was back in her car in less than five minutes. And despite being gone that short period of time, Ajali was greeted by a wet ticket plastered against her windshield. Damn!

At home she changed from her damp clothing and into a comfortable pair of baggy slacks and an oversized tee. The shirt belonged to Bryce. She sniffed, hoping for a whiff of him, but the shirt had been washed and now smelled like mountain-fresh fabric softener. Oh, what she wouldn't give to lie next to her man and sniff the scent that was uniquely his, all night long.

Motivated by that desire, Ajali set up the two candles, lit them, sat in her chair and began deep breathing. She counted backward from ten to one and then began telling her body to relax. Her face began to tingle. The tingling sensation moved down to her chin and neck. Then the darkness behind her eyes became even darker and darker until she felt plunged into complete blackness. She felt weightless and began to lift. The impulse to fight the ascension was strong, but she let go and allowed herself to float until once again, she found herself hovering above her body.

How strange she looked sitting in the chair. She'd never seen the top of her head without the benefit of a mirror. She thought about her bedroom and within seconds, her astral body was there. *Ah, so that's how it works. All I have to do is think about where I want to go and voila—I'm there.*

Wanting to check on her body, she imagined herself sitting in the living room. Instantly, she was above her body again. She looked peacefully asleep in the chair. The experience was incredibly strange, but also fun in a creepy sort of way.

Then she remembered the serious business she needed to attend to and focused her thoughts on Bryce.

Like a rocket, she felt as if she had shot through the roof of her house. She heard a loud whooshing sound and then soft music. Bryce's bedroom looked like it had been hit by a tornado. During her first visit, she'd been so focused on his apparent despair, she hadn't paid attention to the appearance of his apartment.

Ajali was appalled. His laptop was in pieces, scattered on the floor. Clothing had been discarded all over the place. Open CD cases were strewn about. Plates on top of the bureau had congealed food stuck on them. She was astounded. Bryce was a neat, organized person. He would never live in squalor such as this.

But the worst sight of all was Bryce, lying on his back asleep in bed. He was unshaven and looked as if he hadn't bathed in weeks. His hair was matted—terribly unkempt. Despite his disheveled appearance, the love Ajali felt for him poured from her heart. As if her love for him was something tangible that he could feel, Bryce began to stir.

But before he became fully awake, a thick, dark mist seeped from the top bureau drawer. It was a dreadful and terrifying sight. It floated toward the bed and then slowly thinned out and began to take form. There was no depth, just a smoky outline of a woman with huge breasts, an extremely narrow waistline and sensual, well-rounded buttocks and hips. She looked like a pencil drawing of the perfect woman.

Ajali stared at the form of her rival who was hovering only inches above Bryce. The smoky outline now covered Bryce's body like someone had traced the image of a woman on top of him.

Bryce's chest rose and fell rapidly; his breath came out in quick, ragged gasps. His groin began to slowly gyrate. Ajali watched in horror as Bryce panted; his tongue protruded and licked out at the thin air. She wanted to scream when the blanket that covered him was yanked off him by an invisible hand.

Bryce was naked. He had an erection. The smoky outline hovered again. The head area of the smoke woman was in close proximity to Bryce's erect penis. When his face contorted in sexual pleasure, a horrified Ajali realized the demon woman was giving Bryce head.

Propelled by intense jealousy, Ajali instantaneously hurtled to the scene where the crime of passion was unfolding right before her indignant eyes. Now hovering above Bryce's bed, Ajali shouted his name, then forced her ethereal body into the demon mist.

The moment she made contact with the succubus, she heard and felt a crackle in the atmosphere. It was anger. Hatred. Directed at her. But Ajali didn't flee. She stubbornly maintained her position directly above Bryce's bed.

Bryce, jolted from the unearthly coitus, sat up and looked around, confusion creased his face. He called out, "Eris!" The sound of his voice was an agonized plea.

Despite her awareness that Bryce wasn't himself, that he was possessed, hearing him plead for the resumption of sex with someone—*something*—other than her was a powerful blow to Ajali's self-esteem—a blow that sent her reeling to the other side of the room.

Seconds later, she was back inside her body sitting in the chair. Her mission had failed. Feeling helpless, she covered her face and cried into her hands. Her man was possessed, obsessed and pussy-whipped by a fucking demon, and there was nothing she could do.

The black and white candles flickered as if to remind her that there was still hope. On her next trip, she would not try to do battle alone; she'd call on the Goddess Kali to help her conquer the demon and reclaim Bryce's soul.

Chapter 23

Two days passed and Ajali was unable to reach a level of meditation deep enough to astral travel. Frustrated, she decided to give it one last try. She sat in what she now referred to as her meditation chair, breathed in deeply, counted backward and told her toes and other body parts to relax, but pesky thoughts defiantly ran across her mind.

After twenty minutes or so of trying to relax her body and quiet her mind, she became frustrated, leapt up from her seat and blew out the candles with two exasperated bursts of air.

Then it struck Ajali: maybe she was going crazy. Perhaps the breakup with Bryce was so painful that she'd created this fantasy world of demon possession and out-of-body travel to justify Bryce's callous behavior. Who could expect her to be in her right mind after getting ditched right before her wedding?

She thought about her trek to Marcus Hook in the rain and sucked her teeth. People like Madame Alvenia preyed on the weak and hopeless. She persuaded people to believe there was a remedy, a quick fix for a broken heart. Ajali felt so stupid. Of course, the woman would lead her to believe that unearthly influences had prompted Bryce to leave her. The woman couldn't make any money if she told the truth: *Your man simply stopped loving you; there's nothing anyone can do. He's gone. Accept it. Move on.*

No, telling people the truth wouldn't earn her a dime, and it certainly wouldn't encourage repeat customers or word-of-mouth advertising. What a pathetic fool she'd been.

And that Goddess Kali trick! What a ruse. How could she have been so desperate and dumb? Well, she'd had it with the self-pity. Ajali firmly made up her mind that she was going back to work with her head held high: she'd resume friendships, reestablish her social life...and learn to live again. Without Bryce.

The distinct, acrid odor of smoke from the extinguished candles wafted through the air, a reminder of her foolishness. Ajali turned up her nose, picked up the phone and called Tee.

"Hey, girl," Tee greeted her.

"Hey, what's going on tonight? You going out?"

"Uh-huh. It's Thursday. You know I don't miss karaoke night."

Ajali laughed. "For somebody who can't sing a note, you sure picked a strange favorite pastime."

"Girl, you don't know? Karaoke was invented for people like me. People who can't sing but love holding a microphone and being the center of attention."

Ajali laughed again, picturing Tee holding the mic like a pro, working her body like Beyonce, and using all the facial expressions of Patti LaBelle while singing terribly off-key. "Well, I was thinking about joining you tonight."

Tee let out a yelp of joy. "Aw, we gonna party tonight. Welcome back to the world. I've missed you so much, Aj."

"Thanks, Tee. I'm sick of and tired of being sick and tired. The hell with Bryce. It's time to move on."

"Amen," Tee said.

Slightly tipsy and feeling happier than she'd felt in ages, Ajali waved good-bye to Tee, the designated driver for the evening. She entered her apartment and clicked on the lights, smiling as she recalled Tee's antics: she had greedily hogged the mic all night, performing songs by Mariah Carey, Fantasia and Destiny's Child. Tee also entertained the crowd with some old-school rap; she had the crowd roaring with laughter when she broke into a hilarious rendition of LL Cool J's, "Mama Said Knock You Out."

Ajali washed off her makeup, brushed her teeth. She felt lighter, less weighed down by the pain of the loss. She climbed into bed expecting sleep to come easily for a change.

With her head resting peacefully on a down-filled pillow, Ajali closed her eyes and felt herself drifting off when a sudden foul odor permeated her bedroom. Her eyes popped open; she sniffed the air. "What on earth?" she asked aloud. From the corner of her eye, she noticed something move. She bolted upright and strained to see in the dark. A dark shadow moved along the wall and inched toward her bed. The shadow emitted a rotting stench that caused Ajali to choke and gag.

The shadow sidled up closer and whispered in her ear, "You can't have him; he's mine!" The words, angry as a violent storm, were carried by breath that was rancid and hot. The disgusting odor lingered in the bedroom for several minutes.

Ajali jumped up and turned on every light in the apartment. Terrified, she ran in the kitchen, yanked open a drawer and pulled out a sharp knife. Back in bed, she tucked the knife under her pillow. She knew the blade was an ineffective weapon against her dark opponent. Nevertheless, it provided a modicum of comfort during the long, sleepless night.

Chapter 24

When the sun filtered in at dawn, Ajali allowed herself to sleep. She dreamed of Bryce in bed with the covers pulled over his head, twisting and moaning. He was surrounded by dozens of evil-faced little imps who giggled maliciously and erupted into high-pitched squeals as they jumped from the headboard onto Bryce's blanket-covered head.

In the dream, Ajali cowered helplessly in a corner of Bryce's bedroom while the horrid little creatures ran amok all over his body, tugging at the blanket, trying to snatch away his only source of protection.

His anguished cries were muffled, but Ajali clearly heard him call her name. Her love for Bryce felt stronger than ever and she was emboldened to come out of hiding to defend her man. She swatted at the little demons, but it seemed that with each bunch that she knocked aside, a larger number would run up the side of the bed, stronger and more evil than the pack she'd overthrown.

She swung and swatted until she was exhausted but to her horror, hundreds of imps were scratching and biting through the blanket. Pinpoint-size red specks gradually appeared. Ajali touched one of the tiny red dots. It was blood—Bryce's blood.

"Oh, my God," she cried out. "They're going to eat him alive." Paralyzed with fear, she screamed, "KALI!"

Kali didn't appear in a dramatic swirl of smoke; there was no drumroll or any fanfare at all. She simply materialized and raised her sword. The imps now shrieked in fear and scurried and scattered, running for cracks and crevices like roaches that had been doused with insect repellant from a can of Raid.

With sword in hand, Kali stood beside Bryce's bed. Bryce trembled beneath the covers.

"His days are numbered," Kali said in a harsh tone. "You." She pointed her sword at Ajali; her eyes, filled with fiery rage, bulged frighteningly. "You deserted him; you left him unprotected."

"But I..."

"Silence!" Kali flung back the covers; Bryce was turned on his side, curled with his balled fists pressed into his cheeks. His teeth chattered as he mumbled incoherently as if delirious. It was a sight so pitiful, Ajali instantly reached out to comfort him.

"He cannot see, feel or hear you," Kali informed her sternly. "Your touch, although tender and filled with compassion, will not release him from Eris's vile shackles. You've wasted precious time with frivolous activities... dancing, merrymaking and weakening your spirit with poisonous intoxicants..."

"What poisonous intoxicants?" Ajali frowned uncomprehendingly.

Kali's nostrils flared angrily as she sent Ajali a telepathic image. Ajali saw herself sitting at the bar laughing and talking and drinking vodka.

"You squandered precious time while your loved one suffers at the hands of one of Satan's whores."

"I'm so sorry, Bryce." Ajali fought back tears. "I really thought I was going crazy; that I had dreamed all this stuff."

"You are on the landscape of dreams at this very moment, but does that fact make what you've seen less real?"

Ajali shook her head.

"Your physical body lies sleeping in your bed, correct?"

Ajali nodded.

"The dream landscape is as real and as significant as your waking landscape. In fact, much more can be accomplished on this realm, where time and space do not limit what you can accomplish. Now, speak no more. Behold!" Kali turned Bryce over onto his back and Ajali uttered a small scream.

His penis was ravaged with oozing blisters and boils. His scrotum was discolored and swollen to the size of an eggplant. "Oh, Jesus," Ajali exclaimed and covered her face, for it was an unbelievably grotesque sight.

Kali softly touched Bryce's genitals. He winced and uttered a pitiful groan. "When Eris first introduced your young man to unholy copulation, he tried his best to thwart her efforts, but she is a force too strong for mortal man and soon he craved the depravity of the act. He's almost depleted of all male life force. He is dying. Yet even in his current state, the succubus continues to visit his bed, demanding more of his infected manhood."

"Infected? Bryce is infected?"

Kali simply turned her bulged eyes on Bryce's genitals. Maggots crawled out of his abundant pubic hair.

Ajali recoiled in disgust and let out a whimper.

"Those are her pets," Kali said, pointing her sword at the maggots that slithered in quick retreat. Some disappeared back into the forest of dark pubic hair and others burrowed into the raw lesions on Bryce's penile skin.

"He cries out; he pleads for mercy, but Eris continues to drain him." Kali sighed and shook her head. "All this suffering and you find reason to frolic in the night."

"What can I do right now?" Ajali asked, contrite.

"You must reclaim the female life force she has already siphoned from you."

Ajali grimaced.

"Your last encounter strengthened the evil one. She grows stronger every day. She weakened your spirit and caused you to doubt yourself. Your doubt gave her complete and unchallenged dominion over this one." She pointed to Bryce. "He is close to death."

"How close?" Ajali's voice was an agonized whisper.

"It is up to you."

"Please, Goddess, tell me what to do?"

"Do you believe that you are a goddess?"

"No, I'm just a human being."

"You are a woman; thus, you are a goddess. Believe. And fear not the evil one. Now, come close."

Ajali hesitated, and then edged close to Kali. Kali softly recited a prayer and advised Ajali to repeat it twice, which she did. And after reciting the prayer, she was overcome with a feeling of peace.

"Eris cannot touch him when he is shielded by prayer. The Prayer of Protection will keep him safe when you've assumed your ethereal body while in a meditative state."

"What will happen to him when I'm not in meditation?"

"Eris will debilitate him further," Kali uttered softly—regretfully. Then her voice grew strong and serious. "She'll laugh at his cries of pain and ride him until she's drawn out the last drop of his spermatic fluid. When he's depleted, she'll call forth her tiny banshees and allow them to feed upon him." Bryce moaned as if feeling the full effect of Kali's words.

Although she was just a visitor on the landscape of dreams, Ajali felt the same emotions she'd feel if she perceived this horror in the physical world. She was so nauseated, she had to sit down. Perched beside Bryce, she bent over him and lovingly wiped perspiration from his face and then whispered the prayer.

He stopped moaning, shifted his position and began to ease into what appeared to be a peaceful sleep.

Kali's lips relaxed into a smile. "Do you see the healing effect of prayer?"

"I do."

"Repeat the Prayer of Protection throughout your waking state. Meditate five times a day until he is out of harm's way."

"And once he's safe...she'll go away. Right?"

Kali gave a noncommittal grunt. "She'll leave *him* alone but she'll need to finish what she started with you in order to attract more prey."

"Kali, you're scaring me. What do you mean she'll have to finish with me? I thought she needed my life force to give her the strength to attack Bryce."

"Eris wants a human form. She has a small portion of your essence, giving her the shape of a woman, but not the flesh, bones and blood."

"How do I defeat her? Is there another prayer?" Ajali asked anxiously.

"Once the young man is safe, you must take back your feminine life force and send Eris's wicked spirit back to the Dark Realm."

ris overheard everything the two biddies said. Everything except the prayer, of course. When they'd started rattling that prayer off, self-preservation instinctively kicked in and Eris shut down all her senses.

Now they were gone. Finally. She glanced over at Bryce. The sun outside shone brightly, but with the curtains drawn, the room was as pitch-black as midnight. Still, she saw him clearly. With her indigo eyes blazing upon him, Bryce promptly discharged a succession of mournful mumblings and pathetic moaning sounds. He seemed to realize, even as he slept, that his Earth life was soon coming to an end.

True to his former self, the Stovall man was a spineless weakling who had become quite useless to Eris. She liked her men virile, with gushing ejaculations. Bryce was no longer producing an adequate amount of seminal fluid. He cried and sniveled for the duration of their sexual encounters—a ritual that was supposed to fill her with immense satisfaction as well as supply her with the male life force that was necessary for her strength and survival. The amount of semen that she was able to siphon from him had dwindled down to barely a dribble. The man was truly worthless.

She brightened in remembrance of the snippet of enjoyment she was able to gain from the Stovall man. Mmm, how she delighted in licking the wounds on his male appendage with her fiery forked tongue. Oh, the thrills she derived when he screamed in agony. The anguished sounds he emitted often brought her to convulsions of orgasmic pleasure.

But besides that, he was dull, dull, dull. Disgusted and weary of him, she dismissed her former notion of becoming his bride. How could she possibly benefit from marriage to such a sickly and feverish man? He slept and moaned incessantly—how pathetic.

Besides, why should she limit herself with this Stovall weakling when she was a powerful goddess, destined to be worshipped by legions of men?

Eris decided to allow Bryce's heart to continue to beat for as long as she needed him alive. When she acquired a body—the moment she drew breath into her human form, she'd siphon his last bit of male essence and rejoice when his insignificant life ended.

And, of course, she'd seize the precious wedding ring from his bureau drawer.

On the day that he expelled his final breath, she'd feel so vindicated and overjoyed, she'd have a great celebration, and later, in the moonlight, she and her imps would dance together on his grave.

Her musing made her feel victorious and beautiful. She caught a glimpse of her silhouette on the wall and nearly swooned from the sheer joy of seeing the form of her soon-to-be curvaceous body. It was perfectly shaped—lovelier than even her last lifetime on Earth. Eris cupped and caressed the outline of what would soon become a set of full, sumptuous breasts. She turned and admired the features of her round hips and high protruding ass.

Ah, such loveliness should be worshipped by more than one man. When she acquired her next body, she promised herself she'd have an entire harem of unworthy male beings whose only purpose in life would be to worship and adore her. And most important, the male harem would be required to satiate her ravenous sexual appetite.

Using her third eye, she spied on Ajali, who awakened with a start. Ajali looked around her own bedroom and then helplessly traipsed into one room after another. Finally, she absently wandered into the kitchen, picked up the phone and speed-dialed Bryce.

Eris's eyes gleamed with interest when Bryce's answering machine clicked into gear. She watched Ajali open her mouth, preparing to leave a message. But instead of hearing Bryce's recorded voice, Ajali was greeted with an awful crackling sound followed by the hiss of Eris's discarnate voice. "He's mine!"

Ajali gasped and stared at the phone in shock and horror.

The vibration of Eris's loud laughter sent what felt like a high-wattage jolt of electricity up and down Ajali's arm.

Ajali screamed and dropped the phone, which made Eris shriek with devilish glee.

Scared of getting another electric jolt, Ajali refused to go near the phone that lay on the kitchen floor. Ajali paced worriedly back and forth from the kitchen to the living room. She hadn't expected Bryce to pick up, but had hoped the sound of the ringing phone would maybe chase away those nasty little creatures just in case they were nearby, tormenting him.

With such frazzled nerves how could she possibly sit still enough to concentrate on meditation? Biting her nails, she paced some more. She thought about her dream and those nasty sores all over Bryce's penis. And those maggots. *Oh God! Poor Bryce. I can't leave him there defenseless; I've got to get him out of there.*

Without giving it another thought, Ajali threw on a pair of sweats and a shirt. Luckily, she'd been too traumatized to return her set of keys to his apartment on the day he dumped her.

She parked in front of Bryce's building, turned off the ignition and then it dawned on her that she wouldn't be able to lift Bryce out of the bed or get him outside to her car; she'd need help. She looked up and down the block, but the neighborhood was pretty deserted. She walked around the corner and spotted a man loitering in the parking lot of Shop Rite supermarket, asking shoppers if they could spare some change. He looked to be in his mid-thirties and other than possessing that unbathed and haggard look of the homeless, the man looked healthy as a horse.

Smile in place, Ajali approached the man. His return smile was wide and even a bit cocky as if he expected Ajali to offer him a hot meal, some money and some wild sex.

"What's up, ma? You lookin' good, baby. Whatchu gon' do? Can you help a brother out wit' some change?" His tone and demeanor had changed from beggar to a man getting his mack on. She needed his immediate assistance and didn't have time to look or feel indignant.

"I need a favor."

The man frowned and reared back as if she'd invited him to a job fair where he was required to fill out a slew of employment applications.

"I need you to help me get my sick fiancé out of his apartment and into my car. He lives right down the street." She pointed to Bryce's apartment building.

"And what's in it for me?" the man asked, suspicion etched all over his face.

"Uh...Twenty dollars?"

The man did a quick dance step that informed Ajali that he was delighted by the amount of the monetary offer. "All right, baby girl. I'm wit' it. My name's Donnie."

She told him her name and steered him toward Bryce's building. Ajali started off at a normal pace, but the thought of Bryce being tortured by little demons quickened her steps until she was nearly trotting.

"Yo, what's the rush, ma? You running like dude's about to drop dead or something."

"Well, he's really sick," she said, looking back at Donnie, who didn't seem to be trying to keep up. "Could you hurry up, please? I'll throw in an extra ten bucks, okay?"

The promise of more money was just the incentive to get Donnie to match her speed and jog along beside her.

"Dude ain't all big and fat or nothin', is he?" Donnie asked breathlessly when they ran up the steps that led to the front door. "'Cause I ain't trying to break my back; you know what I'm sayin'?"

"No, he's not fat," she answered absently as she dug around inside her purse for the set of keys to Bryce's apartment.

Her sense of smell didn't operate during meditation or while on the dream landscape, but the stench hit her the moment she cracked the door to Bryce's apartment. The chain was on from the inside, but the smell seeped through the opening.

"Dayum!" Donnie scrunched up his face and vigorously fanned it.

Being that he could use some freshening up himself, Ajali thought the homeless man had a lot of nerve. Still, she needed his services so she had to be polite. "He's sick," she said with a sad smile followed quickly with an apologetic shrug. "Can you break the chain?" She looked at Donnie hopefully.

"Breakin' and enterin'? I ain't trying to catch no case, ma. Now, you said you was gon' pay me to lift old boy up and help him to your car..."

"Fifty dollars. I'll give you fifty dollars." She anxiously tried to peek through the slight opening, hoping Bryce was up and about and hopefully—feeling better.

"I hear you talkin' but right about now, you gon' have to show me the money."

Ajali was hesitant about pulling out her wallet. "Do I look like someone who would jam you? I'm an honest, law-abiding—"

"Then call the superintendent or somebody and tell 'em to let you in homeboy's apartment the legal way."

Donnie wasn't dumb, Ajali realized. She slipped her hand inside her pocketbook and stealthily extracted a twenty. "Here. I'll give you this now and you'll get the rest after we get him in my car."

"Bet!" Donnie said and snatched the money. "Now stand back, baby girl." Donnie leaned back and lifted his leg like a kickboxer and gave the door a hard thrust. The chain popped and Ajali burst inside the apartment.

"What the fuck! Goddayum, it stinks in here," Donnie complained as they walked down the hallway. "You sure homeboy ain't dead up in here?"

Ajali shot Donnie a murderous look. "Don't say that." Now frightened, she started running and calling Bryce's name. When she reached the bedroom, she let out a sigh of relief. He was trembling and moaning, but he was alive.

Demonstrating his discontent with the repugnant odor, Donnie entered the bedroom with the top of his filthy shirt covering his mouth and nose. Only his eyes were visible and they were bugged out in disbelief. "What the fuck happened to dude?" he asked with his neck stretched, refusing to come too close to the bed.

"Come on, Donnie, I need you to help me," Ajali pleaded. "He's really sick; I've got to get him out of here."

The blanket that covered Bryce was stiff from dried perspiration, semen, and blood, so Ajali hurried to the linen closet to get a clean sheet. But when she lifted the blanket and saw the horribly swollen, purplish-colored scrotum; and the oozing sores and tiny bite marks that covered Bryce's body, she was certain Donnie would settle for the twenty he already had in his pocket and haul ass out of the apartment.

Thinking quickly, she threw the clean sheet over the soiled blanket. "Come on; let's get him out of here."

Standing rooted to the floor, Donnie rolled his eyes up to the ceiling in thought. "Yo, dude looks like he might need some CPR or something. Maybe we shouldn't move him."

"Come on, Donnie!" Ajali shouted. "Please. Don't you want the rest of the money?"

The mention of the word *money* worked like the snap of a hypnotist's fingers bringing a subject out of a trance. Donnie put one foot in front of the other until he was standing at Bryce's bedside, assessing the situation.

"Why's he all skinny and shit? He got AIDS?"

"No! He just has a bad case of the flu."

"What? That SARS shit?"

"No! Just an ordinary virus, now come on. Just help me lift him, okay?"

With his shirt still covering his mouth and nose, Donnie lifted Bryce up like he was nothing more than a sack of potatoes. Ajali stayed close by his side, making sure the sheet didn't slide off. As squeamish as Donnie was acting, he was liable to drop Bryce if he saw his wounds.

"Whoa!" Donnie stopped mid-stride; his eyes narrowed suspiciously. "Don't tell me homeboy is all naked and shit?"

Unfortunately, the blanket and sheet only covered the top of Bryce's body.

"I know that ain't dude's naked bony ass rubbing up against my arm?"

Ajali was silent; she didn't know how to respond.

"Aw, man. This shit is fucked up. Why ain't you put some drawers on homie?" Donnie shook his head. "I shoulda known better than to trust a big butt and a smile," he said, using a line from an old school song.

Had the situation not been so grave, Ajali would have laughed. But she was busy holding the door open for Donnie and then had to rush to keep up with him, sticking close to his side as if he were carrying precious cargo that couldn't be out of her sight for one second.

And in her center of the universe, Bryce *was* the most precious cargo in the world.

With the promise of even more money, she persuaded Donnie to get in the car with her and carry Bryce inside her apartment. After they'd gotten him into bed, she thanked Donnie. She cast a glance around the kitchen and noticed the telephone lying on the floor. Still terrified of touching it, afraid of another electric shock, she asked in a voice as casual as she could muster, "Would you mind putting that phone back on the base?"

"Anything else, Your Highness?" he grumbled as he did so.

Biting a fingernail, Ajali watched like a hawk, praying Donnie didn't get jolted by an electrical shock. To her great relief, he replaced the phone without incident.

"No, that's all. Thanks again. I really appreciate your help," she said sincerely. She emptied out her wallet, giving Donnie ninety more dollars. She would have gladly given him more if she'd had more cash on hand.

Chapter 26

*E*ris transformed herself to colorless moisture, which she cooled down to body temperature to attach herself to Donnie's sweaty forehead. Disguised as perspiration, Eris had hitched a ride to Ajali's apartment.

When Donnie bent down to pick up the telephone, tiny beads dripped from his forehead to the tiled kitchen floor.

One drop pulsated with life and separated from the small pool of sweat. It slowly worked its way to the base of the refrigerator, where it adhered itself as a thin layer of condensation. Although it was undetectable by the human eye, the patch of moisture undulated and writhed with delight.

In the bedroom with Bryce, Ajali tried to get her bearings. But the move had agitated Bryce; his breathing had a raspy quality and he kept moaning something awful.

What should she do first?

Pray!

The word just popped in her head. She was excited and nervous at the same time. The prayer would help Bryce, but could she remember it? She got a pad and pen and sat next to Bryce and started writing the Prayer of Protection as she spoke each word. She looked at the written words and nodded her head. Yes, she'd remembered it word-for-word.

Ajali recited the prayer over and over until Bryce finally became still and peaceful. Then she braced herself and pulled back the covers. "Oh no!" she groaned aloud and threw the covers back over him. His injuries looked much worse than they had appeared in her dream state. Bryce's penis was not only afflicted with boils, bruises, welts and open sores, but there were also tiny, deep gashes on his inner thighs, chest and shoulders.

She was afraid to take a look at his back, but calling forth all her courage while she again recited the prayer, she turned Bryce over to examine him. She bit down on her lip to hold back the tears. His back was mutilated with innumerable deep perforations. Teeth marks, left by those savage little imps.

Having no medical training, Ajali was in over her head—but if she put Bryce in the hospital, Eris and her team of ghouls would surely kill him before the doctors could even come up with a diagnosis.

No, she had to keep him right there with her, under her watchful eye, protected by her prayers.

Ajali gathered the necessary materials to nurse Bryce, then fetched a basin of warm soapy water. She softly bathed his face and then commenced to clean his wounds. Starting with his genitals, she bravely inspected his pubic hairs, hoping not to find the maggots she'd seen in her dream. There wasn't a trace of the nasty creatures. Kali had called them Eris's pets, so maybe they were somewhere with Eris.

Whatever the case, she was ecstatic that Bryce was no longer infested with those disgusting-ass maggots. After cleaning the wounds that covered his genitals and other body parts, Ajali spread a topical antibiotic on each and every bite, blister and bruise. She recited the prayer throughout the procedure and Bryce did not stir or grimace in pain.

Encouraging him to drink liquids, she put a straw in his mouth, which he reflexively sucked, ingesting small amounts of water; when she switched to apple juice Bryce greedily took in an entire cup. Ajali beamed like a proud mother. She carried the cup back to the kitchen, wondering what she'd give him for dinner. She spotted a can of chicken broth in the cabinet and nodded in approval.

Finished administering to her man for the time being, Ajali ran water for a badly needed hot bath. Immersed in sweet-scented, bubbly water, she pondered her situation. She'd have to battle the demonic entity to get back her essence.

She felt fine. She wasn't weak or ill as one would expect after being robbed of something as important-sounding as female essence. Ajali surmised that she must have an abundance of the stuff. Still, according to Kali, she had to get it back. It gave Eris the strength she needed to wreak havoc upon Ajali and Bryce's life and future happiness.

Oh well, she'd deal with that during meditation, she decided as she sank deeper into the soothing bathwater. But an image of Bryce alone in her bedroom prompted her to sit up and recite the prayer aloud. Feeling that he was fully protected, Ajali allowed herself to relax.

After her bath, clad in cotton pajamas, she went into the living room, lit the black and white candles and sat in the meditation chair. She closed her eyes and began to deep breathe and count backward. When she reached number one, instead of being in a relaxed state, her nose started inching. She scratched it and started the process again; this time, when she got to number four, her scalp began to itch. She just couldn't concentrate.

"That's it; I'll try again later," she said as she rose from the chair and peeked in on Bryce. He looked better already. She padded into the kitchen and opened the can of chicken broth, heated it in the microwave for just thirty seconds and took it to the bedroom, where she lovingly spoon-fed Bryce.

If Eris ever touches a hair on his head again, I'll kill that demon bitch...or die trying, Ajali vowed as she kissed Bryce's cheek. As sick as he was, it was so good to have her man back.

With the constant recitation of that damning prayer, Eris couldn't get within an inch of Bryce. It didn't matter; he didn't have much left to give. Besides, she had the salty taste of another man in her mouth. Donnie. The bum's essence was a part of her now and she wanted...no, needed more.

She'd changed her molecules to accommodate the move to the new location so she was stuck in her current state for a while. Once she regained her strength and ability to transform from liquid to a gas, she'd pay that interloper, Donnie, a nocturnal visit and penetrate his dreams.

Chapter 27

*E*ris tried to block the sound of Ajali's prayers, but it was becoming increasingly difficult to shut out the incessant babbling. When at last her form congealed and thickened into a dark, gaseous, feminine structure, she eased out a crack beneath the window pane with a craving so intense she could hardly enjoy the moonlight she loved so much.

In shadow form, Eris slid along cars, the sides of houses and apartment buildings. She ignored her growing hunger, her craving for testosterone, as she reveled in the freedom of being one with the black sky.

There was no point in rushing; finding Donnie would be easy. His scent would lead her to him. She licked her lips in anticipation; his essence would soon give her the strength to battle the female—her nemesis, who'd somehow called forth Kali—a powerful warrior, but no match for Eris's superior, conniving mind.

Eris's laughter shrieked across the sky and then landed softly—a tender whisper inside Donnie's ear.

He sat slumped against a wall in an alley, asleep. He slept so deeply, in a realm so strange and mysterious, Eris could not get through. Donnie's slackened mouth stretched into a smile before he gasped and took his last breath, succumbing to the peace he sought from the needle that protruded from his arm.

Eris screamed, and it was an eerie cat-like sound. She felt robbed, humiliated, betrayed. She snarled at the man, wishing she could kill him; but alas—Donnie was already dead.

Having gone an entire earth day without an infusion of life force, Eris was desperate for prey. She had to go back to the Stovall man and his woman until someone else unwittingly summoned her into their life.

Back in Ajali's apartment, Eris couldn't believe her stroke of good luck. Ajali was asleep. No prayers and no burning candles; she had left the Stovall man defenseless. Eris hovered over him, but he had become bare bones with a minimal amount of testosterone—not enough to strengthen the body she was forming, not enough to do much of anything. But the woman... The portion of the woman's essence had given Eris her womanly form. Growing impatient with battling over meager doses of female essence, Eris quickly devised a new plan.

Bryce was back to good health and good spirits. In fact, he started whispering words so loving in Ajali's ears; he was bringing her close to tears. Tears of joy. He kissed her and softly bit her ear; calling her "Beautiful" like he used to do.

"I've missed you and I missed all the things we used to do." He climbed on top of her, pressing his hardness into her pelvic area.

"Baby, are you sure it's okay? Are you healed...you know...down there?" Ajali asked, uncertain that Bryce's wounds could have healed so quickly.

"Don't worry about that; I want to love you in a different way. Relax, Beautiful. Open your legs," he whispered seductively.

It was too good to be true. Bryce, back to his normal sexy self. She wanted to ask if the wedding was back on, but decided to save that question for later. Bryce dove under the covers and Ajali shyly parted her legs. He hadn't even touched her and already she was grunting, moaning and gripping the sides of the pillowcase while squeezing her eyes closed tight.

It had been so long since Bryce had made love to her, her juices were flowing embarrassingly out of control.

When his tongue lightly touched the soft flesh between her thighs, she jumped as if hit by a stun gun.

"Calm down, baby," he said soothingly.

"I can't," she moaned. "Oh Bryce, it's been so long."

"This is an exotic flower. These are the flower's petals," he said as he gently spread her moist vaginal lips. "Fresh, sweet and dewy from morning rain."

"Oh damn, Bryce. You sound so sexy, your voice is torture. I can't take this shit—hurry, Bryce. Fuck me."

"No, baby. I have to take care of my flower." He slowly inserted a finger and sucked it. "Mmm. Sweet honey."

Ajali twisted in agony. She whimpered his name.

"Now spread your flower for me." Bryce place Ajali's hands on her womanhood. "Spread it for me," he requested as he got down on his knees and covered her with his mouth. He sucked hard, giving her a mixture of pleasure and pain. He stopped and looked at her. "Ajali, can I have some more?" he asked in a calm voice.

She nodded her head frantically. "Yes, Bryce. Yes!"

"Can I have all of it?"

She nodded a wild affirmation.

"Spread it, baby."

She stretched herself as far open as she possibly could. And this time Bryce inserted his tongue, which went deeper than ever before, hitting corners never touched before, sucking out her goodness, all the while rubbing her clit with his finger.

Or was it his finger? Ajali stiffened and sat up and watched with wonder while Bryce slurped between her legs like a starving man. His hands, she noticed...both hands were pressed against her hips.

"Bryce?" she uttered, terrified. But he didn't hear her, he continued to lick and suck. His tongue was inside her, so what was rubbing against her clit?

"Bryce!" She grabbed one of his hands, pulling it away from the side of her hip. Finally, he looked up—but was faceless with a darting forked tongue.

Ajali awakened. She felt disoriented but was comforted by the feeling of holding onto Bryce's hand. Shaking away the feeling of her awful dream, she cast a glance downward and screamed. Bryce was sound asleep in his usual curled position—with both hands balled up to his cheeks.

Panting in terror, she looked from Bryce to the horrible disembodied hand, which had traveled with her from the nightmare realm. In a matter of seconds the hand began to fade and then quickly disappeared back to the abominable place where it belonged.

Ajali was mystified as to what had actually happened. "Bryce," she whispered, searching his face for glimmer of confirmation that they had made love. She touched his warm, damp forehead with the back of her hand. His breathing was ragged and uneven. She didn't have to check his wounds to realize that he was still sick, much too sick to have spoken so clearly and coherently during her dream. The man lying next to her still needed her care and wasn't capable of giving her sexual pleasure.

Something shameful and unholy had been done to her as she slept. Mystified, Ajali swung her legs off the bed. Scratching her head, she padded to the bathroom.

She eased onto the toilet seat, unaware that she was chafed and raw until she released a stream of urine. It burned so badly she nearly jumped off the toilet seat.

"Oh my God, what's going on?" she wondered aloud as she tilted her body to one side in an attempt to endure the burning until she finished. She dabbed the tender area gingerly with tissue paper that normally felt cottony soft, but now felt as hard and painfully abrasive as a Brillo pad.

With her pajama bottoms gathered around her ankles and her legs gapped slightly apart, Ajali toddled over to the vanity closet and took out a handheld mirror. She bent at the waist to examine the tender area.

The inside of her vagina was beet red with protruding milkwhite sores. Ajali's hand trembled; her eyes closed involuntarily at such an appalling and offensive sight. Then, hoping against hope that her imagination was running wild, she took another look. Lined in an even row on both inner vaginal lips were sharply pointed, evil-looking things that looked like a set of tiny, razor-sharp teeth.

Ajali gave a frightened cry. And then began to whimper, pitifully. Eris! The demon bitch had violated her—infected her genitalia with her long, vile tongue.

She heard Bryce groan and felt a wave of panic. Was he being tortured again? For Bryce's sake, Ajali quickly pulled herself together, resolving to examine herself again later. Maybe the lesions inside her vagina would disappear like the disembodied hand she'd held when she awakened from the dream. She stood up, pulled up her pajamas, washed her hands thoroughly and rushed to Bryce's bedside.

The friction from walking fast was very painful.

Chapter 28

The dead junkie had given Eris a bright idea. He'd gone directly to his bloodstream for the fix he needed, thus she went straight to the source of the female life force she desperately needed. She'd sucked out Ajali's essence and the results were swift and amazing.

Eris had a body! She couldn't see her reflection in a mirror but the body parts she was able to see with her blazing indigo eyes were a work of art. She was truly flawless, an ebony goddess.

She ran her hands over her breasts, tummy and waistline and released a satisfied sigh. She was perfectly sculpted—a beauteous sight to behold.

Although she was in the bedroom with Bryce and Ajali, they couldn't see her, for she made certain her new feet were planted firmly in the invisible realm.

Eris touched her hair, an abundance of wild, coarse coils—her crown and glory. No longer satisfied sharing her living quarters with such a dreary and monotonous couple, she began to formulate a plan to go out in the world and find a dwelling place of her own.

She gazed at the spiritless pair huddled together in despair and laughed so loud and at such a high pitch, the sound vibrated and shattered the glass on a picture that hung on the wall. Bending over and muffling her laughter, she watched the woman, Ajali, limp to the living room, butcher knife in hand as she sought out the source of the glass-breaking mischief.

Eris would have loved to linger and have some more fun but she had other plans.

She used her third-eye vision to locate the perfect home. Transforming to mist, she slipped through the crack beneath Ajali's apartment door and streamed out into the world.

None of the professional and real-estate-savvy agents in the entire city of Philadelphia could have located living quarters as perfect for Eris as the cavernous abode she acquired on her own.

It wasn't the fancy palace where one day she'd reside, but it was the perfect temporary residence until she'd gathered all the male and female life force that she required to maintain a permanent earthly body.

It was a decayed and abandoned insane asylum; twenty-seven deteriorated buildings located on the north and south sides of Roosevelt Boulevard, all connected by tunnels. Many of the eerie, ivy-covered buildings were well hidden by trees and a forest of wonderfully wild and high weeds, which were a haven for the insect creatures that Eris would later train as house pets.

Careful not to attract the attention of the patrolling guards, she remained misty; she'd materialize into her gorgeous physical body later when the sun went down.

Excitedly, she toured her spacious dwelling place, roaming all twenty-seven buildings, inspecting every room.

In one of the former patient wards, the old cots were nothing more than rusted skeletal frames, devoid of mattress and bed covering. Debris from caved-in ceilings lay in dusty piles on the floor. Also on the floor was plaster that had crumbled from the walls, glass from broken windows and splinters of wood that had once served as shutters to keep the sun from shining light into this place of unspeakable misery and pain.

Eris could sense the anguish that once dwelled behind these walls and it gave her trembles of pleasure as she journeyed on to the next chamber of her eerie estate. As she floated the sun began to set, darkening the dismal environment even more.

As she desired, her body magically began to take on its human female shape. Eris felt gloriously beautiful, powerful and invincible.

Naked, she strode into the next room. The moment she entered, she winced and issued forth a low growl. She spun around angrily. What was in this room that could cause her such vexation?

Heeding her feeling of extreme discomfort, she observed the environment warily, narrowed her indigo eyes.

There was an overturned broken piano; grimy candleholders; musty old hymnals with the "spine" pulled away. Several pieces of mildewed sheet music were scattered about the floor, and a rickety podium with the peeling painted image of a crucifix informed Eris that she was inside the asylum's place of worship—a chapel.

Her only defense from this house of prayers was that it had been desecrated—violated—and therefore its spiritual power had diminished.

Ha! The foolish believers had beseeched their God to show them mercy. Obviously he didn't. Eris could still hear their haunted cries coming from the floorboards, the walls and what was left of the ceiling, still tormented and pleading for salvation. Laughing cruelly, she trod a few feet through the rubbish.

What's that? She took a few steps closer to the object of interest and then instantly recoiled and gave a furious hiss.

On the floor was a statue of the Virgin Mary. Then Eris noticed that the statue had been defiled, which emboldened her to inch closer.

Eris gave a great whoop of glee. The statue lay on its back covered with filth and debris, but even better, it had been beheaded.

You were so pious, you lost your head! And it serves you right. Pointing at the statue, Eris doubled over in laughter. *Look at you, you so-called virgin, lying in the muck like a two-dollar whore!* Using a shoeless foot, Eris gave the sadly discarded statue a sacrilegious kick to get it out of her way.

Still, being inside a chapel was disturbing. Desecrated or not, this place of worship did not evoke feelings of well-being. Leaving behind a spiteful giggle, Eris fled the chapel and swiftly moved on.

Eris inhaled deeply. She smelled life force. The smell emanated from her own foot, which had kicked the statue. Eris relied on her third-eye vision for clarification.

Someone had handled that statue, had tried to straighten it, had tried to give the Virgin some dignity, but in touching the statue a portion of life force was left behind. That life force was now attached to Eris's foot.

Seduced, Eris hurried toward the strong masculine scent, which was tantalizing her. It came from another building. Taking the quickest route, she traversed a long steam tunnel in the basement. Sloshing hastily through the slimy, knee-deep water of the catacombs, Eris was anxious to apprehend her prey.

Finally, she reached the end of the tunnel, the scent was so strong she become woozy. With blazing indigo eyes, she located her target in the dark— a homeless man, sound asleep inside a padded room. Remnants of his life surrounded him: a pile of tattered clothing, empty liquor bottles, empty cans of sardines, Vienna sausages and other canned meat. There was a flashlight on the floor, and pornographic magazines.

Covered with a green wool blanket, the man drooled as his head lolled drunkenly. One hand possessively clutched a nearly empty bottle of whiskey. In a deep, intoxicated sleep, he was unaware that Eris had joined him.

She slithered under the blanket, taking with her the slime from the corroded tunnel. She ripped open his pants at the crotch. She released his soft member and caressed it. A smile played at the corner of the sleeping man's lips and then his member awakened and became stiff.

Shaking with excitement, Eris couldn't decide the manner in which she'd siphon the male elixir from the homeless man. Deciding to try out her new female organ, Eris mounted the man and rode him until he reached an explosive orgasm. It pleased her that the vagrant had provided a substantial supply of his masculine liquid. But she needed more.

She felt his fingers tangle into her hair; his rough fingers touched her face. "Goddamn. I thought I was having me a wet dream, but you real." He touched her face incredulously. "You staying in here, too?"

Eris didn't answer.

"Where your clothes at? It gets cold in here at night." The man gave her a long look and noticed the dried sewage on her legs. He shrugged. He'd seen worse in the years that he'd been homeless. He'd trudged through the tunnels himself.

"You don't talk much. You one of them deaf-mutes? Hot damn. I done lucked up and got me a woman who won't give me no lip." The homeless man smiled wistfully.

"Don't worry; I'll help you find yourself something to wear. Now come on, get up under these covers." The man looked up at the padded ceiling. "I done hit the jackpot. Yes, indeed." He looked at the ripped crotch of his pants and shrugged. "You was horny, huh? Snuck up on me while I was 'sleep. Well, come on. It's a lot more where that come from. Yes, indeed. I done hit the jackpot tonight."

Eris didn't say a word. She got under the covers and took him in her mouth and gave a hard suck.

"Hey. Watch that. Feel like you using too much teeth. Suck on it slow and gentle, baby. Go 'head. I ain't had a good blow job in a while." He closed his eyes and relaxed against the padded wall.

Eris sucked softly, making him purr. She added some pressure, making him moan, and let him slide in and out of her mouth as the man humped hard and fast against her face, trying to get back into the soft moist place.

Then she opened her mouth wide taking in everything...his dick *and* his balls.

"Goddamn, you good, girl. Come on, baby," he said with a hard thrust. "Take it all. Suck that dick, baby. Aw, yeah. Suck my balls. Ooo, goddamn, goddamn, goddamn!" The homeless man was briefly silent and then he asked, "Do you swallow, sweet thing? You gonna swallow all this good cum?" He didn't wait for Eris's answer. He started thrusting faster. Breathing like a dragon, he worked himself up to the inevitable eruption.

He came so violently, he made sounds similar to one who's been touched by the Holy Ghost. The man sounded like he was speaking in tongues. Finally, after depositing the last drop of semen, he let out a long, satisfied breath and relaxed. His dick remained inside Eris's mouth.

Eris began to move her lips.

"Whoa, whoa, whoa..." The man tried to sit up but with Eris refusing to release him, he surrendered and slumped back down. "Give me a few minutes, all right? You about a frisky somebody; I done gushed up a geyser and you still want more. Lord, I must be in heaven." He smiled and closed his eyes.

Eris made sucking movements with her lips.

"Hey! That's enough for right now!" he shouted, irritated. "You done wore me out." He tried to ease himself out of her hot mouth. But Eris put suction on him that informed him that she intended to have her way.

"Come on, baby. What's wrong with you? I gotta rest a while." He used a pleading tone because he now sensed something was wrong with the mute woman. The man was beginning to feel afraid of her.

Eris started making slurping sounds as she sucked on his flaccid penis. Too tired and too scared to get an erection, he appealed to her common sense. "Come on now, quit it. I done came twice. I ain't no superman or nothing." He tried to use a firm tone, but the tremble in his voice revealed his fear, which only served as an aphrodisiac for Eris. "I can't just keep getting it up every few minutes. I gotta get some type of rest," he went on. "Now come on and get some sleep. We can do something in the morning."

Still holding onto his private part, she looked up and smiled. With her indigo eyes shining upon him she resembled a cat with a mouse in its mouth. The man let out a terrified yelp.

She could have drained him quickly, but she chose to take it slowly. His agonized screams lasted at least ten horrible minutes as Eris slowly siphoned semen, blood, veins, arteries, mucocutaneous tissue, urine and water. The outer flesh lay flat and empty, resembling a brown cigar wrapper, stripped of the tobacco filling.

Satisfied, Eris wiped the side of her mouth, pushed the dead man away and rushed back though the catacombs. Revitalized and strong, now she had the strength to finish touring her abode. Who knew what delicious treats lurked in corners and hallways? Perhaps she'd stumble upon a midnight snack.

Chapter 29

When the FedEx deliveryman rang the doorbell, Ajali scribbled her signature and snatched the package from his hand. Ripping open the box, she gazed at the small tube—the medication she'd ordered from an online pharmacy. In the bathroom, she read the instructions. Unwilling to even glimpse the hideous outgrowths, she carefully applied the cream without the use of a hand mirror. Her fingers were her eyes. She quickly dabbed every disgusting protrusion with the medication while praying that the treatment worked. She needed a miracle healing.

The vulgar outbreak of warts between her legs was Eris's diabolical work. Since her prayers along with a topical treatment was working well for Bryce, Ajali prayed this meditation would heal the ghastly outbreak. She wanted to sit down and focus on what she hoped would be a miracle healing.

But she had other pressing business to attend to. Nagging business. The two-week vacation time Bryce had taken for the wedding and honeymoon that never happened was almost over; his employer would be expecting him to return to work in a few days. The need to call his job and provide a logical explanation for his absence was hanging over her head like a dark cloud.

The cancelled nuptials were public knowledge; a call from the jilted bride would definitely raise suspicions.

I'll ask Tee to make the call. Giving a sigh, she changed her mind. Tee would require a drawn-out explanation that Ajali wasn't prepared to give. Even if she were so inclined, she honestly couldn't explain her problems; she had no idea why that awful sexually deviant entity was out to destroy her and Bryce. And Tee would try to have her committed for even talking some trash like that.

She could just hear Tee: *Let me get this straight...'cause you're telling me some really creepy shit. You expect me to believe that Bryce is being haunted by some dead woman. And she was sexually molesting Bryce so bad, she drained him of all his masculinity? You tryin' to say Bryce can't produce any more sperm? You're telling me he has to rest to replenish his supply. Okay, I see,* Tee would say, while not really seeing. *But help me out here,* she'd continue, *you said the ghost molested you, too, so what you're telling me is the ghost chick is bisexual. Right? And she tricked you into thinking she was Bryce while you were 'sleep—she tricked you into letting her give you oral sex and now you got warts?* Tee would shake her head and say, *Girl, if you ask me, you're letting Bryce drive you straight-up crazy. A cancelled wedding is not the end of the world, now snap out of it and get yourself some help. Seriously, Aj. You need help, girl!*

Realizing she couldn't go to Tee for help, Ajali pushed Bryce's job dilemma to the back of her mind and went about her morning routine.

Bryce's ability to swallow had improved. She had taken him off the liquid diet and was now feeding him soft foods. While she spooned oatmeal into his mouth, Bryce opened his eyes and gazed at her briefly. In his eyes, she saw love. She hadn't imagined it, and that look of love was enough to motivate her to settle down and meditate. Meditation was not only an outlet to astral traveling. Kali had told her that it would help her get in touch with her higher consciousness—that part of the self that was wise and all-knowing. If ever there was a time that she needed answers, that time was now.

Pleased that Bryce seemed at peace after being washed and fed and having his wounds cleaned and dressed, Ajali surrounded him with the Prayer of Protection. She softly padded to the living room where she lit the candles and sank into her chair, counting backward until she felt totally relaxed and weightless.

She found herself on an isolated beach. In the distance she saw a small child—a little girl, left alone on the beach. She looked to be about three or four years old. Ajali began running toward the abandoned child. Upon approach, she noticed the little girl was crying.

"Don't cry, honey. Are you lost?" Ajali felt an inexplicable feeling of love for the beautiful child, who looked remarkably familiar.

The little girl shook her head.

"What are you doing out here by yourself? Where's your mommy?"

"I was looking for you."

"For me?" Ajali was shocked. "Do I know you? What's your name, sweetie?"

"We don't use names, but if I'm born, you're going to name me after someone very special," the little girl replied, wiping away tears and producing a gleaming smile.

Ajali crinkled her face in confusion. "What do you mean?"

"I'm your future daughter. If I'm born in this lifetime, you're going to give me a name that has a special meaning."

"What do you mean, if you're born? If you're my future daughter..."

The little girl's face took on a troubled look. "You have free will," the child said with wisdom beyond her years. "There are many roads in life and you're able to choose which roads you travel. If you don't get back on the road that will lead you to me, I won't be born."

Ajali got down on a knee, bringing herself down to the little girl's level. She cupped her face. "I thought you looked familiar. You look just like Bryce." Ajali's tone was filled with joy and wonder.

"They were preparing me for birth on Earth, but something happened and you're not safe now. We're not sure if I'll join you in this lifetime." Tears rolled down her cheeks, again.

Ajali was aware that in an altered state, there is often a shift in reality, causing peculiar events to appear routine and perfectly normal. "Oh, honey, don't cry." Ajali gave her a comforting hug; she didn't want to let her unborn child go.

"I love you, Mommy. But I'm afraid for you. I think something bad is going to happen to you." The little girl wept softly.

"I love you, too, sweetheart," Ajali said and meant it with all her heart. "There's nothing to be afraid of. Mommy and Daddy are going to make everything turn out all right in *this* lifetime."

"Are you sure?" the child asked with a sniffle. "I'm scared of that mean lady. She doesn't want me to be born."

"Does she bother you?" The motherly instincts Ajali never knew she possessed surfaced and she felt as fierce as a mother lion.

"No, she doesn't know about me. They keep me hidden."

"Who keeps you hidden?"

"The angels; they protect me. Your prayers protect me, too."

Now Ajali started crying. "Tell them I said thank you."

The little girl smiled. "That's funny. The angels wanted me to thank you for your prayers. They say that your prayers help protect me."

"I thought I was praying for your daddy; I didn't know about you."

"It doesn't matter; your prayers protect me, too. If Daddy survives, I'll survive." The child kissed Ajali and started backing away. "Don't worry, Mommy; Daddy's friend can call his work for him." Ajali reached for her, but the child was picked up by a low cloud that floated up high into the sky.

"I love you, Mommy." The child's voice was carried by an ocean breeze. She was gone, but she'd left Ajali with a solution to her problem.

Ajali opened her eyes. Although she was back in her own living room and sitting in the meditation chair, the taste of her sweet child's kiss remained on her lips.

The love she felt was unconditional, pure. Unlike any love she'd ever known. She'd protect her child's right to life with every fiber of her being.

Ajali closed her eyes and brought to mind an image of her beautiful little girl. Thanking the angels for her child's safekeeping, she made a promise to go to any lengths, to do whatever was necessary to bring her and Bryce's daughter into a safe and loving world.

The phone call to Justin, Bryce's good friend and intended best man, turned out to be a good decision. Surprised that she could string together lies so quickly, Ajali told Justin that Bryce had eaten some sushi and was unaware that he had gotten a tapeworm.

"Over time, he became sick and disoriented. His untreated symptoms resulted in some really erratic behavior. Canceling the wedding was just one of many bizarre behaviors," she explained sadly. "He was delirious, Justin. But he's doing so much better, being under a doctor's care and taking antibiotics."

Thankfully, Justin bought the story. He not only called Bryce's employer, but since a mere friend wasn't allowed to request extended sick leave for an employee, Justin even went so far as to pretend to be Bryce when he spoke to the Human Resources representative.

"Yeah, I was starting to worry about my man," Justin told Ajali over the phone. "The few times I was able to reach him, he sounded like he was on drugs. Then his answering machine started kicking out the craziest messages." Justin laughed. "Your call is right on time, Aj. I had just made up my mind...today I was going over to his place prepared to kick the door down if I had to."

"I appreciate everything, and I'll be sure to let you know when he's well enough for a visit."

"I can't help asking, but um...is the wedding back on?"

"Not officially. We haven't set a date. We'll probably just go to a justice of the peace." Ajali felt she spoke the truth. Bryce still loved her; she knew that with all her heart. He'd been bewitched and that *witch* wasn't getting her claws into him ever again.

Chapter 30

At first she was alarmed by the low rumble in her stomach; she thought her new body was malfunctioning, and then she remembered the sensation—it was called hunger. And she was famished. For food.

Eris gave a broad smile. Her body was functioning perfectly. As soon as she was certain that it would no longer require male or female life force—the moment she could rely on her body to sustain itself—she would leave for Virginia to collect her jewels and begin life anew.

Thinking rationally, she realized she was unwilling to sell her jewelry; parting with her beautiful treasure was unimaginable. An affluent male was what she needed. A bewitched devotee who'd ensure prolonged financial independence. Acquiring a loyal and generous lover would be easy.

A full moon and a private room was all she required to make a man grovel at her feet, betray his wife, desert his family, and adorn her with the finest jewelry while signing over to her the deed to the family estate.

Casting a spell on a man was easy, but keeping him bewitched required guile and cunning.

She wouldn't make the same mistake she'd made with Arthur Stovall. The price had been too steep. Feeling rage at the memory of being burned alive sent blue-tinted sparks flickering in the dark catacombs as she waded through the sludge and slime.

Eris found the kitchen. Like everything else in the abandoned place, it was a pigsty, and there was nothing but rodents roaming about. Rodents didn't suit her new human appetite.

Naked, with muck-covered legs, she left the building and made her way through tall grass, parting it with long, purposeful strides. Leaves, grass and insects were instantly affixed to her sticky legs. She didn't notice and didn't care. Her only concern was food.

Spotting a security car that patrolled the abandoned asylum, Eris waved her hands over her head and began running toward the road. "Help me, please help me. I've been raped." She looked back in fear as she pointed at the building she'd just left. "A madman dragged me in there, but I managed to escape…"

The patrolman reached for his radio.

"No! Don't call anyone. I don't have any clothes on; I don't want to be seen like this. Can you help me…please?" She shined her eyes on the security guard and sent him a telepathic image of the two them entangled in hot sex in the backseat of the patrol car.

Thinking that he'd come up with the idea, his mind immediately went to work on a way to encourage the strange naked woman to give him some quick no-strings-attached sex.

"I'm starving," she said, allowing her body to swoon against the car.

"Okay, I'll tell you what. Get in the backseat, but you have to lie down on the floor; I can't let anyone see you back there. I'm gonna drive you over to the Boulevard and grab you a burger or two…"

"And clothes. I need clothes," she added.

"Now that might present a problem." The security guard took his cap off and scratched his head.

Eris sent him another, more powerful telepathic image. The driver's-side door was wide open. He saw himself sitting on the edge of the seat, facing outward, his feet planted on the ground while Eris, her knees scraping gravel, performed oral sex.

Again, believing he'd come up with a really kinky idea, the security guard whispered, "Be quiet, I'm gonna call my wife." He pushed the numbers to his home. "Hey honeybunch. Listen, do you still have those boxes of clothes you were gonna donate to Goodwill? You do?" He looked back at Eris and winked. "No, I'm not taking them anywhere this time of the night, but it just so happens that we picked up a slew of vagrants and they're about to be hauled off to the city shelters and you know me with my soft heart…some of those homeless people are women with nothing but the clothes on their back. I figured you could make a donation to those poor women." He listened to his wife for a few moments, turned and gave Eris a thumbs-up.

"Food first," she insisted when he hung up the phone.

"Okay, but we gotta hurry up before my supervisor comes back on patrol." He backed out, in what seemed like two seconds, he was pulling up to the intercom at McDonald's. "What do you want?" he asked Eris.

"Anything. Lots of it."

He gave her a curious look. "Three double cheeseburgers, two small fries."

"Will that be all?" asked the mechanical voice.

"No!" Eris exclaimed. She pointed to three colorfully displayed photos of food items.

"Add a Big Mac, a grilled chicken salad, and a large Coke to that order," the security guard added reluctantly. He pulled up to the window and begrudgingly gave the attendant a twenty-dollar bill.

Eris ripped the the large greasy bag from the guard's hand and tore into the meal, stuffing large portions into her mouth. Making sounds similar to a wild animal, Eris devoured the food in just a few minutes and quickly guzzled the beverage.

The security guard's startled look suggested that picking her up was perhaps a bad decision.

Eris's telepathy was strong. She heard his thoughts and put him back on track with another erotic image.

She hunched over and curled up, making herself so small she'd be undetected from the eyes of nosy neighbors when he parked in front of his house. He went inside; and with her third-eye vision, she watched the security guard kiss his wife in gratitude. He even gave the unpleasant-looking shrew a wink and a flirtatious pat on her backside as he eased out the front door.

Hoisting two large boxes into the trunk, he drove Eris back to the deserted insane asylum.

The images Eris had sent the guard changed drastically. They were together in the backseat but instead of engaging in wanton sex, Eris whispered in his ear, "You're mine now. Do you understand?"

Trance-like, he nodded dumbly.

In the next scene, Eris was the one seated in the driver's seat while the security guard was positioned on his knees.

The female juices she'd siphoned from Ajali overflowed and streamed down her leg. "You're sick," she told the man. "You don't feel well."

"I'm sick," he repeated.

"What do sick people need?" Eris asked, her voice hypnotic.

"Medicine," the man replied.

She knocked his cap onto the ground and rubbed the top of his head. Scooting forward, she parted her legs. "I've got the medication you need." With a finger, she swiped the juices that trailed down her thigh and held the finger to the guard's lips, offering him a taste.

He opened his mouth willingly and sucked Eris's finger. Withdrawing her finger, she asked, "Feel better?"

The guard gave a hesitant nod, as if he weren't sure.

"Still sick?"

"Uh-huh," he said, sounding terribly ill.

"Do you need more of my very special medicine?"

He nodded.

Eris guided his head to her thigh. "Lick," she whispered. He licked and licked, moving upward until he was at the spot where the supply was in abundance.

He stuck his tongue in the sticky pool. One taste and he was hooked like an addict. And Eris intended for the security guard to be a faithful servant—at her beck and call for as long she needed.

Eris pulled his head away. "This healing elixir will make you feel better. But it's rare; it's limited. You must drink slowly and savor the taste."

He did as he was told...savoring the taste until Eris was satisfied. A human orgasm caused her body to jerk as if hit by a thousand electric jolts.

Swearing he felt much better, and thanking Eris profusely for the miracle treatment, the security guard drove her to a motel on Roosevelt Boulevard.

With a fiery glint in her eyes, she telepathically persuaded the guard to use his credit card to check her in for a seven-day stay, which he did with the sincere promise to bring her food three times a day.

Chapter 31

"Aj."

The sound of her name jerked Ajali awake. Bryce was calling her and this time it wasn't a dream.

"Yes, honey. I'm here," she said, lifting up on an elbow and smoothing back his hair. "Are you hungry?"

Bryce grunted.

This morning was the first time he'd spoken a word. And his first word was her name. Ajali grinned as if it were Christmas. She could see a healthy glow coming back to his face. Bryce was going to survive. *They* were going to survive.

The visit with their unborn daughter made her will to overthrow the evil force stronger than ever. Ajali was determined to win the battle and she would *not* die trying. Her opponent would die. Ajali would slaughter, mangle, disembowel, behead and exercise all types of medieval torture on anything and anyone who stood in the way of her family's future happiness.

Feeling empowered by Bryce's increasing health, Ajali got out of bed to make him breakfast. Maybe he was ready for scrambled eggs? She looked back at Bryce; in that short time span, he had dozed off again.

She cracked eggs, whipped them and prepared to scramble them. Suddenly she felt a discomfort between her legs that she couldn't help but associate with the warts that had somehow miraculously healed. Ajali frowned in fear. *Had they come back?*

Trying to ignore the feeling that something was wrong, shaking away the thought that the she-devil had returned to her bed, Ajali fed Bryce the two eggs she'd scrambled, a half-cup of applesauce, and six ounces of water, which he still had to drink through a straw.

She tried to focus her attention on how well Bryce was doing. He kept his eyes open throughout most of his meal, so she engaged him. "You look so good today. You're getting stronger and healthier every day." Spooning scrambled eggs into his mouth, she said, "I made something special for you; something with some flavor. I know you're getting tired of all that oatmeal," she said cheerfully as she fed him. There was a lilt to her voice that she no longer felt. She was worried, but was trying to disguise her fear.

Bryce looked at Ajali. His eyes projected remorse and pain. He looked at her imploringly and said, "I'm sorry, Aj." His voice was weak, barely a whisper.

So much had happened, so much had been lost, but it wasn't Bryce's fault. "It's not your fault, baby," she assured him. "This thing that has happened to us is some sort of dark force—something supernatural," she explained awkwardly. "But we're not going to let evil win. We're going to get stronger and together, we're going to win." She'd said a lot and Ajali wasn't sure if Bryce's mind was totally intact, if he'd been able to comprehend the significance of her words. It didn't matter; there were three words that were understood in every language. "I love you," she said and broke down and cried. She hadn't meant to, but the tears were drawn from deep reserves of emotions...love, pain, fear and the determination to win.

The feeling of Bryce weakly patting her back sympathetically should have been documented as a major breakthrough, but knowing that something really bad was happening to her—inside her—it was next to impossible to appreciate or find any joy in the moment.

When Bryce dozed off, not wanting to wake him, not wanting him to know how very frightened she felt, Ajali crept silently to the bathroom.

She inspected her private parts with a hand mirror. Thankfully, the warts hadn't returned, but something else was undeniably wrong. Her vagina felt dry; so dry it hurt to walk, to sit, to use the bathroom. Perhaps the dryness was a side effect of the medication she'd used to heal the warts. Yes, that made perfect sense.

Grateful that there was a plausible explanation, she applied a lubricant between her legs and tried to take her mind off her latest baffling medical condition.

Ajali settled into the meditation chair. The candle fire danced. She could feel her skin tingling all over. Something important was about to happen.

In a matter of seconds, her spirit left her body and lifted out of the chair. Without a destination, she thought of her daughter, hoping to be guided to her heavenly home, but instead she found herself flying through the sky above traffic on a highway, heading north. She noticed a street sign. Roosevelt Boulevard. She was puzzled; she didn't know a soul who lived on Roosevelt Boulevard.

In an instant, she was inside a hotel room. A woman—a peculiarly beautiful woman wearing a dark-colored dress was sound asleep in bed.

Instinctively, Ajali knew. This woman was her enemy; this was Eris, the evil one, who brought pain and destruction to every path she crossed.

Eris's eyes popped open like headlights being flicked on. She shrieked and threw back the covers. Prepared to pounce and battle for her life, Eris scratched out at the hovering Ajali; she raised her face and issued a loud, threatening growl.

Anger mingled with fear was an adrenaline rush that enabled Ajali to propel herself forcefully and swoop down upon Eris, screaming the Prayer of Protection repeatedly as Eris crouched down and covered her ears.

In the exact moment that Ajali took a breath, in order to continue the fervent prayer, Eris removed a hand from her ear and slashed her clawed fingers across the air.

Eris hadn't touched her, yet Ajali felt dizzy and weak as if she were quickly losing blood, losing her life force. She tried to flee but lost her sense of direction, bobbing around in a confused circle and then bumping uncontrollably into walls, against the ceiling.

Below her, Eris howled with laughter. "I ripped your silver cord; it can't be repaired. So just remember my sweet one...you and that Stovall man will always belong to me."

Driven by fear, Ajali popped back inside her body. Eris's demonic laughter echoed in her ears. Terrified, Ajali wondered what Eris had done to her; what had she taken this time? Kali had warned her to protect the silver cord that connected her astral body to her physical body. She'd cautioned her that Eris could gain strength from tearing it and extracting life force.

Physically, Ajali felt fine. Well, not quite. She still had that vaginal discomfort, but there were no new symptoms. She inspected her hands, legs and feet; stroked her chest, neck, shoulders and back. Every body part was unscathed and accounted for.

She crept past the bedroom where Bryce slept and warily slipped into the bathroom to look in the mirror to scrutinize her face. She prayed her face wouldn't reveal any visible traces of the failed astral trip.

Ajali gazed in the mirror and gasped. Her knees wobbled and she grabbed the sink. If Bryce weren't depending on her, she would have allowed herself the luxury of passing out.

She was stunned. And deeply troubled. The hair around her temples was streaked with gray. Ajali's frantic fingers began parting sections of her hair. To her utter dismay, she discovered gray roots. Lots of it. And the hair that wasn't gray was dry and brittle...without luster or life.

Another thing...her eyes had that hollow, sunken look like she hadn't slept for days on end.

Oh my God, this can't be happening to me! I'm only twenty-six years old, but I look like a woman twice my age, she thought.

Although she'd touched her body a few moments ago, she'd been searching for a wound or some other type of physical injury, but she now realized her debilitation was of a different kind.

She was aging. Rapidly, it seemed.

She snatched open her top to examine her breasts. Was it her imagination? Or had they sagged a bit? She inspected herself closely and shook her head. They weren't quite as perky; they looked a little droopy. They looked somewhat withered and sad.

Looking downward, she checked out her tummy. It was still flat, but there was a bit of excess skin. *Oh no!*

Ajali had to sit down on the edge of the tub; her eyes darted around worriedly as she tried to fathom what was happening to her. Rocking back and forth, with her head in her hands, it became abundantly clear that Eris was siphoning not just her womanhood—the demon was robbing her of her youth.

A sudden flash of scorching heat engulfed her; perspiration poured from her scalp, neck and chest. *What is this?* she wondered, wiping away the perspiration with a wet washcloth while simultaneously fanning her face. *Am I suddenly going into menopause?*

Kali, she cried. *Kali, please help me!*

But Kali did not make an appearance; she couldn't in the waking state. Ajali was desperate for answers; she needed the remedy for a quick reversal of dwindling youth. Her mind raced and she suddenly recalled Madame Alvenia, the woman in Marcus Hook, Pennsylvania. Madame Alvenia could channel Kali!

Suddenly, hopeful that there was a remedy for this outrageous hurtle into middle age, Ajali called Madame Alvenia and made an emergency appointment. She told the woman she had to see her today!

Chapter 32

*E*ris felt invigorated by the encounter with the mortal known as Ajali. Eris's body was stronger, her femininity enhanced. She doubted if she'd have any more trouble from that meddling mortal. The woman probably didn't have the strength for another battle. Drained of vital female nutrients, the poor thing had probably skedaddled into a corner to lick her wounds and sadly reminisce about her lost youth.

One hard scratch at the female's silver cord had ripped it so severely, Eris was able to quickly extract vital nutrients, which endowed her with heightened sensuality and remarkable beauty. The body she possessed could now last for at least fifty years without having to siphon even a smidgeon of female life force.

But Eris doubted if she'd settle for a mere fifty years. She planned to live like a true goddess forever.

She looked around the cheap motel room and became furious. This was not the proper environment for an immortal goddess.

By the time the security guard knocked on the door, Eris was seething. Tiny sparks flickered in the air.

Eris swung the door open, indigo eyes gleaming with rage.

Looking shell-shocked, the security guard entered the motel room carrying a cardboard tray that contained an Egg McMuffin, hash browns, coffee and orange juice. Crossing the room, he carefully placed the tray on the dresser top. "Enjoy your breakfast," he said as he made hasty steps toward the door.

Arms folded, Eris stood with her back pressed against the closed door.

"Leaving so soon?" she asked in a hardened tone as she pushed in the door-knob lock and slowly slid the upper bolt into place.

Being locked inside the room with Eris frightened the guard. Her icy demeanor terrified him so badly he trembled; his face registered alarm.

She was hungry but the food could wait. A different kind of hunger over-powered her need to eat. She glided over to the bed and languished upon it. "Get over here," she demanded. Tingling nerves and raw sensuality caused her to salivate. "Hurry! Come quick! Indulge me," she ordered him.

She sent the man a series of telepathic images of the sexual acts she required him to perform. Although many of her requests could be considered depraved, she used mind control to deceive him into believing he wanted nothing more than to give her pleasure in the most unutterably perverted ways.

His troubled look was quickly replaced with a smile as he approached the bed, happily prepared to be of service to Eris for hours if she desired him to do so.

Finally sated, two hours later Eris ate the cold food while the security guard sat gazing at her with a look of complete adoration.

"How many of those plastic cards do you have?"

"You talking about my debit card?" he asked, still wearing a dopey smile.

"Whatever it's called. The plastic money you used for this motel. How much is it worth?"

"Oh, not much. Just a couple hundred dollars. My wife keeps all the credit cards."

"How many?"

"Oh, I don't know…about five or six of them—maybe more. She just tucks them away; she doesn't even use them. She calls it emergency money."

"Get them for me. Now."

"Okey-dokey," he said cheerfully. "I'll be back in a flash."

There was no reason to stick around Philadelphia any longer. The Stovall man had no value; she'd taken such a large quantity of his female's life force, it was now safe to travel to Roanoke. She imagined her beautiful jewels and practically swooned at the thought of the life of luxury that awaited her.

She went through the boxes of secondhand clothing. Nothing looked suitable. She'd look better traveling naked than wearing the security guard's wife's discarded apparel.

Eris had watched enough TV at the Stovall man's apartment to know what was in fashion and what was not during these modern times. And the contents within those boxes of junk simply weren't acceptable.

But she had to wear something. She browsed through the items and could not find one decent frock. There was nothing but trousers. Dozens of trousers in different styles and fabrics. She selected a pair made of blue denim. Ugh. Absolutely ugly. And a shirt. Why would a woman hide her femininity with such masculine attire?

When the man returned, Eris was fully clad. And unhappily so. "What did you bring me?" she asked; disdain dripped from her lips.

The man proudly spread out eight bright plastic cards: silver, gold and platinum in color with names of various banks embossed in a bold script.

"How much is all this worth?"

"I'm not sure. I do know that each card has a credit limit of at least five thousand dollars."

"How do I use these?"

"Just sign Bevvie's name."

Eris looked at the name beneath the bank's logo: *Beverly S. Brunson*. She turned the cards over; none were signed. So, with her fancy old-fashioned script, Eris signed the woman's name on each card. Beverly S. Brunson would be the identity she used for folks of a nosey nature.

She didn't trust the simple man to tell her the absolute truth about the fake money. There had to be more to it than simply signing a name. She studied the cards, felt them and then tried to use her third-eye vision to gain more clarity on how to use them. But to her horror, her third-eye vision was not functioning properly. It was blurry; she was going blind. She started to panic, but calmed down. She was totally human now. She'd have to rely on normal vision, her superior intelligence and quick wit.

"Let's go test these cards. Take me to an apparel shop; I need to purchase a few frocks."

Despite Eris's strange way of speaking, the security guard knew she wanted to shop. He took her to Strawbridge's department store and waited inside the car in the parking lot.

Pressed for time, Eris didn't allow herself to be in awe of the huge and brightly decorated department store. The clothing items that adorned one particular mannequin were fit for a queen and Eris couldn't resist having everything on display, from the shoes to the costume jewelry. Shoppers watched, appalled, as she undressed the mannequin. Angry blue sparks and a quick snarl sent them scurrying away.

The store associates whispered that Eris wasn't working with a full deck, but instead of informing security and creating an unnecessary ruckus, they indulged the seeming crazy woman just to get her out of the store.

She spent two thousand dollars on the purchased items. Eris changed into her new clothes in the dressing room.

After dressing, she perused the sweet-scented area of the store where perfumes and colognes were spritzed every couple of minutes. She was beckoned by a consultant at the Iman makeup counter and Eris allowed the woman to magnify her beautiful face with lipstick, eye shadow, eyeliner, mascara and rouge.

The consultant patiently showed her how to apply each item and then convinced Eris to spend over four hundred dollars on beauty enhancements that the woman insisted Eris shouldn't live without. Money was not an object—what did Eris care? She easily handed over one of Beverly S. Brunson's credit cards.

Then the beauty consultant suggested Eris pay a trip to the in-store hair salon, which Eris did, where her coarse locks were transformed to soft and bouncy curls.

Wearing a Donna Karan ensemble—skirt, blouse, belt, handbag, shoes and jewelry—Eris left Strawbridge's looking like she stepped straight out of *Vogue* magazine.

The dutiful security guard whistled in admiration.

Eris ignored the compliment. "Take me to the center of the city; I must have better accommodations."

Chapter 33

Leaving Bryce unattended would have been unthinkable, but under the circumstances, Ajali didn't have a choice. He was no longer in danger; she was.

She'd made a desperate call to Madame Alvenia; the kind woman granted her an appointment for six o'clock that evening.

In just a few short hours, Ajali had developed a bad case of unsightly spider veins on her thighs, which had gone from firm to flabby; stubby hair was sprouting from her chin; and she was retaining water something awful—her ankles and feet were so thick and swollen she couldn't get her shoes on and had to resort to wearing bedroom slippers. Her body temperature fluctuated wildly from hot to freezing cold.

Her heart went out to all middle-aged women who had to suffer through these symptoms of aging, but at least they'd experienced the full range of youth and the process of aging was occurring as Mother Nature had intended—at a normal rate. But for Ajali, the aging process was an assault to her system.

She wasn't ready for the abrupt change. She couldn't accept living the rest of her life in such a debilitated condition. She'd hardly begun to live. There were so many things she wanted to experience—marriage, for one thing. She and Bryce were supposed to grow old together. Have children together.

Ajali grabbed her stomach. She felt a visceral reaction to the concept of never bearing a child. She felt a pang—a deep yearning to conceive the daughter she'd met in an altered state of mind. It wasn't fair. She hadn't even begun to live and now she was aging at a frighteningly accelerated rate.

"I have to leave, but don't worry; I'll be back as soon as I can," she assured Bryce as he slept. Leaning over, she kissed him and then blew another kiss as she softly closed and locked the door.

This time there was no torrential rain outside to hinder her journey to see Madame Alvenia, but there was a storm brewing inside the car. Hot flashes were hitting her every few minutes, followed by a downpour of perspiration that blurred her vision as it ran down her forehead and into her eyes. Her loose-fitting top was drenched and the seat of her cotton slacks was soggy as if the seat warmer were turned up to an extreme high.

Once again, Ajali was soaking wet with her hair plastered to her face as she stood outside Madame Alvenia's door.

"Come in, come in, dear heart," the sweet woman said comfortingly. Ajali had already told her everything about her rapid aging condition...the hot flashes, the gray hair. She'd tried to prepare her, but Madame Alvenia was only human and couldn't help from wincing and biting down on her lip when she saw Ajali's condition.

"Oh honey, come sit down."

Ajali sat at the same table as before. But this time Madame Alvenia didn't offer tea; she knew Ajali was in too much distress to indulge in the polite social custom of sipping tea. She needed to see Kali posthaste.

"Honey," Madame Alvenia said, "I'm going to try to summon Kali, but I can't promise you that she'll come." She gave Ajali a sad smile. "I have no control over these matters. I act as a channel and the best I can tell you is that I'll do my very best to relax and allow Kali to come through."

Ajali nodded and leaned forward anxiously as Madame Alvenia began to deep breathe. Ajali looked down at her swollen fingers that had begun to fidget nervously. She heard a loud burst of air. Startled, her head jerked up.

Madame Alvenia was as still as a statue. Her eyes popped open, her mouth opened so wide, Ajali could see the woman's tonsils. Ajali had forgotten about this unsettling part of the session. Seeing it for the second time didn't lessen the discomfort or her fear.

"I am Kali. I have come." The vocal quality was strange but familiar and oh so comforting.

"She's killing me, Kali," Ajali divulged. "Look at me; I look like an old woman."

"I do not see your physical body; I see your aura and your soul. You are not well; I can sense that there is an injury to the spirit that has manifested into the physical."

"What can I do? I think I'm dying," Ajali blurted fearfully.

"The harm that has been done to the silver cord is permanent; it cannot be reversed." Kali spoke without emotion, which bothered Ajali. She wanted Kali to be angry with Eris—to want to exact revenge.

"Then there's no hope for me?" Ajali asked, teary-eyed.

"There is always hope. Without hope you will surely perish on this Earthly realm."

"What should I do?"

Kali closed her eyes, which was a strange thing for her to do. Her bulging eyes—wide open at all times—seemed to be an essential part of her identity.

Ajali didn't want to bother Kali in case she was working on some kind of reverse-aging spell, but her eyes had been closed for an awfully long time and Ajali was beginning to wonder if Kali had gone back to her home on the spirit realm.

"Kali," Ajali whispered.

Kali's eyes popped open so dramatically, Ajali jumped.

But Kali's face was filled with compassion and warmth. She exuded benevolence—a quality Ajali didn't know the ferocious goddess possessed. Then she recalled that Madame Alvenia had told her that Kali was also considered to be a loving mother.

"The demon Eris is cunning. Her skills in deceitfulness have been well honed over many lifetimes. She's connived for thousands and thousands of years."

Feeling without hope, Ajali sighed and wiped her damp forehead.

"To win this war, you will have to destroy her."

"Destroy her...take her life?" Ajali asked incredulously. "I could go to jail for murder!"

"If not, you'll lose your life and will not bring forth new life into this world."

Ajali thought of her daughter. Her shoulders straightened as she began to feel empowered. "I met my future daughter; I want to give her life."

"Then you must slay the demon."

Trying to kill the powerful Eris was a bad enough thought, but even if she succeeded, Ajali couldn't help thinking about the prison time she'd have to serve. Her lip began to tremble when it occurred to her that she could also end up getting the death penalty.

"There are no Earth laws to protect an entity that is not a human being. She walks and talks as a human, but there is no record of her life. Do not fear Earth justice."

Ajali felt a little better. "How can I...uh...kill her? She's so strong. And I'm growing weaker every hour."

"She can only be destroyed by fire. Only fire can send her wicked soul back to the Dark Realm."

"Fire?" Ajali's voice rose to an alarmingly high octave. She had a disconcerting visual; she saw herself trying to chase Eris down with a Bic lighter. A malfunctioning lighter that only produced an ineffective, tiny flame. With her bad feet she could only manage a slow shuffle as she tried to ignite the demon woman by flicking a Bic that refused to produce anything more than a few sputtering sparks.

She had another extremely disturbing visual of Eris, swatting the useless lighter from her hand.

Ajali didn't like the idea of confronting Eris at all.

"Fear not," Kali said. "I am with you. If you cannot overthrow the evil one, you must summon me."

"I called you before, but you didn't come," Ajali said defensively.

"You must summon me with the Chant of Custody."

"Custody?" Ajali asked meekly.

"You must give me custody of your body if you find that you are losing the battle. Only with your permission can I take custody. But be warned: there's always the possibility that I'll be forced to remain."

Ajali looked at Kali uncertainly. "And what will happen to me?"

"Your spirit will linger between worlds until I'm destroyed by fire. At that time I'll return to a realm even higher than from whence I came. When my Earth days are over, my act of service will elevate my spirit and your spirit will ascend as well."

"Kali, I don't want to lose my body," Ajali, shouted. "I want to live out my life here on Earth," she said in a softer tone, but sounded near tears.

"Nor do I desire an earthly existence; but it's a risk we both shall take if you call upon me and grant me custody."

"How do I find her?"

"She'll come to you. Be prepared; she'll need more of your life force."

"More of my life force? You can't be serious? Look at me!" Ajali shouted, her arms outstretched. "She's taken everything. There's nothing left to take from me."

"Be prepared," Kali warned.

Ajali dropped her head in despair, when she lifted her chin; she was once again looking into Madame Alvenia's compassionate eyes.

At home that evening, after she fed Bryce and prepared her tired body for bed, she surrounded the bedroom with lit candles. Matches and lighters were strewn on countertops, the nightstand and the kitchen table; in her purse, the pockets of her robe, her pajamas and most of her clothes. She was ready for Eris.

The burning flames of the candles gave her peace. As she adjusted her aging body into a comfortable position, she caught a glimpse of herself in the mirror, illuminated by candlelight. She gave a sharp cry. She and Bryce looked like two senior citizens huddled together in bed.

Chapter 34

The Crowne Plaza hotel, located in the heart of Center City, was the perfect location for Eris. Using Mrs. Brunson's credit card, she checked in with the poise and confidence of a seasoned world traveler.

"May I help with your luggage?" the concierge inquired.

"My bags were delayed at the airport. Please let me know the moment they arrive," Eris replied.

Never would have anyone suspected that Eris's last Earth experience was as a slave mistress to the owner of the plantation.

Her lack of sophistication was apparent, however, when she fumbled with the keycard that would admit her to her room. It took exactly five and a half minutes for her to figure it out.

After luxuriating in the whirlpool, she perused the menu and ordered room service. Wearing the hotel-issued robe, Eris admitted the waiter. The meal was delivered by a young, attractive blonde female who wore a uniform that could have easily been worn by a male: black slacks, white shirt and black bow tie. Her long hair was pulled back with a black ribbon.

Exhilarated, Eris took in a sharp intake of breath; the female server presented unlimited possibilities.

Eris lifted the lid on each tray to make sure the provisions were exactly as she'd ordered. She nodded and gave the young woman a winning smile, assuring her that she was pleased. The waiter turned to leave.

"One moment," Eris called, holding up a finger.

Hoping for a large tip, the young woman spun around, eager to be of service.

"I'd like a bottle of your finest wine. I'd be honored if you'd join me." She gave the waiter a sly grin accompanied by a telepathic image of naughty female sex. "What's your name?"

Feeling a sudden and overwhelming physical attraction to the hotel guest, the young woman blushed. "My name's, um, Jaclyn. And...uh, yeah," she stammered, eyes downcast in embarrassment over the lewd sexual images running across her mind. "I can bring you a bottle of wine," Jaclyn managed to say in a normal tone, though it was difficult to restrain herself from fondling Eris's enormous breasts.

"What time will you be finished your chores?" Eris inquired sternly.

The girl looked up at the ceiling for an answer. "Not until eleven o'clock," she said, sounding regretful.

Eris checked the time on the bedside digital clock. Eight thirty-five. "I don't want to wait that long...do you?"

"No," Jaclyn said emphatically, turning a deep shade of red. "I get a break in an hour, I can come back then," she offered enthusiastically.

"Very well. I'll expect you in one hour." Eris turned her attention to the platters on the rolling cart. The young woman stood for a few uncomfortable moments until she realized she'd been dismissed.

"Oh, Okay," Jaclyn said, her voice faltering as she backed away. "I'll see you later."

Eris didn't bother to even grunt an acknowledgment of the girl's awkward farewell. The only sounds that came from Eris were the unusual and exceedingly unlady-like chomping noises she made when eating.

Exactly an hour later, Jaclyn returned with a bottle of white wine.

"I hope you like this," she said with a worried expression. "It's the house wine. And...ah, that's the only bottle I could get away with not paying for."

Eris took the bottle, inspected it. Uncorking the bottle looked beyond her immediate capabilities. "Open it," she ordered, handing Jaclyn the bottle of wine.

Once again, the girl blushed. Her constant red-faced display of bashfulness was starting to irritate Eris.

"Hurry, I'm thirsty. Pour two glasses, undress and join me in bed." Eris flung off her robe and strode naked to the king-size bed.

Jaclyn gave Eris a look of admiration. "You have an awesome body," the young woman said. "Do you work out?"

Eris ignored the question, which made Jaclyn nervous. Her hands began to shake as she handled the bottle of wine.

Propped up by an elbow, Eris viewed the uncorking of the bottle of wine; she found the procedure quite entertaining and enjoyed the popping sound when the cork was finally freed.

Carefully carrying two glasses of wine, Jaclyn walked stiffly toward the bed. She handed Eris a glass and set the other on the bedside table. "Should I take off my clothes now?"

Eris nodded, keeping her eyes locked on Jaclyn as the red-faced girl, obviously ill at ease, disrobed. Excited by the possibility of acquiring even more beauty from siphoning this female's life force, Eris felt a buildup of saliva in her mouth. She swallowed it down with a gulp of wine.

"This is my first time with another girl," Jaclyn admitted, when she discarded her bra. Eris was immediately disappointed by Jaclyn's small breasts.

Jaclyn took a sip of wine, got in bed and cuddled next to Eris. "Being with a woman has been a fantasy for a long time. I never dreamed it would ever really happen," she said with a giggle.

To quiet the silly girl/woman, Eris stroked her soft blonde hair. She pulled off the ribbon, freeing her long hair and began to run her fingers through the silky tresses. Jaclyn shivered,which incited Eris to toy with the young girl.

Eris gently stroked Jaclyn's hair and then suddenly grabbed a handful and gave it a harsh yank, causing the girl to utter a moan. Pulling Jaclyn's hair until her chin tilted upward, Eris ran an onyx-colored finger up and down the girl's white throat. Their contrasting skin tones were interesting. Jaclyn's eyes were closed as she made a continuous purring sound that spoke of utter bliss.

Leaning in close, Eris lightly nipped the girl's neck, causing her to cry out and press her neck against Eris's mouth, yearning for more. Eris licked the neck that was offered; she was no vampire and did not crave blood. She was yearning for female hormones—female life force. She already had a beautiful body and this encounter was not an act of desperation. It was folly; it was also pure greed. Forcing herself to be patient; Eris decided to indulge her carnal desires before draining the worthless serving girl.

Wasting her breath on dialogue was tiresome, thus she transmitted a visual of Jaclyn kissing her feet. Jaclyn didn't hesitate. Swiftly, she was at the bottom of the bed with her glass of wine in hand. She dipped Eris's toes in the cool glass of wine and drizzled some of the liquid on both feet, and then slowly licked the wine without missing one drop.

It was a pleasant sensation, but Eris had another idea.

"Can I feel your breasts?" Jaclyn asked suddenly. There was an innocent quality to her voice that revealed that she was completely unaware that everything she did or even thought she desired came straight from Eris's wicked mind.

With closed eyes and an increased heart rate, Jaclyn fondled Eris's breasts. Eris was so aroused, she emitted a gurgling sound. Had Jaclyn opened her eyes she would have seen the stream of saliva that ran down the side of Eris's chin. Feeling the moistness, Eris wiped away the dribble with the back of her hand.

Now bored with the sensation, Eris pushed Jaclyn's head away and nudged her until the girl was flat on her back. Eris wanted a taste of the girl's small, candy-pink nipples. She licked a circle until the nipple tightened and became rigid. The girl's hands fluttered and flailed; not knowing what to do and being quite out of her senses, she pushed Eris's head, forcing her mouth to press hard against her nipple. Eris bit her so hard, she broke the skin. Jaclyn whimpered; tears flowed from the sweet pain. She twisted her body, offering Eris her other nipple—offering Eris another bite of her pink candy.

Eris punctured Jaclyn's nipple, tasted the blood, but didn't experience a rush; not the kind she got when she siphoned life force. Dispensing with the fun and games, Eris crouched between the girl's legs. Jaclyn trembled and moaned loudly before Eris even touched her.

To achieve instant silence, Eris tightly gripped the girl's hips, holding her in place while her hot tongue jutted inside her vagina. In an instant, Jaclyn went into shock. Frozen in place, her eyes were wide and confused. Times like this, Eris yearned for her former long, forked tongue.

Eris lapped the outer juices while Jaclyn lay stunned like a small animal caught in the grip of a scorpion. And like a scorpion, Eris began to slowly extract the girl's vaginal juices. Opening her mouth wide, Eris sucked out everything that was vital to keeping the young woman alive.

With all life force depleted, the young woman had the value of an overly worn dress. Discontented by her uncomely appearance, Eris pushed Jaclyn's lifeless body off the bed; it thumped loudly when it hit the floor.

Feeling rejuvenated and festive, Eris picked up the wine glass and took a sip. The taste of Jaclyn lingered on her tongue and Eris found the mingled flavors of the human and the tart beverage an oddly pleasant combination.

Not quite up to the espionage involved in disposing of a dead body from a public place, Eris thought it an appropriate time to be on her way to Roanoke. A wardrobe could be purchased upon her arrival.

Eris didn't trust those flying machines; she was human now and if one went down in a blaze, her Earth life would be terminated. Therefore, she picked up the phone and asked directory assistance for the number to the train station.

There was a train departing for Roanoke from 30th Street Station at midnight. Perfect. By the time the staff discovered the girl, the woman known as Beverly S. Brunson would be long gone.

Eris immediately began to prepare herself for her midnight trip to Roanoke. Using the lit mirror in the bathroom, she applied mascara, but noticed something odd. Her eyelashes were coming out at the root and curling around the mascara wand. She let out a small cry, assuming the wand was contaminated. Unable to bear the sight of her beautiful long lashes separated from the lid, she threw it in the waste can. And stamped her feet in fury.

The lashes would grow back, she assured herself as she left the bathroom and walked in circles in the hotel room. Something was on the bed, something dark and foreboding. Covering her mouth in fear, she eased up to the bed and let out another soft scream. The pillow was covered with hair. Dark hair. *Her* hair. Her hand flew to the back of her head. There was an enormous bald spot smack in the back of her head.

Angry blue sparks flickered in the dimly lit bedroom. She tried to understand what was happening. Why was she falling apart? She stomped to the bathroom, where there was a full-length mirror on the back of the door. This time her scream caught in her throat and she literally swooned and had to catch herself by grabbing the doorknob before she hit the floor.

One breast was still full and beautifully sculpted, but the other sagged down to her belly, which stuck out like she'd swallowed a small melon.

She swirled around to get a back view. Her buttocks were horrifying. One cheek stood high and proud, while the other was dented with cellulite and sagged down to the back of her thigh. And on her back was a hideous hump.

Eris was a walking sideshow. Instead of enhancing her beauty, the serving girl's life force had caused her body to become deformed.

Aside from being burned alive, nothing this horrible had ever happened to Eris. There had to be a way to fix it, but what? And how? She had only an hour to get on the train to Roanoke.

"Xavier," she cried out. "Xavier, help me."

But Xavier couldn't help a woman who was blind in her third eye. There was no way to communicate. Amused, he watched Eris falling to pieces and began to giggle while lying in his crib.

Talking to one of her friends on the phone, his young nanny said, "This baby is so straaange. He laughs and giggles all the time, but instead of sounding like a happy little baby, his gurgles remind me of sinister laughter. Like something you hear in a horror movie, totally not the sounds that should be coming from inside a baby's crib."

The baby, thoroughly amused at Eris's dilemma, laughed so hard, tears fell from his eyes. The nanny, now concerned, got up and looked inside the crib. As she wiped away the tears, she noticed that the baby wore a horribly obnoxious grin. He looked absolutely demonic.

Her employers were high-level officials; however, the nanny no longer cared. There was something wrong with their baby—something strange and disturbing. She made a mental note to request her agency place her in another home.

Meanwhile, Eris calmed down enough to figure out what went wrong and was struck with the realization that she shouldn't have mixed the life force of two different females. Male life force could be intermingled because all it provided was strength. But female life force was vital to her very existence and so should never, ever be mixed.

She'd known that. Greed and power had again gone to her head making her forgetful, causing her to make a crucial mistake. And the last time she was haughty and careless, she'd lost her life. She vowed to somehow find a way to right this tragic wrong.

Chapter 35

The disadvantages of possessing a physical form were many. The human body was not only weak, fragile and unreliable, but it was also a cumbersome vehicle for speedy and discreet travel.

Had she not been burdened with the hideously malformed and malfunctioning body she now possessed, her desire alone would have instantly transported her back to the dark seclusion of the asylum, putting significant distance between herself and the hotel's serving girl, whose lifeless body now lay awkwardly wedged out of sight in a small cranny between the wall and the bed.

If she were able to convert to mist, she'd depart the Crowne Plaza in the guise of a sudden rush of wind undetected by the human eye. If she weren't in such a panic and could afford the luxury of traveling in a leisurely fashion, she'd glide through the air as welcome and calm as a gentle breeze.

Fortunately, her ability to communicate with her servant remained intact. Sending her voice telepathically, she summoned the security guard with one word: *Come!*

Mentally sensing his movement, she anxiously tracked his journey from the northeast part of the city until he pulled to the curb in front of the Crowne Plaza hotel.

Like a bandit, Eris moved swiftly through the hotel's lobby and out the revolving door. As if he were escorting her in a stretch limousine, her servant stood outside his security vehicle and dutifully opened the back door.

"Where should I take you, uh, ma'am?"

With her bodily malfunctioning and feeling an increased fear that she'd be forever disfigured, Eris felt cranky and insecure. "Address me as Goddess, you impudent rodent," she spat at the security guard.

"I'm sorry, Goddess, I wasn't trying to be smart; I just wanted to know where you were heading."

Refusing to waste precious breath on an ill-mannered servant, Eris sent the security guard a visual of Ajali's apartment. She was silent for the duration of the ride, communicating her commands with thought transference.

Upon their arrival, the security guard exited the vehicle while Eris remained in the backseat, anxiously waiting.

Using a nightstick, he banged on Ajali's door, loud and long until she dragged her weary body out of bed and down the hall.

"Who is it?" Ajali called out as she peeked through the peephole.

"Security, ma'am." The security guard held up his name badge and thrust out his chest to display his shiny badge. "One of the tenants reported smelling smoke coming from your apartment; are you okay?"

"Smoke?" Perplexed, Ajali frowned until comprehension relaxed the muscles in her face. "I'm burning candles," she explained. The remembrance of why she'd lit candles and the gravity of her plight caused her face to tighten back into a frown.

"The neighbors are pretty worried, miss. They're ready to call the fire department. I know you're tired, but do you mind if I take a look around? See, I have to give my supervisor some kind of report about all this smoke, but don't worry, I'll be out of your hair as quick as I can."

Ajali unlocked and unchained the door.

"Holy smoke! Pardon the pun," he said as he gawked at the numerous candles in the living room. "This place is lit up like Christmas; no wonder the neighbors thought there was a fire." He shook his head disapprovingly.

Tightening the sash to her robe, Ajali started to explain, but before the words could make it to her lips, the security guard's expression switched from quiet displeasure to outright rage.

Shocked into full mental awareness, she realized she'd been so focused on keeping demons at bay that she hadn't thought about the criminal-minded humans who continually search for prey. How stupid of her to have allowed a potential murderer to enter her home under the guise of security when her apartment building had nothing more than an intercom system; there *was* no patrolling security team.

Her brain went into frantic mode and tried to transmit a signal for her to cry for help but shock sealed her lips shut and silenced her scream.

He pointed a gun at her and held a warning finger to his lips. "Be quiet or die," he whispered without emotion. "Now, come with me."

Come with him? Where? she shrieked in her mind. *Why does he want to take me somewhere? What kind of burglar acts like this?*

Wearing an angry expression, the man jerked his head, silently ordering her to walk out the door. But Ajali didn't move. She couldn't. She felt a wave of regret and turned her head. Helplessly, she gazed toward the bedroom where Bryce slept.

I'm sorry, Bryce.

"Move your ass!" the man snarled through gritted teeth.

Though she'd been cautioned to keep quiet, Ajali, desperate, risked speaking in a whisper. "I have money—and jewelry." She twisted off her engagement ring and offered it to him. "Here, take it," she said pleadingly.

Ignoring her plea, the man yanked Ajali forward. He pressed the gun into her back and escorted her out the door.

Clad in a bathrobe and cotton nightgown, Ajali, terrified of being brutally raped and murdered, was forced out of her apartment and led outside into the night. She didn't have on shoes, socks or slippers; her swollen bare feet trudged haltingly to the waiting car.

The security guard spoke quietly to a woman inside the car, then he shoved Ajali into the backseat. To her utter amazement, she was face-to-face with the mistress of doom. Ajali gasped in horror. She felt her bile rising. Her stomach did multiple flips. She opened her mouth but a horribly deformed hand clamped her lips shut before she could let out a frightened scream.

"Be silent or die now!" Eris said harshly. "Do you understand?"

Ajali promptly nodded. *Dear God, this can't be real; it has to be a dream.*

"Good," Eris said, and removed her hand. She smiled at Ajali; her indigo eyes seemed to flicker and emitted sparks. "Greetings!" she said brightly. "We finally meet outside of your dreams and meditative state. What a pleasure!" Eris wore a broad smile.

Outside of my dreams! Crushed, Ajali slumped against the seat. She was not asleep—she was fully conscious—in the midst of a grotesque, waking nightmare.

"I am the goddess Eris, and yes, you are known as Ajali." Eris then gave a contemptuous snort; her lips twisted into a malicious smile. Her indigo eyes took on an odd hue as they began to flicker and glow brightly inside the dark car.

Whimpering in terror, Ajali scooted as far away as possible from Eris and her creepy blue eyes. When Ajali had first encountered Eris while in an altered out-of-body state, Eris had been a dark mist that exuded evil so powerful and combative, Ajali was forced back into her physical body. She'd witnessed Eris become a mere outline of the female anatomy, a state the demon woman had achieved by siphoning Ajali's life force; and then there was the dream state that Eris managed to slip inside and use her obscene lips to deplete Ajali of her female essence.

All of those memories were beyond horrific, but sitting in the backseat of a car fully conscious, with a demon that possessed a human form acquired from Ajali's life force, was unendurable. It was taking every ounce of effort to not give into a well-deserved complete emotional breakdown.

Eris pointed a finger at Ajali. The finger, Eris suddenly realized, had gone crooked. Stunned and repulsed by her curved digit, Eris quickly withdrew her hand and placed balled fists into her lap. "I don't wish to kill you for your life is quite valuable to me. There are, however, many females available to service me," she lied. "With that said, know that I won't hesitate to end your vexatious existence if you attempt to escape. I don't really need *you* since you're obviously wasting away..." Eris gave Ajali a lingering look of revulsion.

Shifting her gaze to her unsightly hands, Eris sighed in exasperation, then continued, "I could easily siphon life force from another female human being but I chose you despite your deficiencies because I prefer to draw from the same stream of life that transferred me from mist to human form."

Suddenly, Ajali's concern for Bryce overshadowed her fear of the demon as it occurred to her that he was left alone in her apartment surrounded by dozens of candles. Not only were there candles in the living room but there were even more in the bedroom. With his strength slowly returning, Bryce was able to shift his position on his own. Suppose he regained even more physical abilities during her absence, suppose he tried to reach for the glass of water on the nightstand beside the bed? His sleeve could become ignited. Bryce could burn alive in her bed.

The horror of it all caused her to tremble and then she began to ramble. "What else do you want from me?" Ajali held out her hands. "Look at me; I'm old. My fiancé is violently ill. There's nothing left to take. Please, I beg of you...please, leave us alone."

"Your words have touched my heart and filled me with compassion," Eris said sarcastically. "Now, please. Speak no more!" She held up her hand for silence and instantly brought it down to her lap. All five fingers, she discovered, were gnarled and horribly twisted.

Ajali whispered the Prayer of Protection. Eris's ears began to buzz. The sound of the prayer filled her ears with what felt like a legion of insects, buzzing and flapping their wings. Unable to bear it, she sent a mental image to her servant.

In an instant, the security guard pulled over. He got out, jerked the screaming Ajali from the car and tied her hands behind her back. Then he unlocked the trunk.

"Please, mister, oh, please don't put me in there," Ajali wailed. "Please, I'm sorry. I promise I won't make another sound."

Mechanically, the security guard stuffed a dirty cloth into her mouth. Shaking her head in terror, her eyes bulging with fear, Ajali mutely testified that she would be good; she'd behave.

The security guard ignored her silent plea. Gripping her neck, he forced her into the trunk.

Ajali was plunged into darkness. Concentrating on survival, she inhaled sparingly, terrified that the air supply would not last. She had no idea where they were taking her; but the jostling, rolling around and bumping she had to endure inside the trunk miraculously loosened the rope until she was able to work her hands free. *Thank you, Jesus.*

The car crunched slowly over what felt to Ajali like a gravelly road and then it came to a slow stop. She could feel and hear her heart pounding like a sledgehammer inside her chest.

The trunk was popped open from inside the car. Quaking, she listened to the sound of her captor's footsteps as he walked to the back of the car. Although the trunk was wide open, it was too dark for the security guard to spot Ajali, who was crouched in a corner of the trunk.

But she could see his shiny badge as he pulled a flashlight out of his pocket. In survival mode and acting on pure instinct, before he could flick on the light, Ajali swung the tire iron with all her might. She leapt from the trunk of the car. Fueled by fear and the will to survive, Ajali, though aching and aged, moved with the speed of a cheetah and the agility of a leopard.

Running for her life, she sprinted over gravel and dirt and around shrubs and trees and bushes without giving a thought to the fact that there were no shoes on her feet.

She put every ounce of the youth she'd retained into her flight for life. She ran without destination; hoping desperately to find someone who could help her—save her. But the only sounds of life were the sounds of night creatures. She heard crickets courting, birds taking flight—some sang from treetops, some shrieked. Insects flew in her face, creepy crawlers scampered beneath her bare feet, but Ajali kept running. She felt as if she were lost in an inescapable dark jungle. With her eyes widely stretched, she searched for a sign of humanity.

She didn't see the small incline, but she felt it when she stumbled and began to roll down an endless steep hill. Finally, when her rolling body came to a halt, she jumped to her feet, surprised that nothing was broken or cut, astonished that she was intact. And then she saw it—the building in the distance. Though it was dark inside, she ran toward it with hope and relief as if the building gave off a shining beacon of light.

As Ajali drew closer to the building, her heart dropped. Protecting her face as she made her way through high scratchy weeds that stood like sentries in front of the abandoned brick building, she grimaced and put her hand to her mouth to stifle a cry. This was no beacon of hope; the building was old and decayed. Her eyes swept the desolate area and fell upon a number of dark, seemingly abandoned buildings. *Where am I? Is this an old college campus?*

Had she not heard the sounds of tires rolling and a car engine humming in the distance, had she not been frightened by the thought of being discovered by the car's searching headlights, Ajali never would have entered the foreboding building, but there was nowhere else to hide.

Inside the pitch-black and creepy building, she felt along the walls. They were rough and emitted an unpleasant musky scent. Not knowing where she was or where she was going was beyond disturbing, yet she couldn't stop. She needed to find a room—a nook or cranny where she could safely hide from the demon and the lunatic in case they discovered the building and came inside looking for her.

After a few feet of plodding along and using her hands to guide her, Ajali realized she was in a curved hallway. The hallway gave off an eerie vibration as if woe and sorrow seeped from the walls.

Frightened of her pursuers and terrified of the hall, she moved along quickly until she finally felt an opening—a doorway to a safe place, she hoped.

Chapter 35

Warily, Ajali entered a room that was an enormous open space. She couldn't make any sense of her environment. Despite the darkness, the vastness of the room left her feeling completely exposed. She stretched her eyes, trying to adjust to the pitch-black nothingness. Ajali sliced the air with her hands, frantic to find something that would give her a sense of her surroundings.

Feeling vulnerable and terribly afraid, she crept ahead uneasily, turning her head this way and that, expecting the demon to grab her at any moment.

Ajali shivered in fear, knowing she could not win a battle if she tried to fight Eris with her bare hands. With that thought, she clawed at thin air, searching for something—anything she could brandish as a weapon. Finding nothing, she continued to move with caution; having no sense of direction, she was startled when she bumped into a wall.

Ajali jerked around and desperately felt along the wall. It was very different from those in the hallway. This surface felt like ceramic tiles. Some were still smooth; however, neglect and decay had taken a toll. Most of the tiles were cracked with jagged edges or encrusted with unknown material. Trying to loosen a jagged tile to use as a weapon, she put forth tremendous strength to rip it off the wall. But when her fingers sank into a moist, moldy substance, Ajali gave a small yelp and snatched her hand away.

The sound of her own voice startled her. Frightened that she'd given away her hiding place to the two crazies chasing her, her hand left the safety of the wall. Retreating in fear, she backed into something hard. She spun around; groping in the darkness, she discovered steps and long metal seats.

Bleachers. She was in a gymnasium or an auditorium. She now knew with certainty that she was in a college or someplace that provided education.

Her pondering was cut short by the sound of a door opening. Griped by intense fear, Ajali could hardly breathe. In a stooped position, she tiptoed away from the bleachers and slowly slid along the wall. Something hard stubbed her toe, but she didn't make a sound. The pain brought tears to her eyes; she grimaced and found herself reflexively bending over to soothe her injured toe.

Her butt touched something. She felt a railing. Stairs. She had stumbled upon a set of steps. With nowhere else to go, she ascended the creaky, metal spiral stairs. Halfway up the horribly winding staircase that led to God knows where, she collided with a spiderweb and had a sudden change of heart.

Being chased by a demon who wanted to deplete her of her youth was terrible enough, but if she was greeted by a nest of spiders at the top of the stairs, she'd need wings to escape. So holding tightly on the rail, Ajali carefully backed down the stairs.

When she finally came to the bottom step she reached out to her left and was flooded with relief when her hand touched a door. A closet! Could it be a closet—a place to secret herself away from the exposing glare of the security guard's flashlight when he came barreling into the wide-open space?

No! It wasn't a closet at all; the door led to another room. As she tried to decide if this was a stroke of good luck or an ominous threat to her security, she heard fast-moving footsteps. Still surrounded by darkness and paralyzed by fear, Ajali had to literally pinch herself, hoping to wake up from this nightmarish hell.

Running in the dark, she fled the room and soon found herself knee-deep in water. As Ajali waded through the slimy, rancid water, which felt and smelled like sewage, a light shone and voice called out, "There she is!"

She looked back in horror and tried to run quickly but the thick swamp-like water caused her to tread sluggishly, as if in slow motion. The shine of the flashlight revealed that she was in a watery tunnel that led to only God knew where. Again, she looked back in terror and what she saw made her heart lurch in terror. Ajali's was so frightened, she gulped a burst of air.

Then the pounding inside her chest became ominously quiet. It seemed her heart had come to a complete stop.

The man with the flashlight sloshed through the murky water. On his face was an expression of unreserved disgust as his light shone upon the pool of knee-deep muck and waste.

As fast as a speedboat, the demon woman plowed through the cesspool, zooming past the lagging security guard. With teeth bared, she salivated; her eyes glowed and discharged a flurry of angry sparks that flickered in the dark tunnel.

In a matter of seconds, Ajali heard panting and then felt hot breath burning the back of her neck. She tried to run faster but stepped on something—a rock, a piece of metal or maybe a shard of glass. She screamed in pain and at that moment something grabbed the sash of her robe. Deformed hands wrapped around her waist, limiting her motion. Ajali ripped herself from the demon's grip, limped a few steps and then toppled over into the murky abyss.

She came to inside a dimly lit room. Stretched out on a metal table, she looked around questioningly. Her robe and nightgown were drenched—covered with slimy muck. Her tormentors were not in sight and her first instinct was to bolt for the door, but that wasn't possible: her hands and feet were fastened tight by leather restraints that were attached to the table's side railings. Three flashlights illuminated the room, which seemed clinical like a doctor's office or a hospital room. Maybe this was an old hospital. But no, why would there be a gym inside a hospital? Perhaps it was a former medical or nursing school.

What is this place? She turned her head from one side and to the other as she tried to make sense of her environment. *Escape* was the operative word and it would be helpful to know her exact location in the remote chance that she got ahold of a phone.

And then it became crystal clear. Everything fell into place—the abandoned buildings that seemed to be in the midst of a forest, the long hallways, even the gymnasium. She wasn't inside any college or university; she was inside Byberry! Byberry: she'd read about and had heard stories told in horrified hushed tones about the former mental hospital. *The state had to shut that place down; they treated those patients like animals. Tortured them with shock treatments and lobotomies. The staff didn't keep them poor people clean and didn't feed them properly. Hundreds, maybe thousands died from pure neglect. You know they say that place is haunted by the ghosts of all those tortured souls.*

When Ajali was in high school, Byberry was considered a fun place to visit at Halloween. Students would come back to school spinning wild tales of being chased through the tunnels by the spirit of an ax-carrying mental patient named Stanley.

But her predicament was not make-believe; though she wished with all her heart that this was a nightmare, it was not. Ajali was wide awake.

Captured and in restraints, Ajali knew it was only a matter of time before her captors returned to siphon more of her dwindling life force.

She lifted her head as far as she could. Her poor legs, mottled and dis- colored by unsightly varicose veins were further defaced with multicolored slime. One of her feet throbbed so badly she was surprised it wasn't smeared with blood. Her foot must have been sprained, she surmised; or worse, she had broken a bone. Whatever, the prognosis did not bode well for escape on foot.

Suddenly, she heard movement; her eyes darted anxiously as she struggled in vain to release herself from the leather restraints. The sound of voices grew closer. Terror-stricken, Ajali bucked and thrashed to no avail. Shackled to the padded table, there was nothing she could do but await her untimely and unnatural demise.

Eris walked briskly into the room; the guard trailed behind. The dreaded moment had finally arrived yet Ajali was filled with a strange sense of relief. She was tired to the bone and weary of mind; resigned to her fate, she prayed death would be painless and swift.

"Ah, so cat and mouse is the game you like to play," Eris announced brightly. "Then play we shall. I am the cat and you are the mouse." Eris sidled up closer to Ajali.

Ajali thought at first that fear had caused her eyes to blur for it seemed that Eris's body was horribly misshapen. In the shadowy room, Eris's humpback looked eerily like a cat arching its back; her disfigured hands looked clawed, but it was the thick grayish drool that ran down the side of her chin that filled Ajali with quivering trepidation.

Like a cat, Eris climbed up on the table, making a low growling sound as she straddled her prey. She clamped her knees against Ajali's waist and looked into her captive's terror-stricken face.

When Eris brought her grinning face closer, Ajali flinched when she noticed that one of her eyes was missing its lashes. Worse, Eris's eyes held a look of pure evil.

"Please." It was useless to beg, she knew, but the word escaped Ajali's lips involuntarily.

"Please?" Eris repeated tauntingly. "Are you requesting that I show you mercy? That I spare your life?"

"Yes, spare my life. I beg of you," Ajali said urgently, hoping against hope that that perhaps Eris would show her mercy—allow her to live.

But Eris curled her lips into a sneer, communicating that Ajali's predicament was hopeless. "You weren't very considerate of *me*, were you? You have the life force that I need. Instead of relinquishing it freely, you forced me to chase you—hunt you down." Eris paused and gave a coy smile. "I must admit, under normal circumstances, I do appreciate a good chase." Then her expression changed to a mask of anger. "But I don't have the time or the vitality to run through muck and mire in pursuit of you." Eris spoke through gritted teeth, and then pressed a disfigured hand to her head. "Oh, you've been such an exasperating little twit."

With certainty, Ajali knew the death planned for her would not be humane; Eris would indulge herself for extended periods of time, causing Ajali to suffer in a whirlpool of agony for hours, perhaps even days. Petrified, Ajali yelled at the top of her lungs, "Help! Somebody help me, please." Trying to break free, she pulled at the leather restraints, thrashed and twisted on the torture table, to no avail.

Physically aroused by Ajali's fear, Eris decided to frighten her nemesis out of her wits. In an act of sexual indulgence, Eris sent Ajali a fleeting image accompanied by the feeling tone of having the very last breath sucked from her lips. Giving a live demonstration, Eris bent low and kissed Ajali, transferring vile slobber from her lips to Ajali's mouth, causing Ajali to gag.

A loathsomely familiar long tongue forced its way inside Ajali's mouth and licked her tongue. Eris's tongue was no longer a human organ; it had reverted to its demon form.

Ajali squirmed and thrashed in misery as she felt the hot and horribly long tongue slowly begin to separate. It licked the roof of her mouth and at the same time it stroked her gums.

There was no opportunity to scream, for ever so slowly her breath was seeping from her body. Just before Ajali lost consciousness, Eris removed her mouth and watched with interest as Ajali gagged and gasped for air.

With Ajali's breath, she had reshaped and restored the appearance of her hands. Eris held her hands up to her face and regarded them. She gave a cry of delight when she saw that her fingers were no longer gnarled and crooked.

Admiringly, Eris studied her palms and then the tops of her hands. "Look," she said, displaying her hands for Ajali to see. "They're lovely again, aren't they?"

"Yes, they're really beautiful," Ajali quickly complimented, while still gasping for breath. She was surprised and relieved that she was still alive after having the air sucked from her body. She raised up as far as the restraints would allow. "Now, can you untie me?" she asked desperately. "You have what you wanted, don't you?"

Eris laughed without mirth. Her self-satisfaction had lasted only briefly. "I need to rejuvenate more than a pair of hands. So, be still; stop squirming. I have to extract more."

"No, please. Don't," Ajali begged. Petrified, she twisted her body away from Eris and reached out toward the security guard, who stood stock-still, zombie-like.

"Mister, don't just stand there. Do something. Help me," she yelled at the guard, her eyes traveling to the gun stuck inside his waistband. "She's gonna kill you, too. She's a demon. You have to shoot her and then set her on fire." Ajali knew she was ranting like a mental patient who hadn't taken her medication, but she had to at least try to get the man to snap out of his stupor. Maybe he'd do something if he understood that they were both in terrible danger.

The security guard did not blink or move a muscle. As if hypnotized, he stood frozen in place. His eyes were wide open, staring into space.

Eris hissed and then flicked out her serpent-like tongue. Ajali recoiled at the grisly sight. She screamed, shook her head frantically and tried to throw herself off the table. But the restraints kept her locked in place. With defeat in her wide brown eyes, Ajali fell flat on her back. She closed her eyes and quietly wept.

Greedily, Eris lapped the salty tears that trickled from Ajali's eyes. She hummed as if in rapture; her refrain was out of time with Ajali's plaintive wail. The discordant melody stimulated Eris; she enjoyed the disharmony of their song. She writhed against Ajali's frail body as she licked all the moisture from her victim's eyes.

Eris licked her lips and brushed her fingertips against both her eyes. Her lashes had returned, thicker and so long they curled over, while Ajali was left with burning dry eyes, blurred vision and lashes singed by a scorching hot tongue.

I love you, Mommy. It was the voice of a child, whispering softly in Ajali's mind. A reminder to fight—not just for her own life—but also for the life of her unborn child.

A calm feeling washed over Ajali—a measureless peace. But it was not the tranquility of one who acquiesces to death. She closed her tearless eyes and prayed to God to spare her life, pleading with the spirit of her future daughter to forgive her if she lost this fight.

And on the wings of angels she sent her undying love to Bryce, the man for whom she'd risked her life.

"What are you doing, little mouse?" Eris inquired, head tilted to the side. She looked upon Ajali with amused fascination. "Are you drawing in more life force for me?"

Ajali frantically inhaled air through her nose and her mouth. Gulping in as much life force as she could contain, preparing for battle, Ajali closed her eyes and prayed her soul would not end up imprisoned in limbo.

Reciting in her mind the Chant of Custody, Ajali bravely and soundlessly summoned the Goddess Kali.

Chapter 37

*A*jali's wide, unseeing eyes and lolling tongue signaled the coming of the Goddess Kali, but Eris misinterpreted the sign. She saw a woman whose life was quickly ebbing. Desiring more of Ajali's life force, she knew she had to quickly revive her.

"Come!" she shouted to the security guard, her shrill voice awakening him from an entranced slumber.

In a matter of seconds, he stood by Eris's side. "Yes, Goddess?" He rubbed his eyes and squinted in bewilderment as he examined the dying, shackled woman.

"She needs to breathe! Relinquish the breath from your mouth. Give her life," Eris barked at the security guard.

"You want me to give this woman mouth-to-mouth? You think my breath is gonna bring this woman back from the dead?" He scratched his head, confused.

"Yes. And be quick about it, fool. Hurry, you idiot," she berated him. "Make haste before she dies!"

The security guard had CPR training; he carried a card in his wallet to prove it, but he'd only practiced on a dummy. Never had he resuscitated a human being. Not wanting Eris to know that he wasn't really qualified, he dramatically inhaled, bent down and pinched Ajali's nose—and bellowed in alarm when the woman suddenly broke free from the leather restraints and bolted upright.

With the strength and the swiftness of a superbeing, Ajali—now Kali—

leapt from the table and ripped off the side rails. She rubbed the two pieces of metal together; the sound was deafening, as she quickly crafted one of the metal pieces into the shape of a sword.

Mumbling a chant, she endowed the crudely formed instrument with the power and fury of her goddess sword. In an instant, Kali wielded a dangerously sharp and mighty weapon.

Eris snarled and took a defensive stance, ready to do battle with an old foe. "So, it's you!" Eris let out a chuckle. "Greetings, Kali. Do you intend to use your sword to take off my head?" she taunted.

Eris was crafty; but Kali was quick. In addition, being the source of fertility, it was her nature to fight fiercely for the life of Ajali's unborn child.

Hurriedly, Eris sent an image of Kali clumsily stumbling and dropping the powerful weapon.

Kali didn't speak. She moved in a slow circle, swinging the sword upward to block the deceptive image Eris attempted to implant in her mind. Kali then lowered the sword from her head and wielded the weapon defensively.

In a split second, Eris launched another image of Kali bowing in devotion and submitting to Eris's will. Kali hastily blocked it.

Desperate, Eris summoned all her power and telepathically urged Kali to return Ajali's body back to the table—to willingly relinquish her remaining womanhood.

The image seemed to hit Kali with the force of a thunderbolt. Kali froze, then looked confusedly at the sword she held, staring at it as if it had materialized out of thin air. Dropping the sword as if it suddenly radiated fiery heat, Kali turned slowly and lifted herself up on the table.

With a cocky grin, Eris leisurely approached. "Tell me, Kali," she said, peering into the woman's bewildered face, "has the mighty goddess succumbed to my inescapable desire or am I now dealing with the mortal called Ajali?"

Kali opened her mouth but did not speak; instead she exhaled strong gusts of air as violent as a windstorm. Eris was thrown off her feet and sent sprawling by its force.

"You deceitful, ugly bitch!" Eris screamed as she scrambled to her feet.

With bulging eyes and protruding tongue, Kali picked up her weapon of war. "You!" She pointed to the security guard who cowered in a corner. "Leave us!"

"No! You are my servant; do not leave." Blue sparks flickered as Eris turned hateful eyes on the security guard.

Obeying Eris, the man froze in place. "What do you want me to do, Goddess?"

Kali rubbed the makeshift blade against the side rail. The room filled with an ear-piercing sound of metal scraping against metal. Sparks ignited. Popped and crackled in the air. "Her spell is broken," Kali said. "Now go... Run for your life. Stay, and you will surely die here."

The security guard looked around in amazement. "What the fuck is going on?" He demanded. "Are you people crazy? This is private property and you're violating a city code."

"Go!" Kali ordered and released a mighty roar. She flung the side rail; it whirred above the guard's head, hit the wall and clanged down to the floor.

He ducked; his hands flew to his face defensively. Then the security guard took off running, his heavy footsteps pounded against concrete and wood until at last his steps could be heard no more.

Eris faced Kali without fear. "Your mere sword cannot harm me." She laughed at the goddess. "If you cut off my hands, I'll regenerate a new pair; if you take off my head I'll be momentarily inconvenienced, but I won't rest until I'm fully restored. So have at it, Kali. You're out of your league," Eris scoffed. "You, with your ridiculous nurturing tendencies—you're no match for me. I am the Eris, the Goddess of Discord! I thrive on destruction."

Kali wielded her sword in a circular fashion above her head as if preparing to cut, maim and slaughter her enemy. But then, instead of lashing out in a quest for bloodshed, Kali stopped, bent and retrieved the discarded piece of metal and began grinding the sword and side rail together. A sputtering spark evolved into a small flame.

Eris cried out as thick white smoke billowed into the air.

Kali advanced, waving the flaming sword. "Your wicked spirit has caused enough devastation. I shall cleanse you now with purifying white fire. "

"Keep away," Eris hissed. Backing away from the pure white flame, she snarled and beared her teeth, snapping at the air like a vicious, trapped animal.

Determinedly, Kali pressed forward.

"Keep awaaay!" Eris screamed.

Quickly now, Kali advanced toward the screaming and retreating demon, she drew in a deep breath and sent forth a great burst of air that howled throughout the room, sending dust and debris swirling about. A strong gust slammed the open door shut.

"I offer you death." Kali's voice boomed above the howling wind. "I offer you rest and eternal peace with this purifying white fire." She advanced again. "Or I can send your corrupt soul back to the Dark Realm. It is your choice. Choose now!" Kali demanded as the fire spread, sending up sheets of flames that encircled the spitting and hissing, fallen goddess.

"Eternal peace or damnation? Ha! You offer me nothing! I'll stay right here on Earth and reign supreme," Eris retorted. Now emboldened, Eris attempted to walk through the circle of fire, but Kali stepped forward and issued forth another burst of air.

Her breath fanned the flames, which now stretched and swayed, rhythmically dividing into dual shades. The white flame was now joined by blue, the color used for perpetual banishment. The two flames flared and danced together as Kali swung her sword.

Surrounded by raging fire, Eris raised her head and studied the ceiling, as if considering the possibility of sprouting a pair of wings. Her blue eyes were wide circles of fear. Shouting curses at both Kali and Ajali, she bumped against the wall, banging it with her back, trying to break through.

As the blaze of white flames dwindled down to just a tiny spark, the blue flames grew. Roaring blue flames rushed forward and gathered at Eris's feet. She looked down in horror as the flames rose to her ankles and then ignited with the hem of her designer skirt.

Like a ball of fire, Eris shot across the room. Trying to extinguish the damning fire, she frantically brushed against the door, the wall. Finally, consumed by fire, she dropped down and rolled along the floor.

As Eris burned, Kali sensed that the portal to the higher realm was slowly closing. Kali withdrew her essence, and reached upward toward the higher realm.

And with her soul liberated, it was Ajali who witnessed the writhing Eris as she burned alive. "Burn, you despicable demon," Ajali shouted at Eris, who screamed in anguish. "Go straight to Hell, Eris. And stay there!"

Smoke mingled with evil created an appalling scent. Choking and holding her breath, Ajali trudged toward the door. Before she exited the smoke-filled room, she gave the demon one last look. But Eris was gone. The body she had formed with treachery and deceit was now nothing more than a smoldering heap.

Using a flashlight left behind by the security guard, Ajali found her way out of the building without having to slosh through the tunnel.

A back door, no doubt blown open by Kali, led Ajali to the outside world. Standing in the midst of weeds and shrubs, Ajali prepared herself for a long walk back to civilization. She heard the sound of sputtering static and looked down. To her amazement, there lay a two-way radio, obviously dropped by the bewitched security guard.

"Is anyone there?" she shouted into the walkie-talkie.

"Byberry security. Over," said a voice.

Those few words informed Ajali that the person she had connected with was professional and efficient. "I need help. I'm lost. I'm standing outside one of the buildings. Please, can you help me?"

"Which building? Over."

"Um." She looked around and went back to the building. "I don't know—there's no name or anything."

"There should be a letter and a number. Over."

She squinted and shined the flashlight and there it was: N-3.

"I'm outside building N-3. Please hurry; I've got to get out of here."

"Ma'am, I don't know what you're doing out here, but you're not authorized to be on the premises. I'm going to have to report you. Over."

"Fine. Report me. Just help get me out of here. I'm a freelance writer," Ajali lied. "I was going to write an article about the condition of Byberry today. But, uh…I've changed my mind; it's too spooky in there. Now will you hurry, please?"

"Sure. Now, that walkie-talkie you're using belongs to the security company. Neal Brunson said he'd dropped it on the grounds. The way he hightailed it on out of here, you woulda thought he'd just seen a ghost," the man said with a chuckle.

"Please hurry," Ajali replied.

The security patrolman, a man in his late sixties, had retired but worked the security job to supplement his income. He drove up to the building where Ajali stood, forlorn. He gazed at her with tired eyes and shook his head reproachfully.

He got out of the car, slammed the car door and approached. As he drew closer, his eyes widened in bewilderment. "What the heck are you doing out here in your bathrobe? Is that the way you dress when you're investigating a story?" There was no malice or sarcasm in his tone, just a natural curiosity as to why she was out in a desolate area barefoot and wearing a bathrobe.

She'd been through so much; she didn't know where to begin. She was too exhausted to string together more lies, but the truth, she knew, would be hard for the security patrolman or anyone else to believe.

She was so exhausted; she felt her facial muscles twitch as she struggled to keep it together and not collapse into a total meltdown. "I thought…," she stammered, "I thought I had a good lead. So, I rushed out—" her voice faltered, she brushed burning tears away.

After getting a better look at Ajali's condition, her grimy nightclothes, her startling gray hair, the security patrolman gave her a look of compassion. "Something in there scared you half to death, huh?" He squeezed her shoulder sympathetically.

"They say it's haunted," he added, squinting at the building. "There might be some truth to the rumors, I don't know. I just do my job. I tell the thrill-seekers this place is private property—it's off limits. I warn them that entering any of these buildings is breaking the law. Sometimes they listen, sometimes they don't. What can you do?" he asked with a shrug.

Ajali's mouth formed into a fatigued smile.

"I don't think there'd be much point in reporting you for trespassing. Looks like you've been put through the wringer. Yeah, I'd say you've had enough excitement for one night. Come on, little lady. Get inside the car," the security patrolman said kindly. "I'll call a cab, so you can go home."

Home! Ajali felt her heart quicken with gratitude.

Worried sick about Bryce, Ajali ran up the stairs of her apartment building. Only when she reached the front door did she remember she didn't have the keys to the outer door or the key to her apartment. It was the middle of the night, too late to ring anyone's bell, but she had no choice. She had to buzz her neighbor and ask to use the phone to call Tee. Tee would come to her rescue with the spare set of keys.

She looked down at her gook-covered legs and thought about her aged body and gray hair. *Oh Lord! What will I tell Tee?* Ajali didn't have a clue. She'd piece together a convincing story when Tee got there with the keys.

At the moment, her main concern was getting inside her apartment to find out if Bryce was all right. Holding onto the positive image of a beautiful life with Bryce, Ajali firmly pressed her neighbor's bell.

"Hi. Mrs. Daniels. I'm sorry to disturb you—"

"Who is this?" the neighbor yelled over the intercom. "I guess I'm not supposed to get any sleep tonight."

Ajali was too desperate to feel embarrassed at being perceived as a public nuisance. "It's Ajali Logan, uh, I live next door," she explained. "Listen, I locked myself out of my apartment and I was wondering—"

"Well, *you* listen," the neighbor said in a chastising tone. "The next time you decide to run out of the house in the middle of the night, I hope you and your fiancé don't think you're going to bother me all night!"

Ajali frowned in confusion. How did Mrs. Daniels know about Bryce?

The buzzer sounded suddenly. Ajali yanked open the door and ran up the two flights of stairs. When she reached the top she saw the most wonderful sight. Bryce stood in the doorway of her apartment with his palms up, mouth agape, shaking his head in bewilderment.

"Bryce!" Ajali screamed and ran toward him, colliding with him with such force, he had to place a hand against the door frame to steady himself. She hugged him tight. "Oh Bryce! Bryce! You're all right. You're alive!"

"Aj! What's going on?" He gently pulled away from her and regarded her with a frown. Beginning with her uncombed hair, his eyes roamed past her soggy robe and nightgown, down to her filthy legs and grimy feet. Raising his head, his baffled eyes beseeched her to give him an explanation.

Obviously Bryce had no memory of the awful events he'd experienced. Sighing heavily, Ajali shook her head and gave him a sad, weak smile. "You don't remember anything?" she asked him.

He shook his head and furrowed his brows. "I remember having trouble sleeping. I remember having to take sleeping pills..." He paused and grimaced at that memory. "I think we had an argument over something..." He touched his forehead, trying to think. "I feel like I've been in a coma or something; my body feels stiff and sore—like I've been lying in bed for a long time."

"You have," she told him. "Come on, let's go inside."

At that moment, the neighbor's door swung open. "So, everything's fine and dandy now. I see you two have made amends," the woman scoffed. "Like I said before—the next time you decide to run off in a huff, you two had better leave me out of it, you hear?" Mrs. Daniels slammed her door.

"She had to buzz me in; my keys are here," Ajali explained as she and Bryce went inside the apartment.

"And I woke her up when I knocked on her door, asking if she'd seen or heard you leave." Bryce paused and gave Ajali a skeptical look. "Where were you; what happened? I was just at the point of calling the police when

I heard footsteps. That's why I was standing in the doorway...praying the footsteps were yours."

"Bryce," she said softly, her expression tortured. "I feel like I've been to hell and back. But it's over now. You're healed; hopefully, I'm healing..." Her voice cracked.

"Aj, come here, baby. What's wrong? Tell me, what happened?" He hugged her tight and Ajali, wanting to keep a grip on her emotions, dug deep to find the strength to not break down and cry.

"What do you mean, I'm healed and you're healing? What are you talking about?" Bryce looked at Ajali as if nothing she'd said had registered.

"You were sick, Bryce. Really sick. Don't you remember anything?"

"No." Bryce held his palms skyward. "Like I said, my body's sore, but I don't feel sick, but you..." He looked Ajali over and winced. "Aj, you don't look *sick*— You look like you've been in a war, Baby, please tell me what's going on?" he asked, with a wide sweep of his hand that told Ajali he needed many answers including an explanation for the numerous candles.

It surprised her that most of the candles still burned, hours after being lit.

"Bryce, so much has happened; I don't even know where to begin." Her tone was somber. "As you can see," she said, frowning down at herself. "I need to take a shower." Ajali gave Bryce a wan smile.

"No, you need a long hot bath." He pulled her into his tight embrace, swept her up into his arms.

Her eyes watered, she buried her head into his neck. As Bryce carried her into the bathroom, she finally allowed the tears to spill.

Chapter 38

*I*mmersed in sudsy warm water, Ajali relaxed and closed her eyes. The whistling teakettle, the clatter of dishes and the sounds of Bryce's movements in the kitchen added to her sense of comfort and well-being.

"Thank you, Kali," she whispered. "You made this possible," she said in acknowledgment of the Goddess Kali's role in her newfound peace.

Ajali ran her hand over her entire body. Miraculously, her youth had been restored. A quick look in the mirror before stepping into the tub had revealed a head of dark brown hair without one strand of gray. She'd examine Bryce later; however, she felt intuitively that she'd find his genitals unblemished—willing and eager to perform.

Bryce came in the bathroom and carefully set the steaming cup of tea on the countertop. "I remember," he said in a somber tone. He sat on the side of the tub, picked up her bath sponge, submerged it in water and began sponging her neck, shoulders and chest.

Ajali raised her gaze, expectantly.

"I remember everything now," he said. Worry lined his forehead, his handsome features darkened. "And I wasn't totally honest with you when I cancelled the wedding." He paused.

Patiently allowing him to gather his thoughts, Ajali closed her eyes and waited.

"There *was* another woman, Aj. But she wasn't real. I thought I was going crazy. I was engaged to be married but I was having an intense sexual relationship with a strange woman..." Bryce shook his head. "We were having sex in my dreams. But then the dreams became nightmares." His voice, low and whispery, held a mixture of pain and humiliation. "The sexual encounters became depraved; disgusting. I was afraid to sleep; that's why I started taking those pills. I'm so sorry, baby. My existence had become a living hell."

The hand that bathed Ajali stopped. "I handled the breakup horribly. Dishonorably," he admitted. "But how do you tell the woman you love that you've allowed yourself to be seduced by a ghost?"

Ajali opened her eyes and looked at Bryce's face. "You didn't have to," she said. The water splashed gently as she repositioned herself. Looking Bryce in the eye, Ajali said, "She was a wicked spirit, Bryce. She wanted to possess a human body."

"How do you know?"

"I met her, too."

He gave her a look of wide-eyed disbelief.

"I did," Ajali repeated, nodding. "In the most horrible way you can imagine, Eris introduced herself to me."

"Eris!" Bryce whispered, recognizing the name.

"Yes, Eris. Initially, she appeared in the form of black mist. But she clearly wanted a human body and for that she needed your essence as well as mine. In time, she intended to take our lives." Ajali inhaled deeply. "Baby, would you hand me the cup of tea? This story is going to take a while."

As Bryce rose, Ajali started telling her side of the story, beginning with the day of their cancelled wedding, when feeling bereft, she'd purchased a self-help book that she thought would bring her peace through meditation.

Midway through the story, Bryce interrupted, "Hold on to that thought, baby. The water's getting cold and you're shriveling up like a prune," he added with a sympathetic smile. Holding up a large, fluffy towel, Bryce gestured for Ajali to stand. He wrapped her inside the towel and swooped her up into his arms.

As she neared the conclusion of her harrowing tale, Ajali took a deep, shuddering breath as she described Eris's burning death. She was so relieved that she lay safely in bed, encased in Bryce's arms.

"We're going to set a new wedding date. As soon as possible. Is that okay, baby?" Bryce asked and nuzzled her neck.

"Uh-huh," she responded. "As soon as possible." Exhausted, Ajali yawned and burrowed her behind into the curve of his body; it felt so good, she moaned. There was a time when lying in bed with Bryce was normal—routine. But now Ajali was enlightened and appreciative of everything good in life; something as simple as lying in bed with Bryce felt like a gift from heaven above.

And the sun, as if assuring her of a bright new day, began to peek through the bedroom window.

Ajali and Bryce's wedding was a small affair with Bryce's best man, Justin, and Ajali's maid of honor, Tee. Being three months' pregnant, Ajali's wedding gown felt more than a little snug. It was tight and uncomfortable; but determined to wear it, she'd held her breath while Tee struggled with the zipper.

Both Tee and Justin said she had a glow. "An angelic glow," Tee added, tilting her head curiously. Had they known the physical and emotional torture Ajali and Bryce had survived, they'd realize that the couple's very existence was a miracle.

When the minister finally said, "I now pronounce you man and wife. You may kiss the bride," Bryce and Ajali clung to each other for so long, Justin coughed, and Tee cleared her throat as a reminder to the married couple to wrap it up.

"Uh, do ya think y'all can hold off and save some of that energy for the honeymoon?" Tee said, laughing.

The moment the ceremony ended, Ajali rushed to the chapel's changing room and with Tee's help, wiggled out of the confining dress. "Here you go, Tee," she said, cradling the wedding gown in both arms. "I'm leaving this in your care; I'll pick it up when we get back."

Pummeled by a hail of rice, the newlyweds could only laugh and throw their arms up defensively as they ran to Bryce's car.

"The way you look—that glow...You're so beautiful. I'm going to do everything in my power to make sure you stay as happy as you are right now," Bryce promised as he stole a quick glance at Ajali just before the red light changed to green.

She was so overwhelmed with the glory of life—the wonder of being in love and having that love returned. There were no words to convey her feelings, so she simply smiled at her husband. Looking out the window as they drove along Island Avenue, headed for I-95 South, Ajali couldn't stop thinking, *We're really married; Bryce is my husband—I'm his wife!*

Now comfortable in a pair of loose jeans, Ajali reclined in the passenger seat, peacefully enjoying the view during the ride. Every few seconds, her eyes would dart from the window to her hand. She couldn't keep her eyes focused on the scenery; she was so enthralled with her amazingly beautiful wedding band. Wearing the engagement ring and wedding band together produced a dazzling effect and she was mesmerized by the brilliance and exquisiteness of both rings.

"Honey, I think we should look at that property my father left me," Bryce commented as they traveled along the highway, en route to Delaware. They'd selected a bed and breakfast for their weekend honeymoon that was located in Rehoboth Beach, a quaint little town.

"The old plantation?" she asked with a chuckle as she turned her gaze toward Bryce.

"That old plantation is really worth a lot of money, Aj. I don't know why you never took it seriously."

"I just don't want to see you hurt if it turns out to be worthless," she said, trying to placate him.

"I'm a mortgage broker; why would I not have my facts straight?"

Ajali shrugged. She just couldn't get past the fact that a mansion in ruins, knowingly left to a black family by a slave master, sounded like a far-fetched dream. She considered the story as family legend. Something never proven.

It seemed to Ajali that the story of this great mansion was a bedtime story—a fairy tale Bryce's father had told him when he was child.

"You're in for a big surprise," Bryce said with a knowing smile. "I really think we should give the property a look before we put it up for sale; who knows, we might want to keep it."

Ajali gave Bryce a long "you've gotta be kidding" kind of look. Then, turning playful, she said, "If our property is really worth a lot of money, then we can both afford to take another day off from work, right?"

"We sure can."

"Okay. So…after our honeymoon," she said with a wink, "let's just keep driving south and take a look at the home of your ancestors."

"All right. But don't be surprised if you fall in love with Roanoke."

Ajali burst out laughing. "Me! Fall in love with the South? You're kidding, right?"

"Stranger things have happened," he said. And though he spoke in jest, they both fell quiet for a brief moment, silently agreeing that their notion of reality had drastically changed.

Bryce and Ajali arrived at the oceanfront Victorian bed and breakfast just before sunset. Breathless, Ajali admired the beauty of the mansion, the lush, green manicured lawns and the beautiful flower gardens.

"Oh, Bryce, this place is lovely," Ajali said, in awe. "Look at the porch with the old-fashioned rockers," she said, pointing. "So sweet and quaint."

"It sort of feels like we just stepped into another era," he replied as he parked the car.

"Good evening, Mr. and Mrs. Stovall," they were greeted when they stepped inside the vestibule.

"Good evening," Ajali and Bryce returned the greeting.

While Bryce transacted the business of checking them in, Ajali drifted off in thought. Blushing, she lingered in the moment of hearing herself referred to by her new married name. *My name is Mrs. Ajali Stovall! I love it!*

After a five-course dinner in the mansion's elegantly decorated dining room, replete with antique furnishings and magnificent oil paintings, the newlyweds took an evening stroll. Holding hands they stopped to marvel at a charming lily pond.

"We could have taken a cruise or honeymooned on a Caribbean island, but neither of those expensive choices could have competed with the romantic ambience of this place," Ajali said, waving her hand.

"I agree. We picked a perfect place to celebrate our marriage. But you know something, Aj?"

"Hmm?" she said, looking up at Bryce, love shining in her eyes.

"You know that feeling called déjà vu?"

"Uh-huh..."

"Have you ever felt it?"

"I feel it right now."

"I felt it the moment we pulled into the driveway. This mansion reminds me of somewhere I used to live, but that's impossible, because I've always lived in Philadelphia; I've never even visited the South."

"After what we went through, after what we survived; I no longer believe in the word *impossible*. Bryce, nothing is impossible; belief is the key. I know that magic truly exists in everyone and everything."

Bryce pondered her words and then nodded in agreement. "I really like the feeling of living in a mansion."

"Me, too," Ajali replied eagerly.

"And I'm feeling anxious about seeing our plantation."

"Bryce!" Ajali exclaimed, her eyes filled with wonder. "Wouldn't it be a miracle; if we discovered your family's old plantation really has some value? I mean...can you imagine coming up with enough money to create something similar to this!"

No longer able to keep the secret to himself, Bryce gave Ajali a sly smile. "Aj, the acres of land surrounding the plantation are worth a couple million, and I'm the only surviving Stovall heir."

"A couple million! Bryce!" Ajali squealed. "Why didn't you tell me?"

"I *did* tell you."

"I mean, why didn't you *really* tell me? You knew I didn't take you seriously when you casually mentioned that the plantation you'd inherited was worth millions."

Bryce winked at Ajali. "I sort of enjoyed the fact that you were doubtful.

And now that you know the truth, I want you to think of the ownership of the *valuable* property as a wedding gift from me."

Touched, Ajali looked at Bryce with complete adoration. Pressing her body into his, she lifted her head and gave him a quick kiss on the lips.

"That's why we're going to take that trip to Roanoke. We can sell the property or restore it to its original splendor. It's your choice...And I know it's a hard one to make," he said kiddingly. "A Northern girl moving down South and all..." Bryce gave her a cocky grin.

"I'm sold," Ajali said, laughing and throwing her hands up in surrender.

Bryce nodded and looked off in thought. "Our creation," he said, turning back to Ajali, "will have a different twist."

She looked at him expectantly.

"It'll be like a homecoming," he continued excitedly. "You and I, the descendants of slaves, returning to the plantation. Triumphant survivors— with our heads held high—the mistress and master of our own fate."

Chapter 39

*A*fter dinner, the newlyweds settled in their plush honeymoon suite. Enjoying the atmosphere as well as their closeness, they lay on the heavily carved mahogany four-poster bed, facing each other, cuddling in peaceful silence. Wordlessly, Bryce massaged the back of Ajali's neck. "Mmm," she uttered. He continued to massage with one hand while the other caressed the soft satin fabric of her cream-colored negligee. His hand moved from her waistline down to her sumptuous hips, which had become rounder and more feminine with pregnancy.

What started as a gentle kiss on her lips moved to her neck, where Bryce deeply inhaled her scent. Ajali drew in a shuddering breath as Bryce's mouth traveled to her chest. And then to her full breasts. With both cinnamon brown mounds cupped in his hands and pressed together, Bryce kissed them adoringly. When his tongue swept across this once forbidden territory, she uttered a small mew and shivered with pleasure.

He teased the hardening nipples with the tip of his tongue and then licked them until they resembled small berries. She cried out in passion, but Bryce, unwilling to release this double chocolate treat, opened his mouth and hungrily sucked one breast and then the other.

"Oh Bryce…," Ajali uttered, her voice a hoarse whisper. "Bryce!" She called his name again, her tone now rising to an urgent pitch. When she felt his warm lips trailing down to her stomach, her body tingled. Her breath quickened, small gasps expressed emotions her voice could not form into coherent words.

He nibbled on her tummy; his fingers flitted to her mons, delicately separating her slippery folds. Undulating hips rocked forward, telling him what she needed and Bryce, happy to pleasure her, licked a path from her tummy to the spot that ached with desire.

Ajali's fingers, desperately needing something to hold on to, found his shoulders and gripped them tightly.

Taking his time, Bryce kneaded and then bit her thighs. Ajali whimpered and writhed. Now tending to her growing arousal, he slipped his long middle finger inside her wetness as his tongue stroked her clit. He licked it until it became swollen and slippery.

Moaning loudly, her hips rocked forward. "I need you, Bryce," she said, her voice escalating in pitch. She tugged at his arm as she spread her legs wide, urging him to take her.

Bryce entered her slowly, tenderly. Ajali lifted her legs slightly, encouraging him to hold her legs up high and take her with wild abandon.

But he didn't lift her legs as she urged him to. "I don't want to hurt the baby," Bryce whispered.

Defiantly, Ajali pushed upward, taking what she needed. Caught up in her rapture, Bryce plunged in, burying his thickness deep inside her.

He slowed his pace and looked in her face with penetrating eyes and then cupped her cheeks. "I'm gonna love you just like this, baby, until the day I die." His voice was deep and throaty.

Stroke after stroke, Bryce declared his love while Ajali, beyond aroused, surrendered to the passion and finally erupted in volcanic shudders. But Bryce didn't let up; he continued moving at the same rhythmic pace until he joined her in that nether land where bodies and hearts connect as one.

"I want some ice cream, Bryce," Ajali said, shaking him awake.

"You're kidding," he said, sounding groggy.

"I'm not," she said, shaking her head and wearing a woebegone expression. "But the good thing is," she added in a sudden bright voice, "you don't have to go out and get it."

Bryce lifted his head and squinted at the bedside clock. "Aj, it's after two in the morning. Where am I supposed to find ice cream at this hour in this little town?"

"Call the hostess." Using a tiny and very sweet voice, Ajali formed the sentence as a question; however, she and Bryce both knew she wasn't kidding. She was being uncharacteristically demanding, but had the good manners to be nice about it.

Ajali couldn't help it; the baby was making her want the ice cream. It was late; she cringed to think of how the person on the other end of the phone was going to feel about bringing a bowl of ice cream to their suite. She felt a little better when she remembered that after dinner, the hostess had reminded them, "Don't forget, Mr. and Mrs. Stovall, just pick up the phone if there's anything we can do for you."

Still, she absolutely could not pick up the phone and make what would seem like a diva-type request.

Bryce had to do it.

Just in case the person on the other end of the phone let out a loud gasp when she heard what was being requested of her, Ajali conveniently went to the bathroom while Bryce made the arrangements. Not wishing to see the sleepy face of the person she'd disturbed with what seemed like such a frivolous request, she felt a strong desire to stay within the confines of the bathroom until the treat was at her bedside and the hostess, no doubt clad in a robe and slippers, had trekked back to her own bedroom.

The sound of the flushing toilet and running water drowned out Bryce's voice as he spoke for what seemed to Ajali as an unusually long time. She hoped he didn't have to plead or haggle with a disgruntled night-staff person who perhaps wasn't as cheery as the hostess who'd greeted them when they'd arrived.

Guiltily, she crept out of the bathroom as Bryce was hanging up.

"Are they bringing it?" she asked uncomfortably.

"Yes, you little coward. You hid out and left me to face the firing squad alone."

"No, I didn't. I had to pee. For real," she said, laughing.

Two sharp raps on the door sent Ajali diving under the covers with her back turned toward the door. She absolutely hated being such a bother; but it wasn't her. It was the baby.

"It's the baby," she heard Bryce explain when he opened the door. "My wife's pregnant and craving."

Ajali cringed even more.

"Not a problem," a sweet-sounding woman said. In two seconds the door closed and Bryce was tapping his fingers against her covered head.

"You can come out now."

She threw the covers off and sat up.

"She said the ice cream and chocolate sauce are both homemade."

Ajali squealed in delight as Bryce scooped up a spoonful of ice cream, dripping with chocolate. He hand-fed her every spoonful of the most delicious dessert she'd ever eaten.

"Baby, it doesn't get any better than this," she told him.

"Yes, it does," he promised.

Chapter 40

*S*teeped in Southern charm, the Stovall mansion was renovated true to the tradition of old Virginian splendor. It had taken three and a half years to complete, but for Ajali and Bryce, the final results were worth every second of time and every cent of the fortune they'd spent to refurbish the mansion. The completed project exemplified the opulence, grace and grandeur and replicated an era gone by.

Inside the mansion was a world of exquisite antique furnishing, a dramatic carved oak staircase, brick fireplaces, imported marble, parquet floors, handwoven Persian rugs, crystal chandeliers, high ceilings, and stained-glass windows, as well as the French walnut mirror from Ajali's apartment. The whimsical purchase of the mirror made sense now. Perhaps she had a slight gift of prophecy and had known the mirror would fit perfectly in her future home.

Outside, a circular driveway, bordered by green foliage and colorful raised flower beds, warmly greeted guests. In the center of the driveway was a spectacular cast-iron multitiered fountain.

Acres and acres of beautifully landscaped grounds surrounded the mansion. Brilliant emerald greenery went as far as the eyes could see with splashes of color from a variety of flower gardens and fruit trees. A winding rose-lined path was indeed a visual treat. Along the path were secluded whimsical gardens, a small bridge that crossed a running stream, a series of weeping willow trees, a duck pond and beautifully crafted garden benches.

However, the couple's most cherished creation was their daughter, Kali, named after the goddess who had protected them after they had unknowingly conceived their child.

Kali had Ajali's complexion and beautiful light brown eyes; she had Bryce's facial features and his wiry sandy-colored hair. She was an utterly beautiful child, blessed with the divine qualities of the goddess for whom she was named.

An adventurous and daring little child, Kali seemed to possess her namesake's fearlessness. Despite her delicate beauty, Kali was neither prissy nor prim. She was a ball of energy; a rambunctious and zestful child who kept her parents in a state of dread, fearful that her high-spirited antics would cause her to get hurt.

Contractors were hired to construct the replica of a two-level castle as an elaborate playhouse for Kali, whom Bryce and Ajali often referred to as "Princess." Giving her a castle for a playhouse seemed most fitting for their little princess.

The castle was furnished with a throne. There were majestic costumes for Kali to wear. But Kali never was still long enough to sit on her throne and she quickly grew tired of pretending to be a princess.

Outside the castle was a wonderful play center with an authentic musical carousel, a swing set, a sliding board, a seesaw, a sandbox and jungle gym. Being such a vivacious little thing, athletic and full of exuberant energy, her playground was Kali's favorite place. There she could climb, run, leap and swing and not worry about breaking any of the fragile, precious things her parents happily bestowed upon her.

Bryce, never handy with workmen's tools, was determined to improve his skills in order to plant with his own hands a tree outside the playhouse. The tree stood at the exact height as his little princess. Together, he and Kali had selected the precise site where the tree would be planted.

"You and this tree will grow together," he'd told his little girl.

"It's a magical tree, so don't be surprised if it outgrows you by leaps and bounds," Ajali added.

"My tree is magical?" Kali asked, enchanted by the notion.

"Yes, it is, sweetheart. There's magic in everything," her mother said.

The day of the planting was a special occasion shared between Bryce and

Kali. Following the instructions that came with the tiny tree, Bryce proceeded to dig a hole as deep as the rootball and twice as wide.

The soil around the hole was hard and Bryce had to loosen it up a bit while Kali, impatiently holding her little shovel, kept asking, "Daddy, when can I dig?"

"In a second, Princess. Daddy has to make sure the soil is nice and soft," Bryce explained, as he chopped the dirt with the blade of the shovel.

"Hurry up, Daddy, I wanna help."

Peering through the kitchen windows, Ajali periodically checked up on their planting progress. Observing the two people she loved with every ounce of her being filled her with tremendous joy. The last time she'd looked out the window, Bryce and Kali both were perspiring, but too involved with the task to stop for a drink. From her observation, the hole still wasn't very deep; therefore, a refreshment break was in order.

Smiling as she made lemonade, Ajali had to admit that life didn't get much better than this.

"Is it my turn yet, Daddy?" asked three-year-old Kali, anxious to use her brand-new child-size shovel.

"Okay, go ahead, Kali. Dig right here, where I softened the soil." Bryce put his hands over top of Kali's small fists, which were wrapped tightly around the handle of her shovel.

"I can do it!" she said in protest, but gave her father a gleaming smile.

"All right, go ahead." Bryce had to force himself to take a few steps backward. He was overly protective and realized that would become a big issue as his independent daughter matured.

"Bryce! Kali!" Ajali called from the spacious wraparound front porch.

"We'll finish later, sweetie. Mommy's calling us for lunch."

"Aw, Daddy. I didn't get a chance to make the hole deeper. I don't wanna eat lunch."

"We're not hungry, Aj," Bryce called out.

Ajali didn't know why Bryce thought it was lunchtime. But unwilling to exert her vocal cords again, she decided she'd take the beverage outside to them. Humming happily, she placed the pitcher and three tumblers on a tray.

"Okay, Kali. Go ahead. Start diggin'," he said with a loving smile.

Kali dug in and lifted bits of earth. "Look at me, Daddy!" she squealed.

"I see," he said indulgently. "You're a very strong little girl."

"Look, inside the hole, Daddy. There something hiding in the ground."

Taking a step forward, Bryce peered into the hole and saw dark wood peeking through the earth. "Didn't I tell you this would be a perfect spot for your magical tree? It's not even planted yet and you've already found a hidden treasure," he said teasingly. "Stand back, Kali, let's find out what you've uncovered."

Eager to please his daughter, Bryce started digging fast. Shoveling the soil that surrounded the hard object, he could tell that it was square-shaped and made of wood. Curiously, he dug beneath the wood and lifted it from the ground. Bryce was surprised to discover he'd unearthed a large, square wooden box.

Stooping, he picked up the box. "What have we here?" he asked, dramatically lifting the lid, expecting to find worthless junk.

The box was filled to the brim with dazzling jewelry from gold belt buckles to pearl hatpins. Quickly weeding through the jewelry, Bryce found a carved cameo brooch with gold bezel, diamond hair pins, an array of glimmering rings, earrings and pendants made of crystal, sapphire, emeralds, rubies and diamonds. Gold bangles and bracelets adorned with every precious stone imaginable were also in abundance inside the box.

"Ooo, Daddy!" Kali screamed and jumped up and down in glee. "Give me, Daddy," she insisted. "It's my magical box."

"What are you two shouting about?" Ajali asked as she approached carrying the lemonade tray.

"We found a treasure chest!" Kali shouted.

Bryce presented the box to Ajali. Ajali placed the lemonade tray on a bench. "Oh my God," she exclaimed when she peered inside the box. "This beautiful jewelry was buried in the ground?"

"Yes, it grew inside the hole where me and Daddy are gonna plant my magical tree," Kali informed her parents, pointing to the ground.

Grinning and shaking his head in astonishment, Bryce hung an emerald necklace around Kali's neck.

"This is absolutely incredible," Ajali said. "A miracle! You read about people finding buried treasures, but..." Then she furrowed her brow. "You know, Bryce... I've heard about Southern whites who hid their valuables during the Civil War. These jewels probably belonged to your ancestors. So Kali's correct; the jewelry is rightfully hers."

"Let me hold the treasures, Mommy."

Ajali carefully handed Kali the heavy wooden box. "Be careful, Princess... It's heavy."

"I'm strong," Kali said, struggling to hold the heavy box.

Bryce, Ajali and Kali sat on the garden bench, all making sounds of wonderment as they explored the glittering contents of the box.

"Bryce," Ajali whispered. "Those jewels look like they're worth a fortune; should we get them appraised?"

Bryce nodded. "That's a good idea."

"I promised my little princess magic, but I'm honestly starting to feel a little spooked. This is uncanny. Look at this..." He waved his hand expansively over the box of jewelry. "How can this be possible? If my suspicions are correct, I'm certain those jewels are worth a king's ransom. I just don't get it." Bryce had a look of uneasiness on his face.

"You're acting like finding a little magic is a bad thing," Ajali commented.

"It's just that we already have so much of everything. We don't need anything else. Perhaps I'm being foolish, but something about the unearthing of this jewelry box doesn't bode well. It doesn't feel right."

Kali, busy digging in her treasure, wasn't listening to her father's apprehensive words spoken in a low tone.

Smiling, Ajali nudged her husband with an elbow. "Honey, I know it's just hard to believe how our life together just keeps getting better. But you can't start doubting our miraculous lives. What did I tell you I learned from my experience with the Goddess Kali?"

Bryce smiled as he recalled the words Ajali spoke after their wedding; after their horrific ordeal was behind them.

"Nothing is impossible; belief is the key. Magic exists in everyone and everything," he recited.

"Do you believe it?"

"Yes,' Bryce said in an awed whisper.

"Then stop worrying, we're living a miraculous life and we deserve every bit of it." Ajali glanced at their daughter. "Right, Kali?" she said and nodded her head reassuringly.

"Right, Mommy." Kali had no idea what her mother was talking about, she was too busy clipping on a pair of dangling pearl earrings. Kali shook her head, smiling as the dangling pearls swung from her ears. Then she looked at her parents with the wise expression of someone beyond her years. "You're right Mommy; we're survivors. We're blessed."

Ajali and Bryce exchanged curious looks. It wasn't the first time Kali had spontaneously uttered words of wisdom and they doubted it would be the last.

Chapter 41

THE DARK REALM

*W*ithout Xavier's companionship and sage advice, the Dark Realm was unbearable, far worse than before. Eris, disgusted with the corroded environment, and revolted by the ménage of grotesque beings who squabbled and shrieked endlessly, had tried to construct a cavern similar to the one Xavier had created. But she did not possess his superior abilities.

Why hadn't she accepted Xavier's initial offer to join him on Earth? Stubbornly and oh, so foolishly, she'd refused to assist him with his well-planned scheme—his vendetta against the earthly parents he'd selected. Now, instead of reeling from the thrill of earthly pleasures, she was contained once again, inside this abominable place.

She felt so forlorn, so regretful. And so angry, she flailed about and kicked the soot, sending up a swirling dark tornado. "Xavier!" she cried out. "I know you can hear me. Help me," she called. "Get me out of here!"

Using her third eye, a skill she'd reacquired, Eris watched her former companion contently gurgling in the arms of his nanny. She waited for a sign from him, a telepathic message. But Xavier ignored her, as if he'd not heard her pleas.

Eris, momentarily distracted by the screams and wails inside the tumultuous dwelling, sighed and then turned her attention back to the Earth. And now, her third eye wandered until she located her target. She fixed a glowering gaze upon the disgustingly ever-joyful Stovall family.

And what is the cause of such merrymaking today? Eris's third eye roved, looking for the source of the family's glee. Her wandering gaze halted and then widened in horror. Her jewels; her precious treasure, were in the hands of that abominable Stovall child!

Livid and needing an outlet for her rage, Eris lashed out and clawed a male creature in close proximity. Now, two depraved souls scuffled in the soot. Amidst a frenzy of snarling, biting and scratching, Eris managed to tear at and then rip off her opponent's phallic appendage. As the creature howled in rage, she held the dripping prize over her head, screaming triumphantly before taking a huge, satisfying bite.

Meanwhile, Xavier, while being rocked to sleep by his nanny, observed Eris with his third-eye vision. He arched a brow and nodded his head in approval. Eris was a remarkably ruthless warrior. It would benefit him enormously to have Eris as a co-conspirator in his diabolical scheme.

"Oh my God," yelled his most recent nanny when she saw the baby's odd expression. With a shudder, she dropped him in his crib and scrambled toward the phone.

Timing, wicked one. You were never patient. You've no choice in the matter, now. You must abide in the Dark Realm. When I require an accomplice in my plan for catastrophic political upheaval, I'll provide you with the keys to unlock the doors of hell.

"I can't do it," the nanny yelled into the phone. "I can't deal with this weird baby anymore," she told her supervisor at the employment agency. "You'd better send someone else to take care of him—and I mean, now!" the nanny exploded, looking back at the infant with terror-filled eyes.

Her mouth dropped open incredulously, when she discovered the infant conversing to himself. "Listen to me! I have to go! This *baby* is actually mumbling; he's talking to himself like he's freakin' possessed." The young woman paused and listened briefly to her employer. "Oh, yeah?" she responded. "Well, you can't fire me because I freakin' quit!"

Upon hearing the door slam, the four-month-old-demon baby slithered to the crib's railing and eerily pulled himself upright. Craning his neck, he peered at the window and caught a glimpse of the nanny backing her car out of the driveway as she made an erratic, however, speedy escape.

The demon threw back his head and screamed: "I hope you kill yourself, you fucking cunt!" Squeals of the malicious laughter echoed throughout the resplendent but doomed home.

Author Bio

ALLISON HOBBS resides in Philadelphia, PA. She is a former singer and member of a female trio known as Brown Sugar. A self-taught folk artist, Allison's prolific body of work portrays scenes of black Americana. She received a Bachelor of Science degree from Temple University. Allison is a national bestselling author with four published works with Strebor Books, including *Double Dippin'*, *Dangerously in Love*, *Insatiable* and *Pandora's Box*. Allison has been featured in several periodicals, which include *Romantic Times* magazine and *The Philadelphia Tribune*. Her next novel, *Gold Digger*, will be released in July 2007. Visit the author at www.allisonhobbs.com

Gold Digger

by Allison Hobbs
Available July 2007 from Strebor Books

One

Had her guard been up, Milan would have sensed something was amiss, she would have noticed while gliding into her reserved space that there were more cars than usual in the company parking lot. But seduced by the unseasonably spring-like weather, and still basking in the afterglow of a succession of mini orgasms and one major, body-quaking orgasm the night before, Milan felt lighthearted and carefree. It was February, but her mind was already on a new summer wardrobe, a new hairstyle with bronze highlights, and perhaps a new car. Something sleek and elegant—a Jag or a Ferrari. And breast implants.

Smart, competent, and accomplished, she damn well deserved a bigger set of boobs. But with a low tolerance for pain, she doubted she could suffer through surgery or the agonizing healing process afterward. So, on second thought, she decided to forego breast augmentation altogether; she'd start wearing bras with more padding to give the illusion of a bigger bust line. Her extra dollars would be spent on something totally unrelated to pain—like the pricy Anchor pendant, with its brilliant round diamonds that swung from a delicate platinum chain—that she'd been coveting at Tiffany's.

After a successful nine-month stint as the Executive Director of Pure Paradise Renewal Center and Day Salon, twenty-six-year-old Milan Walden was earning more than she'd ever dreamed of and would soon be eligible for a substantial salary increase. The Board of Directors was decidedly pleased with Milan's inventive ideas and vigorous campaigns to promote the spa's beauty and wellness services. They were particularly impressed with the quarterly profits.

Under Milan's helm, profits at Pure Paradise had tripled in nine short months. Business was booming! Though the wealthy elite were the target market, Milan had innovatively devised beauty renewal and well-being programs to fit the budgets of women from all economic brackets.

Of course, Milan had the good sense not to integrate the well-to-do with the hopeless bottom feeders. No, no, no. The stream-lined programs for those of modest means were scheduled on specific days and time slots, not to mention that the less fortunate were herded down to the lower level—unseen by discriminating eyes.

Milan looked forward to her performance review. Certain that her salary would more than double, she smiled wistfully as she envisioned indulging herself with all the fabulous material things money could buy.

Not bad for a gangly black kid from the Richard Allen Projects, she thought with smug satisfaction as she breezed through the automatic sliding glass doors. She caught a glimpse of her reflection as she passed the mirror which hung above the security station and had to admit that she looked damn good.

Impeccably swathed in a textured well-cut pantsuit, a pair of beaded mules, a colorfully trendy leather briefcase, and expensively coiffed hair, Milan's fashion and beauty sense had changed her ugly duckling status to that of beautiful swan.

Brimming with pride and absolutely pleased with her life as well as the glorious sunny day, which she perceived as a divine design to complement her charmed existence; Milan failed to notice the serious expression of the usually smiling and solicitous security guard as she whisked past him.

When she approached the company's reception area, the woman who sat behind the desk greeted Milan with a strained smile and a weak, "Good morning." The woman was Milan's exact age, with a nice figure and appealing facial features. However, being a lowly receptionist was probably as far as she aspired; the poor envious creature would never come close to reaching Milan's level of success. Feeling superior, Milan smirked at the receptionist as she briskly walked past. *Don't hate!*

A few moments later, as she floated toward her secretary's desk, Milan couldn't imagine why she could smell the overpowering and sickeningly sweet fragrance of potpourri that wafted throughout Pure Paradise but was unable to detect even a hint of the wonderful aroma of her morning cappuccino.

Her secretary, Sumi, who also served as the center's tour guide for prospective clients, was completely incompetent, but being a young and flawless Eurasian beauty, Sumi was excellent advertising for Pure Paradise. Desperate women in their forties, seeking to stave off the destruction of time, flocked to Pure Paradise where they were promised youth and rejuvenation with massage therapy, aromatherapy, yoga, Pilates, facials, seaweed wraps, colonics and even journaling sessions for crying out loud. What a crock! But thankfully for Milan a sucker had been born every minute during the wild 'sixties. Bless those grungy, down-with-the-establishment hippies for prolific breeding and for producing such materialistic and narcissistic offspring.

"Sumi," Milan hissed, banging her chic lime-colored Italian leather briefcase on Sumi's desk. "Where's my Cappuccino Grande? You know I can't begin my day without my caffeine fix."

A look of extreme discomfort crossed Sumi's pretty face. "Someone snatched it," Sumi explained, her voice an apologetic whisper.

"Someone snatched it?" Milan echoed. "Who?" she screeched. In search of a cappuccino thief, she whirled around and assessed her secretary's work area in anger and disbelief.

Sumi pointed toward the executive office—Milan's office. Just as Milan cut her eyes in that direction, the door flew open. A stern-faced board member emerged from Milan's office and beckoned her.

Utterly surprised, Milan's jaw dropped. "Good morning, Mr. Billings," she said, quickly composed. "What a wonderful surprise," she said in an unnaturally high-pitched voice.

"Yes, good morning, Milan." He gave her a tight smile and then with a pompous lift of his chin, he said, "We'd like to have a word with you."

We? Milan mouthed the word as she turned her head to meet the wide doe-shaped eyes of Sumi. She grasped the handle of her briefcase and glared at her secretary, willing the frazzled girl to enlighten her.

"The Board," Sumi finally responded. "They're all in there."

"All of them?"

Sumi nodded gravely.

What the hell? With panic mounting, Milan cleared her throat, donned a twitchy smile, and walked woodenly toward Mr. Billings. Wheels turned quickly inside her head and then it dawned on her—the Board wanted to reward her for her amazing accomplishments. They probably wanted to present her with a monetary bonus a few months before her scheduled performance review. A genuine smile now replaced the painful spastic grin. With a feeling of great relief, Milan traipsed inside her spacious office and offered a cheery "Hellooo" and animatedly waved a hand at the Board members as if they were all the best of friends.

Six entirely Caucasian Pure Paradise Board members were convened. They all sat stiffly on the sofa, settee, and two chairs. The Board's chairperson, Dr.

Kayla Pauley, a nice-looking and stylish forty-something dermatologist, sat behind Milan's desk, wearing a black Armani jacket and sipping the stolen cappuccino. Milan was reminded of how much she disliked the sickeningly self-assured Dr. Pauley, still she gave a delighted smile that welcomed the insufferable woman to her desk—and to her badly needed morning java.

Milan cast a hopeful glance at one of the male Board members who sat in one of the cushy chairs. Not only did he refrain from offering her a seat, the man had the gall to give Milan a look of contempt and then fixed a pleasant gaze on Dr. Pauley.

Irritation coursed through her body and threatened to make an appearance on her face, but she shook off the feeling and graced the Board members with another forced smile. She supposed their solemn expressions and the stifling doom-and-gloom atmosphere was merely a façade, a necessary preface to glad tidings.

Dr. Pauley set the container of cappuccino upon the desk. "Good morning, Milan. I guess you're wondering why we're here." Dr. Pauley leaned forward in Milan's executive chair and began shuffling papers.

Milan nodded absently as she glanced disapprovingly at the blood-red set of lip prints left on the cup. *Her* cup! Despite the monetary compensation she was about to receive, Milan couldn't help feeling violated. Why did Dr. Pauley have to ruin the moment by brazenly guzzling her cappuccino and sitting at her desk?

"It's been brought to our attention," Dr. Pauley began slowly. "That you haven't been…how should I put it?" She paused briefly and then exclaimed with an extravagant wave of her hand, "Milan, we've discovered you haven't been forthcoming."

Say what? Milan kept her bright smile frozen in place for surely she had mistaken the word *forthcoming* for *rewarded*. Of course the Board was gathered to show how much they appreciated her. Her performance at Pure Paradise was stellar. They couldn't possibly have convened to accuse her of—what? Theft? Embezzlement? Why did white people always think blacks were prone to steal? How dare they even suggest that an intelligent, attractive, polished and educated woman such as she would take something from Pure Paradise.

Hmm. On second thought, she had pocketed dozens of those cute little pastel-colored bottles of Hawaiian hand lotion. Sudden fear made her heart pump a zillion beats per second. *Oh hell!* she thought with relief and calmed down. The product was included in the gift bags—giveaways for new clients. *You can't steal something that's being given away.* She had a notion to inform the stuffy Board members of that fact, but held her tongue. In Milan's opinion, the real thief was Dr. Kayla Pauley, the coffee-snatching, desk-stealing hussy.

Without a doubt, the Board had made a mistake, and Milan was prepared to loudly protest any wrongdoing on her part. "Exactly what are you trying to say?" Milan inquired. Her broad smile morphed into a don't-mess-with-me-before-I've-had-my-coffee scowl.

Taken aback by Milan's sudden intimidating presence, Dr. Pauley drew back and nervously reshuffled the papers.

"Milan," Mr. Billings said, rising from his position on the settee. "It's come to our attention that you falsified your credentials."

Milan's mouth went dry. Her rising panic escalated to full-blown terror. She swallowed and took a peek at the papers on her desk. She squinted at her resume, scrutinized it as if there was some kind of mistake. But her name was right there in bold letters as well as her educational background. There were other papers on the desk. One was embossed with the University of Pittsburgh logo and another boasted the Temple University logo.

"There is no record of your ever receiving a bachelor's degree from Pitt or an MBA from Temple." Now emboldened, Dr. Pauley leaned forward. "Milan, your position requires a degree from a four-year college at the least. Our records indicate that your education is limited to a high school diploma…," Dr. Pauley said, shaking her head and scanning the papers in annoyance. "Until you can provide the proper documentation, we're going to have to terminate you immediately."

Dr. Pauley's words were chilling. Milan's knees, damn them, knocked together uncontrollably. She hadn't heard what she thought, had she? She definitely needed a moment to process the information. "I know I don't actually have a degree, but obviously I'm a strong, dynamic leader. "My experience speaks for…," she stammered.

Before she could utter another word, Royce, the security guard, appeared. He glowered at Milan briefly and then said gruffly, "Come with me, Miss Walden."

Milan's jaw dropped. "You're kidding!" She twirled on her heels and faced the group of seven. "Is this necessary? My accomplishments here have been huge," Milan said, fighting for survival—trying to reason with the Board. "I put in thirteen-hour work days and I've made this company a small fortune…" She paused to catch her breath. "And now you're treating me like a common thief."

"Please leave the premises, Milan, or security will have to forcibly remove you," Dr. Pauley said, unmoved by Milan's outburst. Slowly and gracefully, she picked up the phone. "Sumi, please pack up all Milan's belongings."

Milan opened her mouth to further defend herself, but she felt faint; the words necessary to halt this travesty of justice, escaped her.

Smiling wickedly as she swiveled toward Milan, Dr. Pauley said, "We'll forward your belongings to your current address. Hopefully, that isn't a fabrication as well."

The next three minutes were a blur of embarrassed gasps, chuckles, and outright slurs from subordinates who apparently felt Milan had it coming. A minute or so later, she sat inside her car, stunned and trembling, but very reluctant to leave Pure Paradise. Driving away obliterated her chance of being available should the Board come to their senses and reconsider their absurd decision to fire her. As far as Milan was concerned, keeping her around—college degree or not—made good business sense.

Royce had brusquely escorted Milan through the sliding doors and returned to his station. From his vantage point, he could see that she was making no attempt to vacate the company parking lot; the once-friendly security guard stepped outside. With an angry expression, he motioned for Milan to get moving.

Could the day get any worse? Her mind was spinning, her head throbbed, and she felt queasy. She really needed something to calm her down. She imagined Dr. Pauley and realized that what she needed was a goddamn cup of coffee!

Blinking back tears, she pulled herself together, turned on the ignition, and careened out of the lot. The car, seemingly on automatic pilot, was pointed in the direction of the nearest Starbucks.